The Pleasing Hour

The Pleasing Hour

A NOVEL BY

Lily King

ATLANTIC MONTHLY PRESS ❦ New York

Published simultaneously in Canada
Printed in the United States of America

FIRST EDITION

Library of Congress Cataloging-in-Publication Data

King, Lily.
The pleasing hour : a novel / by Lily King.
p.   cm.
ISBN 0-87113-754-2
I. Title.
PS3561.I4814P58   1999
813'.54—dc21   99-25528

Design by Laura Hammond Hough

Atlantic Monthly Press
841 Broadway
New York, NY 10003

00 01 02   10 9 8 7 6 5 4

For all of my families

I

Plaire

❦

PLAIRE IS NOT A WEALTHY TOWN. IT IS NOT ONE OF THOSE IMMACULATE, ROMANTIC villages described in books about the south of France. Its streets are not made of cobblestones or clogged with visitors in the hot months. It does not have red cliffs, or châteaux, or the carapace of a fortress. The churches are unremarkable, the café terraces viewless. In the afternoon the narrow streets grow sinister, blackened by enormous shadows with clawed edges that slowly scale the pitted stucco walls. Half-dead ivy creeps down to meet them. Even at two o'clock on a bright spring day, you can turn down one of those streets and all light and heat will be gone. You will have to wait until your eyes have adjusted to move on. Through the slats of closed green shutters above, you can hear music or the sound of water in a basin or heavy plates being stacked or unstacked. The grocery bags will start to cut into your fingers, and the two miles back will seem, from that dark street, unachievable. But once you reach the valley, and Lucie Quenelle's farmhouse appears on the next rise, there seem to be seven suns stretching across the sky, each one celebrating your return.

She is waiting for me in the garden. I can see her straw hat twitching as she swats at something. At the sound of my sandals through the grass, a smile appears just below the hat's brim. It does not feel like penitence to be here with this old woman, though I know it should.

Once she sets me to work on the table grapes with her, it doesn't take her long to start in with more questions. She has so many, mostly about Nicole.

"She was very careful as a child, deliberate. Is she still?"

"Yes." I try to be curt, entirely uninterested.

"And so equable."

"Yes."

"Perhaps you are too young to know exactly what I mean."

"Perhaps," I say, feeling too old to argue.

She's teaching me how to rewire the trunks of the vines to their posts. Beside her quick spotted hands, mine work clumsily.

"Would you say she's happy, Nicole? Would you say she married the right man?"

"I don't know." But she wants more. She will not stop until she's wrung me dry. "He's not a man I would have married," I add.

"Why not?"

I can't think of one word to throw her off.

"It's hard to pinpoint, isn't it?" she says, furrowing her entire face. "But there's something about this Marc Tivot. A man should never make you feel old."

"She looks half her age," I say, deliberately misunderstanding, veering away. "She's in good shape. She's healthy, nimble—"

"Nimble! Where did you learn a word like nimble? Sometimes you surprise me with the words you know. How is it that you can have such an extensive vocabulary but absolutely no memory for the definite articles?"

"I don't know. It's just a block I have," I say, embarrassed my errors have been noticed already.

Nicole's daughter, Lola, always insisted it was obvious. *Look,* she said, running to the table she had just set, *a knife is masculine and a spoon is feminine. Look at them. You can just tell. Look at this plate. It's a girl's face. And this glass, it's a man. Can't you see it?* Lola had bangs and a birthmark on her ring finger and pronounced my name, Rosie, with the best unrolled *r* in the family.

"Here. Not so tight. Please," she says with sudden impatience. "You're strangling the poor thing. And look down here. His roots are being pulled up."

"Sorry." I let go the vine.

"I love this earth." She squeezes a fistful and, when she releases it, it keeps the hollows of her fingers and the sharp peaks between them. I feel her smiling, waiting for me to look up. But I can't receive her at times: her pale eyes, her pressed white collar and the triangle of scaled skin it reveals, her nimble hands working the earth. *Leste.* All my words lead back to that family.

Marc called me nimble during my first week in Paris when I caught the glass at dinner. Their son had knocked it hard off the edge, reaching for the lemon syrup, and I caught it, a full glass of water falling from the table. Marc called me *leste* and the whole family looked at me, everyone but Nicole, like I might work miracles.

"Look at you. You're freezing," she says, leaving a hand on my bare leg. "The body is so beautiful when it's young. Enjoy it, Rosie."

But I can't feel anything—not her withered hand or the earth she loves or the suns that are still blazing above us—and I know if there's one thing I ache to abandon it is my body.

"You are eighteen, nineteen?"

"Nineteen."

"What on earth could make a child of nineteen so . . ." She studies me for a word that thankfully never comes. "When I was nineteen," she continues, "we moved here, to Plaire. Nicole's family lived right up there, through those trees, which in those days weren't so high. You could see their house, from here, and the sun, as it fell below those mountains. But everything's higher now. Or maybe I've shrunk. I don't know what's different today about the sun and the air, but then the sky would go purple sometimes—not purple, exactly, but mauve. That's what Nicole's mother called it."

"You knew her mother?" It is an odd image, Nicole as a child.

"She was seventeen years younger than me, but she ended up being the closest friend I ever had. She told me that when she was a little girl she'd sit on her grandfather's porch in Roussillon and have tea and cakes during the mauve hour. I never hear the word *mauve* without thinking of her, but the light's changed since then. Anyway, I think it's probably time."

"Yes."

"But we've done quite a lot today. Thank you."

She is giving me room, board, and two hundred francs a week, but she has thanked me every evening of the three weeks that I've been here.

We put the tools and the wire back in the broken basket and follow the path through the roses to the back door. She takes my arm on the steps for balance. "Ah," she says. "Can't you smell the stew? You were right to put in that extra basil." She gives my arm a good tug as if she might be falling, then casts off from me altogether as we enter the house.

After dinner I will write my sister a one-sentence postcard with no return address: *Walked the path van Gogh walked with his bloody ear.* It's a lie—a place Lucie Quenelle has told me about farther south.

In the New Hampshire house with the red door—and the gold slot into which these cards are dropped—live my sister, her husband, and the baby I gave them. All I can hope is when that child has words he will tell them the things I cannot. Perhaps my whole life here in France will spill out of his mouth.

La Rentrée

I SHOWED UP LAST FALL AT 121 PORT DE SUFFREN THE DAY BEFORE THE RENTRÉE, THE day that all French children return to school. Perhaps in Paris alone that day there were ten or eleven thousand other young foreign women showing up on doorsteps, buzzing intercoms, calling from phone booths for the door code they were not given, taking the place and the room of the summer girl who had just vacated. I never became part of that network of women, but I saw them everywhere: at tennis lessons, in doctors' offices, beneath the wide arches of private schools. Wherever I was sent, so were they.

They worked in clusters, met at parks, flicked their cigarettes into the sandbox, kept a loose eye on the kids. They went out at night. They ordered jugs of sangria in small bars packed with foreign women and the men who wanted to meet them. They complained about the families and traded stories of the condescension, the false accusations, the humiliation. They laughed and laughed. They dated Frenchmen and rolled their eyes. Then they fell in love. They told each other everything, rarely in their own language. Sometimes they quit their jobs and got new ones through their agencies. Always broke, they lent each other money. They missed their boyfriends back home. They broke up with their boyfriends back home, succinctly on the phone, digressively through the mail. They sneaked men back to their maids' rooms on the top floor of their buildings, then couldn't get rid of them. They spoke French better and better, with the intent of becoming translators, hotel managers, tour guides, diplomats. French was their third or fourth language. They read Proust or de Beauvoir or Duras and decorated their rooms with prints of Manet, Pissaro, and Gauguin. They mocked tourists who tried to speak French and helped the ones who didn't. They went home for the holidays, then returned to find the Panthéon buried in snow. They studied more French. They were perpetually studying French. By spring, there was nothing left about the kids that was endearing, nothing left about the parents that was a mystery. But they had gotten what they wanted: the words, the vowels and the consonants, the idioms and the intonations that could be gotten only in Paris. They had ripped the tongues from these families and wanted nothing more. They were glad it was nearly time to go. They detached themselves easily at the end of their year, a precise Parisian fluency accomplished, lives ahead of them. If they remembered, they sent a Christmas card each year until they knew their face had lost its definition in the long parade of other foreign girls who had shown up on that doorstep on the eve of the *rentrée*.

I should have been one of them: guarded, flinchless. I should have wanted only a tongue, not safety, not solace. A family will rarely give you those—not your own, not anybody's.

No one had told me it was a houseboat. I approached the long string of them from the stern, reading each name loudly in my head as I passed. *Vanesa* was a forest of squat pines planted in boxes, so many you couldn't see any part of the boat within. *La Liberté* was utterly bare with every window boarded up. *La Chienne* was painted fire-engine red and its deck cluttered with several pairs of shoes, a few rusted bicycles, and an overcrowded clothesline that stretched bow to stern, the middle sagging on the roof of the cabin and on the backs of the two dogs sleeping there.

On *La Sequana*, which was sleek and spare, Nicole stood in the black bottom of a bikini.

I was not used to seeing other breasts. At school, girls had changed facing their lockers, and on overnights they slipped their bras off beneath a nightgown. My sister's breasts were the only ones I knew, and they were the same as mine. But Nicole's were utterly different: perfectly conical and nearly wholly enveloped by dark brown areolas.

She stood on deck, brushing Odile's hair, which rose magically in the breezeless air each time it was released from the bristles. At sixteen, Odile was already a head taller than her mother and had to bend her knees while bracing herself on the railing and grimacing to the rhythm of the hard strokes. She wore a neon-green one-piece. I saw them before they saw me: Nicole jockey-like, quick, and deliberate, her small body in perfect proportion; Odile more languid and willowy but erratic. She flung an arm back toward her mother for hurting her.

Lola, younger by four years, sat waiting on the stoop of the short ramp, fully dressed. She had her head craned in the opposite direction, expecting me in a taxi. Then she heard my step and turned.

"Ah, elle est là!"

I didn't expect her French. Lola's face was so open and her mouth so wide and unpuckered that I didn't expect French to come out of it. It was always a surprise to me, every time, Lola's French.

Her little brother, Guillaume, in swimming trunks too long for his nine-year-old legs, launched himself from the chaise longue toward me. Immediately he was disappointed, which I knew from the expression of expectation that didn't change, as if I might turn into someone else if he could just get close enough. He'd bet his friend Arnaud that his American *jeune fille* would be prettier than Arnaud's new Norwegian one. But I was big and unspectacular, nothing like the cinema samples, and he'd have to give back Arnaud's fountain pen.

I disrupted everything briefly.

The family lined up to kiss me. With Guillaume and then Odile, I aimed for the wrong cheek and ended up butting noses with Guillaume and nearly kissing Odile on the lips, which seemed to horrify her and her profound sense of propriety. Before her turn, Lola told me, "Right cheek first," which clarified everything, and I was prepared for Nicole. No one else seemed to be bothered that Nicole wore no shirt. As we kissed, I smelled makeup and removers, nail polish and toothpaste, and the lingering odor of her younger children—sour milk and butter cookies. The heat had brought to the surface of her skin all of these scents that I never again smelled so strongly, though I never thought of Nicole again without them, just as I never forgot the shape of her breasts beneath her clothes.

Nicole found her silk shirt on Guillaume's chair mashed into a pillow and scolded him in a singsong voice that just made him grin at her. She asked me a few polite questions, which I answered with the simplest expressions I knew. There was something about Nicole, the swift strokes with Odile's brush and now the same movement with her hand to rid the silk of wrinkles, that told me immediately that she was not a person to tolerate mistakes, and I suspected that my four years of textbook French would not hold out for very long.

I had the feeling, from the moment Nicole glanced up and saw me, that I had either arrived too late or too early in the afternoon. There was something distinctly inconvenient about me, which turned out to be a feeling that persisted for several months. It could disappear for long stretches of time, then resurface inexplicably one day as I walked into the kitchen with her dry cleaning or into the living room to call her kids to dinner. She would look at me with that same vague surprise, that attempt to veil vexation. During those first months, no matter how close I came to feel to that family, that look of Nicole's could cast me straight back out to that initial moment on the deck when I wondered if I was too early or too late to begin my life with them.

I followed her down the steep stairs into the house. I'd never been on a houseboat before or been to Paris or spoken French outside a classroom. *A house on a boat on a river in France. A house on a boat on a river in France.* It took a tune in my head as we clomped down the steps and I thought someday I'd sing it to Lola, who liked me already, which I knew by the way she watched beside me with her seal face, her round brown eyes, and hopeful mouth, watching for my reaction to this new world, her world. I wondered if she knew any English, if she would understand *house* or *boat* or *river*. Already I felt that if I said those words—or any words—Lola would understand them all.

I was actually the only one who clomped. Lola bounced and Nicole trotted, gold thongs swatting her heels as she led me down a corridor and pointed without stopping to the children's rooms, bright with rugs, posters, and comforter covers. The beige hallway carpet bled into my room at the end, where there was no vestige of the many girls who'd come before me, only a single bed covered in a washed-out floral fabric that appeared more vividly beneath the glass of the dressing table and on the pillows of the ottoman in the corner. I glanced at this corner placidly, as if I'd often had an ottoman in my bedroom.

Nicole showed me how to open the window and told me I was not to spill in the room or use nails on the walls or eat meals anywhere but in the kitchen. Then she made me open the window myself and repeat back to her the negative commands she'd given. I couldn't remember some of the words she'd used. My comprehension was still way ahead of my recall. Nicole's face said she'd done this a thousand times with the same result. For her I was just another *fille* marking another year, another *rentrée*.

Lola pleaded my case. "Don't worry, Maman. She's understood you." But Nicole looked one last time at the room, as if she'd never recognize it again, and led Lola away to let me unpack.

But Lola and Guillaume were back in my room in a few minutes to model their back-to-school clothes. Lola's were boyish, mostly jeans and soft cotton shirts, while Guillaume's were for a child far younger: wool shorts with tall socks, a shirt with a scalloped collar, plaid overalls. I showed them the pieces of magenta and chartreuse paper I found in a dresser drawer, and they told me it was Sigrid's from two years ago. Because I couldn't understand all of their simultaneous explanations, they resorted to fingers that became scissors, then pulled me into each of their rooms to show me the framed cutouts on their walls.

"And the other girls. How many?" I was wary, in those early days, of full sentences.

"Millions," Lola said, letting her arms flail. "Thirty or forty?" She looked at her brother for verification. She was a spindly, awkward girl in the most awkward stage of her life. I knew from watching her that people had begun to tell her to calm down, to lower her voice, to keep her arms at her side.

"More," Guillaume said.

Their fingers became full of names.

"Pilar!" Lola stopped. "Remember her? She wore Maman's clothes when she wasn't home."

"But Tonia was worse," Guillaume said. "She called Turkey every night and the bill was five thousand francs and she had to work six months for nothing. She cried a lot."

They went through the long list: Vibeke the witch, Begonia the poet, Hélène the belcher. They spent awhile debating if it was Ella or Elsa who ate her cigarettes after she smoked them.

"And me, what?" I finally dared ask.

"You mean what will we say?"

I nodded. Lola shrugged and said something I wasn't sure was a word.

She repeated it. *"Chais pas."*

"What does it mean?"

"Chais pas?" She seemed disappointed, as if she'd had higher hopes for me. *"Je ne sais pas."*

"Chais pas." I practiced. *"Chais pas."*

"How do you say it in English?"

"I don't know," I said slowly.

But she was impatient. "I know, but how do you say it fast?"

"I dunno."

"Dunno," Lola said, in that precise accent she had whenever she repeated me.

"Perfect."

"Dunno," Guillaume tried.

"Dunno," I repeated.

"Dunno."

"Good," I said, but it was a lie to stop the game short and he knew it.

"I don't need to learn English. I'm going to be a priest."

"A priest?" I said, trying to say the word *prêtre* as beautifully as he had and failing.

"We'll say that you aren't very stylish—I'm not either—but that you're very nice," Lola said.

"That you're disorganized." Guillaume looked at my open suitcase and all the balled clothing.

"And that you have a pretty smile."

"And that you're a little fat."

"Guillaume!"

"It's okay," I said. "It's true."

"But you're smaller here." She poked her leg. "And here." She touched her cheek. "And it's very smooth. Look at Guillaume. He already has two *boutons* and he's only nine."

Though I suspected what Lola meant, I feigned confusion to diffuse a moment I thought would be embarrassing to Guillaume. But he showed me the pimples on his chin with pride.

Guillaume left then, but Lola stayed and watched me empty my suitcase. Even as I put things in drawers for the first time, I imagined Lola could already see me packing to go. Lola would treat me kindly, I thought, sometimes even with affection, as if I were a surprisingly pleasant stranger on a long train journey, then bid me farewell, a separation she had always expected and had been through dozens of times before. I felt her watching me, sizing me up against the other faces and suitcases and accents. I figured by now Lola knew exactly how much of herself to give, the extent of the attachment she could afford. What I forgot is that Lola was a child, and no matter how polite and contained and wise she seemed, she did not live within a world of learned boundaries, of hesitation and self-protection, of moderation and mitigation, of meting out and holding back. She lived wholly, fastidiously, and devoutly in the present.

That night we went out for pizza. Since the *fille* was not technically due to start working until the next day, this pizza treat was a tradition in the family on the eve of the *rentrée*.

We took a large table in the middle of the restaurant. It became clear then that Odile was out of my domain. She and her mother sat at one end, only a few feet away but worlds apart from the rest of us, thick in quiet discussion, of which I could understand not one word. Eventually Odile held her sleeve up to her mother, who examined it carefully before resuming conversation. After that I could understand a few things: *soie, jupe, taille.*

Guillaume wanted to talk about clothes too. He asked me if I liked his T-shirt that said BOSTON BAISBALL RED SOCS written in a circle around a football and a flat bat. I nodded, then noticed the streaks of white scarring on his arms and hands.

He saw me looking and said something too quickly. Lola translated. "He almost died once."

Nicole leapt out of her conversation to squelch the topic immediately with two words: "Lola. *Non.*" And that was the end of it.

Guillaume ate his dessert on his mother's lap. Despite the infantile position, his voice instantly changed in rhythm and timbre and became as adultlike and incomprehensible as the other two. Only Lola remained at my level, speaking to me slowly about the unfamiliar cartoon figures that appeared on the paper place mats.

As we walked back along the quai, night had not yet fallen, though it must have been close to nine. The sky was pale green and starless. The river water below seemed not a color but a kind of light, a wan timid light that flickered and then disappeared as a Bateau Mouche slid through with its gaudy necklace of spotlights, inducing a false darkness and shattering the surface of glass.

Lola stayed behind, next to me, though I'd run out of words. I was thinking *This is Paris, this is Paris,* but now that I was finally here I could feel it no more than if I had been walking down a cinema aisle with screens on all sides.

When we reached the barge and filed down the narrow stairwell, the children scattered. Guillaume went straight to the TV in the living room, Lola to her bedroom, and Odile to the telephone in the study. The boat seemed so small from the street, but down inside it opened up into a real house. Nicole told me to make myself at home, then disappeared too. There seemed no place for me to go but to my room. Eventually I heard Nicole in the laundry room—folding the clothes, I guessed, that were dry on the racks. I wondered if I should offer to do it and stood in the middle of my room for a long time, frozen in indecision until it was too late. Nicole knocked on my door when she was through, her head just above the tall pile. I nodded to everything she said, though all I really understood was that she would do breakfast tomorrow but that I should be ready to do something else at ten. She wasn't fooled by my nods but she was tired, too, and simply repeated the time, ten o'clock, when I should be ready. Then she told me to sleep well and shut the door.

One by one I heard the children wash faces, brush teeth, and go to bed.

I removed the remaining things from the pouches inside my suitcase: a paperback, mittens, a flashlight. I examined them peacefully now, these pieces from my room in my sister's house. They bore no marks of the fury and fear with which they had been packed. But when I felt the tiny comb, my hand became too heavy to lift and I sat on the bed beside the suitcase. I was determined to look, though it took me a long time. There were several strands of the baby's fine red hair wound up in the plastic teeth. All that hair. My sister called him Samson and pulled it up with two hands above his head, like she used to do, years ago, when shampooing me. I brought the comb to my nose because I knew it would smell of his scalp and that smelling would hurt far more than seeing. Then I unwrapped a strand and pulled it through my lips, slowly. My cheek had fit perfectly in the soft depression below his crown.

I wound it back on the teeth, set the comb carefully in the pouch, and went to the window. Although I had no sensation of movement, I could hear the faint pat of the river against the hull and, fainter still, the barge ropes straining on their fat cleats. I was relieved by the sky's final darkness and the slow flames of light from the bridge lamps on the water. Another day, however, a day to follow this one, seemed impossible. It had taken all my strength to get this far.

Despite the lingering warmth of the air, a long chill went through me. I undressed quickly and got into bed. The sheets were good, expensive sheets, the kind that always stay slippery and cold, but I already knew sleep wouldn't find me here.

After a long while, someone went into Lola's room next door. She whispered and a man's voice hoarsed back. A father's voice. I'd forgotten about a father. The only word I could make out—and they each said it, Lola first, her father repeating—was my name.

The next morning there were knocks at my door, knocks so swift and hard they were barely discernible as separate sounds. I pulled open the door and saw, in a flicker of a second, Nicole's face fall again with that expression. Its source was unidentifiable; her eyes did not travel; her hands remained at her sides. But there was something in my response that caused disappointment.

As I stepped out into the hallway, I debated whether to shut the door behind me. Not shutting it seemed an invitation for anyone to paw through my things, but shutting it seemed as if I had something to hide. I glanced down to the kids' rooms and, seeing them all open, let go of my door at about halfway, but Nicole reached behind me to shut it firmly, saying something to which I quickly agreed, not having recognized one word in all the sounds. She proceeded ahead of me then, zigzagging down the hall to shut first Lola's, then Guillaume's, then Odile's door, as if to say with each tug that no one but her ever had any common sense about doors.

She wore the kind of pants shaped for shapely women, the kind that matter if they get wrinkled and are sold from hangers, not in piles arranged by waist and length. Into these black pants was tucked a sleeveless green shirt that seemed nearly fluorescent against her deep brown shoulders and arms and the even darker dip of nape below the precise cut of her hair. When we reached the coatroom, a landing halfway up the stairs, she put on a thin jacket and hung a purse on one shoulder. This morning, she explained as we stepped off the barge, she would show me how to shop for groceries.

Up on the street, I couldn't help noticing that people stared at the pair we made. I thought Nicole absurd for dressing up to food shop, for wearing heels and a shiny evening purse that thwacked against her bony hip. It was embarrassing. But after we had walked a few blocks I realized that every woman was wearing heels and carrying shiny purses, even women juggling toddlers, purchases, and sometimes a little dog on a leash. Only in an occasional cluster of tourists moving from one bridge to the next were there women who wore sandals or sneakers or untucked shirts. Though it was only just ten (the thin strokes of a clock reached us from somewhere upriver), the sun beat down fiercely, and I marveled at these women who moved past swiftly in dark clothes and pantyhose, who fit heat-swollen feet into narrow shoes, with neither sweat nor grimace. I wore a T-shirt, track shorts, and flip-flops and was still uncomfortable.

The occasional pulses of traffic stirred up a wind hotter than the air. Nicole moved even more quickly than the rest. I realized that *I* embarrassed *her*.

"*Il fait chaud*," I ventured.

"*Oui, oui. Il fait chaud*," she said, without turning back to me, as if I were one of the men slouching against the river wall trying to get her attention. Then she slowed and said perfectly clearly, as I gained ground, "I adore this heat."

"Me too," I said, which wasn't true, but I didn't know many negatives and negatives made room for a whole conversation and *Il fait chaud* was about as complex as I wanted things to get.

She tried to tell me something else. I thought she said the heat reminded her of her childhood. But when I asked where she was from, she looked at me suspiciously. "I've lived in Paris for nearly thirty years," she said, then added reluctantly, "but I come from a town in the south."

"What town?"

"You've never heard of it."

She veered off the sidewalk, then, and swiftly crossed the street. I hurried to keep up. We passed a café, a dry cleaner's, a pharmacy, a bookstore. At the *oisellerie* there were birds stacked in wooden cages on the sidewalk, black roosters with scarlet crests and tongue-shaped wattles, white doves with long lacy tails. A man in oily coveralls rolled out another stack of square cages from inside the store, this one containing rabbits, white, gray, and cinnamon-colored rabbits, some hugely fat, some with ears so long they spilled onto the floor of their cage. Pigeons flocked, vying for position along the outside slats.

The smell of the cages pervaded the hot sidewalk. I could see how people were avoiding the stench, but I thought it was delicious.

"I'm sorry," I called, when I realized I'd come to a full stop. I hurried to Nicole, who was waiting in the shade of the next awning.

She muttered something, and when she saw I hadn't understood told me simply and slowly that the birds made her sad.

"*Oui,*" I said. I couldn't bring myself to say *moi aussi* again, because they made me elated. They made me feel I lived in a very exotic place, where in a matter of three steps the air could change from the smell of burnt diesel to the smell of a barnyard, where beneath one awning could be a cart of computer manuals and beneath the next a crate of fowl, where the world could shift centuries within a half block.

When we reached the supermarket, she pointed out a row of shopping carts. I removed one and wheeled it to the entrance, stopping on the rubber mat before the closed door.

"What are you doing?" she said behind me, after a few moments. "It doesn't work by itself. You have to go like this"—and she took the cart from me, swung it around, and backed into the door—"like everyone else."

When she was insulting me, I always managed to understand Nicole.

Inside the store she gave back the cart. I headed right, toward the produce, but she quickly steered me left, explaining that fruits and vegetables are delicate and should go on top. It went on like this. She would ask me to pick out pasta or bottled water, and invariably I would choose the wrong type or size or brand. She asked me to get milk and I went toward the dairy section, but that was wrong too. Milk came in unrefrigerated boxes next to the cereal. With each error would come a lengthy explanation of exactly why she bought what she did.

When our number was called at the cheese counter, she receded and I stood alone with the ticket as the woman interrogated me about the cheeses Nicole had named and I now repeated. When it came to how much—in kilograms—of each I wanted, I turned back to Nicole. But she wouldn't help. She stood behind the gathering crowd of women, looking directly through me. A few people began to grumble. I blushed, then began to sweat from all the blushing. Finally I held up a triangle of fingers. When it was all over, I squeezed my way back to Nicole; she said *"Très bien"* without a hint of sarcasm and pointed me toward produce.

I thought this section would be the easiest, but by then I had lost even my ability to judge a good tomato from a bad and was sent back to the crate to empty the bag and start again.

Nicole made me nervous. She made me miserable. I knew if she asked me my own name I would not be able to say it correctly.

In the checkout line I began to worry about getting it all home. I wanted to ask but remembered my French teacher being very particular about the two verbs, to bring and to take, and I was certain I would use the wrong one.

She handed me a check just as the cashier announced the total. It was an incredibly long series of numbers, of which I heard only the number five. It was five hundred and something francs and something centimes.

"Comment?" I asked with mild curiosity, as if I had only missed one numeral.

He repeated the same string of digits and, seeing my pen still poised after the word *cinq,* pointed to the total on the register. I froze. I felt the line grow longer behind me. I didn't know how to write 598,67. I had forgotten. I could hear the sounds in my head but had no letters for them. I felt the blood rushing up again. I could not do it. I could not.

"I don't know," I said to Nicole, and handed her the pen.

"You've got to learn your numbers. You've got to practice," she said, when we were out on the street. "You've got to write each one fifty times."

I wanted to tell her that I'd known my numbers before I walked into the store, that she made me so panicked I couldn't think, that I'd had one slice of pizza since I'd landed in this country and that was nearly sixteen hours ago. It was then I remembered the groceries. We had none of them and were halfway home.

"The food!" I cried, delighted that for once we'd finally done something foolish together.

I laughed too loudly and she told me to *ssss*. She explained something, but I didn't understand until later in the afternoon when all the groceries were delivered in boxes right to the kitchen floor.

Starting the following Monday, she told me, as she showed me exactly where each item belonged, I was to do all the shopping myself. She would sign the check in advance and I would take it to the store alone.

The next morning I got up at five-thirty, turned on a light at the dressing table, and began writing out numbers. I got all the way to *cent quarante-huit* before it was time to wake up the children for their second day of school.

Two Evenings

IT WAS AGREED THAT FIVE NIGHTS OUT OF THE WEEK I WOULD MAKE SUPPER FOR THE children. Their parents often had a dinner engagement, or they ate late at one of the small restaurants across the bridge. Occasionally they passed through the kitchen on their way out as I was doing the dishes: Nicole painted, silked, and stunning; Marc wet-haired and razor-nicked.

Despite his height, his white shirts, bright ties, and custom suits of charcoal or olive, Marc was not a handsome man. I often wondered why Nicole, with her aesthetic vigilance, her swift verdicts on appearance, her intolerance of Lola's best friend Francine and her *tête d'iguane,* and her unconcealed appreciation of the chiseled face of Odile's boyfriend Alexandre, would have selected such an unassuming spouse. But there was something about Marc that kept you looking. His was not a beautiful face—it was too thin, too full of juts and hollows and topped by tufts of wiry, incorrigible hair—and yet you kept looking because if you turned away and looked back it would be changed, still unalluring, but changed. He seemed never to wear the same expression twice, nor ever to match those expressions with his words or movements or the wanderings of his eyes. From the start I studied that protean face, patiently waiting for the one configuration that would make him a handsome man: the static, classic cut Nicole would have married.

Marc worked long hours at the hospital, and when he was home he was usually in his study. We didn't meet until the morning of my second working day, when I found him in the kitchen at six. He was wearing the bottoms of a pair of pajamas and sitting beneath the light of the single lamp that hung low over the table. He greeted me with a routine *bonjour,* as if I were entirely familiar to him, though from his unfocused glance I knew he had not yet seen me. I told him my name and stuck out my hand to rouse him. He stood abruptly and scrambled to gather up all his notes and fat medical books. "Please," I began, but he interrupted.

"I had completely forgotten. The *rentrée*. Excuse me." His long pale chest, flecked with a handful of blond curlicues, flushed a deep salmon color below the pronounced ring of his collarbone. He moved quickly to cover himself behind the stack he made. At the threshold he turned around, startled again to find me still standing there. He peered over his pile of paperwork lodged in every direction between the books, the top sheets secured by his chin. His brow was raised in folds and his mouth on the verge of speech, but he spun around again and vanished down an unlit hallway.

Sunday nights, Nicole had explained, would be different from the rest of the week. We would all eat dinner together, a meal Nicole would prepare with me as helper. After only three days, Sunday was an assault on my routine. I'd quickly grown possessive of the kitchen, where I spent so much of each day. Already I knew it intimately: the smooth cobalt counters, the row of glass cupboards trimmed white by an unsteady hand, the chinked corners of the stone table, and the flaking grooves beneath every drawer handle against which bottles had been pried open. The kitchen was unlike the rest of the house; it contained none of the dark ornate museum pieces of the other rooms around which I gingerly moved. The kitchen, especially on afternoons when the sun spilled through the large southern window or, lingering on the river, kicked up upon the ceiling quavery loops of light, had the feel of a neglected cottage by the sea. But sharing it with Nicole drained it of its peace.

Nicole cooked in a frenzy with no apparent enjoyment. From the earliest stages of preparation, everything was always about to be improperly measured, poorly sifted, badly blanched, or indelicately deglazed. Most of the vocabulary for this work I didn't even know in English, and Nicole's frustration with my ignorance never abated. Only occasionally, in the midst of all her self-created turmoil, did Nicole surprise me. She called the sautéing mushrooms *coquettes* when they popped grease at her, and when I diced instead of julienned the turnips, she said glibly, *"Bon, c'est plutôt à la américaine,"* and threw them in the pan anyway. These moments of forgiving levity were rare, though I was thankful for each one.

When everything was ready, I transferred the food to the platters Nicole had retrieved from locked cabinets and took them out to the long dining room table. I called *"À table,"* and eventually everyone came but Nicole, who finally reemerged after the rest had been seated and served. She wore a different shirt, and the top strands of hair that the heat had coiled were smoothed down. She looked and behaved as if she'd had nothing to do with the making of the meal. She stood behind her chair and exclaimed how delicious it all looked, then, sitting, received with great gurgles of appreciation each platter passed to her. When Marc complimented the tenderloin and Odile the potato *galette,* dishes I was certain they had been eating for years, Nicole deferred immediately to me and I was given a series of insincere compliments.

After a few minutes, the conversations grew too difficult for me to follow. They overlapped or took hairpin turns or were full of words I suspected were names or places but was never sure which. I felt my breathing grow less shallow, and halfway through the meal I began to enjoy the food. They had forgotten me, and I felt snug and warm in my blanket of incomprehension. I had always wanted to go to France to learn the language, but instead I'd come and lost my own. Finally I was free of the need to explain anything to anyone.

But before I could nestle in further, I realized that the whole table was looking at me. Someone had obviously addressed me. "Excuse me?"

"Where are you from in the United States?" Marc repeated, picking out the asparagus from the vegetable sauté.

"From all"—I hesitated. *Over.* I searched for a word: —"places."

His lips parted with another question, but Nicole said, "Ah, the classic American childhood," which seemed to settle the matter.

"I had an American friend once," Lola said. "Do you remember, Maman, when we went to Saint-Malo that summer and we played that game on the rocks?"

"No."

"Yes, and we kept eating all those peanuts and she had a bright blue bikini."

"Your mother doesn't like to remember anything before next week," Marc said.

"That's not true, Papa," said Guillaume.

"Why did you live in so many different places?" Odile asked.

"Her father was in the army, I imagine," Nicole said.

"No," I said.

"Your parents are divorced then," she said.

"My mother is dead." I'd never taken relish in the delivery of those words before. There was a general lowering of eyes in belated sympathy, though Nicole still regarded me with surprise, as if she had not believed that those predictable American lives could end.

Here I'd normally insist that condolence was not necessary for I'd only been a few months old at the time and had no memory of loss. What sadness I felt was for my sister, who had been six. Since then, my father had had a steady stream of girlfriends, and over the years I'd learned little more about my mother than a few expressions she'd had, which my sister imitated when we were children playing house and she insisted, as she always did, on being the mother. *Hot damn!* was one. *Wakey, wakey* was another, spoken softly in my ear after a pretend nap. But the moment had already passed for me to explain any of this, so I kept my head bowed down to my plate and tried but failed to remember any more of my mother's words.

It was then that Guillaume knocked the glass over the edge of the table. I watched my own hand drop the fork and catch the glass just before it tumbled into my lap. A few drops spilled from either side onto my fingers, but otherwise it was still a full glass of water. I'd never had great reflexes or coordination, but my body was still protecting what was no longer there.

"Bravo!" Marc looked straight in my eye for the first time with the face of a usually undelighted child who has finally found something to marvel at. He called me *leste* and Lola helped define the word and everyone but Nicole reenacted the save.

All too quickly, however, I lost the thread of conversation again and they all seemed to drift in their chairs far away from me and I was no longer comfortable in my isolation. This time I struggled to keep up: Guillaume had a new math teacher with some sort of beard; Marc said something about beards that made the children laugh; Guillaume said something else which made no one laugh, though Nicole smiled encouragingly. There was mention of a place they would all go to next Saturday, some château out in the country.

"Even Rosie?" Lola asked.

I felt like the new pet, whose behavior on long car trips was still in question.

"Of course Rosie," Marc answered. He made me feel as if I'd been their only *fille* all along.

"I can't go," Odile announced. "Alexandre called today and asked me to a dinner."

"When? I didn't hear the phone," Nicole said.

"You were upstairs," Odile said.

"When did he call?"

"Around two."

"I wasn't upstairs at two."

"I don't know, Maman. Maybe it was three. But he called. I didn't call him."

And then, after a few unfamiliar words strung together too quickly or spoken too softly, I was plunged back into darkness.

I examined the various styles of speech. Guillaume's was precise, and he was by far the easiest to understand, even easier than Lola, who, when not speaking exclusively to me, tended to ball everything up in her excitement to say it. Odile and her mother spoke in almost exactly the same way, in the tone and rhythm of the women I heard shopping in the specialty shops where Nicole sent me for olives from Nyons or paté from Strasbourg. Theirs were beautiful, fluid voices, devoid of the unanticipated hitches, blunders, and gushes of real people. It was Marc who spoke with all of those. He stammered, then rambled, yet more seemed left unsaid. He was never satisfied when he came to the end of a sentence, as if it were a foreign language for him as well.

Nicole was mouthing something to me, but not in the exaggerated way required for comprehension. Eventually all other conversation stopped, and though her discretion had failed, she still did not speak up. She just gave her plate a little shove and I understood it as my cue to clear.

When I reached the kitchen and saw that the cheeses had been unwrapped and arranged on a plate, I realized that was exactly what she had been saying: *le fromage.*

After cheese, I brought out a raspberry tart that I carried to Nicole, who served the slices from her seat. She cut fat wedges for Marc and each of her children, nothing for herself, and a paper-thin slice for me.

As I received the plate, Lola mumbled something to her mother. Nicole leapt up, yanked Lola out of her seat, swatted her on the rear, and sent her to her room. She came back to her seat and apologized directly to me.

Marc glowered at Nicole, his face crimson, but he said nothing.

"Lola said you weren't as fat as you looked," Guillaume said to me with deliberate slowness.

"Guillaume!" Nicole whined gently, amused, as if he had told a very funny but very dirty joke.

There was a painting on the wall across from my seat that I'd been aware of during the meal. I forced my eye upon it now. It seemed to me a Caribbean scene, though it could have been anywhere with white sand and turquoise water. In the shallows two large women were bent over their washing, their bright skirts trailing in a wave that had just broken. A third woman stood upright, holding her skirt in one hand and the long cloth she was washing in the other. She was turned toward the other two, whose faces could not be seen, and she was laughing. The paint had been applied thickly, and the colors—the piercing blues and whites of the sea, the primary stripes of the skirts, the lean black arms, and the red of the upright woman's lips—had texture and weight. I could smell the soap and the salt; I could feel the clear warm water swirl at her ankles. The bent women were singing. At moments like these, when I was trapped and humiliated during the Sunday dinner, I strained to hear their song.

Much later that night, Lola came out of her room and slipped into mine. She stood beside the bed where I lay with the light on but no book in my hand.

Lola's face was so pale I could see a web of veins at her temple. Despite her long smooth neck and the Snoopy on her nightshirt, she looked terribly old.

She began to cry before she could speak.

I let her stand there a long while.

Go, I thought, *just go.* I didn't want to help her, care for her, grow attached to her. But she just stood there, rolling the edge of my bedspread between her fingers. Finally I stopped their fidgeting with my own.

"It doesn't matter," I said, squeezing hard. *Ça ne fait rien.* It was an expression Lola had taught me that morning, and I'd repeated it again and again because I'd wanted to be able to say one thing exactly like a French person. We had practiced the *r*, the collapsing of the vowels, the hand gesture and facial contortions that went with it. *"Ça ne fait rien,"* I said again, exaggerating everything, and Lola crawled up onto the bed to hug me.

There was so much I would have liked to tell her, but even if I'd had the words I couldn't have spoken then, for the smell of Lola's hair, the weight of her head on my chest, and the small hand gripping my arm made it difficult even to breathe.

As promised, the following Saturday afternoon we went out to the country, to friends of theirs called d'Aubry. Odile had her own party to go to, so we all fit in Marc's car.

On the French highways, signs are blue, not green, and their letters more rounded and shiny white. I was amazed at how quickly the city fell away, replaced on either side of the car by fields, separated by long empty roads leading to villages of which I could see, in the distance, only the tip of a spire or a cluster of flat roofs. I sat between Guillaume and Lola in the back seat. No one had spoken for a long while, and the only sound was the lock on the car's door that Guillaume pulled up and pushed down, pulled up and pushed down. I would have liked to tell him to stop, but my efforts at disciplining Guillaume often displeased Nicole, though if I said nothing she would eventually turn around and scold him herself.

Nicole held the steering wheel firmly in two hands, never changing her grip, not even for bends in the road. Marc sank deeper into the passenger seat, his fingers half laced in his lap unwillingly, as if he could find no better place for them. The loneliness of married life astounded me. They had not exchanged a word for nearly an hour, since they decided who would drive, and now in the lengthening silence and draining light of this Saturday afternoon, the possibility of laughter or any kind of communication between them seemed remote.

"*Arrête,* Guillaume!" Nicole snapped finally, shooting a quick impatient glance at me in the rearview mirror.

Off the highway, the roads narrowed and buckled, then turned to dirt. The d'Aubry château sat abruptly at the end of a driveway of white pebbles. We did not approach the enormous door but followed a path lit by lanterns around to the back of the house. Here there were gardens that led into gardens, each a prelude for the next more spectacular one. There was no way of seeing clearly to the end. The boundary of the first garden, closest to the house, set up with white wrought-iron chairs and glass tables, was defined by scrolled shrubs and a gated doorway at the other end. Three families had gathered for dinner: the d'Aubrys, the Lalliers, and my family, the Tivots.

The two other *jeunes filles* were sharing a cigarette on the rim of the fountain in the middle of the garden. Above them, a pair of granite children struggled with a fish twice their size. Water trickled from its wide mouth down its belly into the pool below. The *filles'* bracelets fell jangling as they took turns raising their fingers to their lips. They both had on black dresses and spoke to each other in a limited but careful French with the crisp overenunciation of the women who employed them. I'd contracted instead Lola's slurred slang: I said *ouai* instead of *oui, bouquin* instead of *livre, bagnole* instead of *voiture,* and often dropped the *ne* in negative sentences. After a series of questions, Mme. Lallier commented on this.

"Hasn't she started at the Sorbonne?" she asked Nicole.

"No, she's not attending classes this term."

Mme. Lallier looked at her inquisitively, for everyone knew there was something illegal about employing a foreign *fille* who didn't go to school.

Nicole ignored the implication. "She studies in her room for hours on end, often before the sun comes up and nearly all day while the kids are at school. I'm sure she'll run rings around those at the Sorbonne by springtime."

Though I'd understood every word, I feigned an unconcerned obtuseness. I wanted no debts to Nicole.

The children had run off together around the other side of the house, and the men stood talking above the bottles of liquor M. d'Aubry had brought out to a table.

Mme. Lallier lustily eyed the plate of stuffed artichoke hearts put down beside her but did not reach to taste one. Though she was the same height as Nicole, she had a long waistless torso and lumpy ankles that made her appear far shorter. "Leyla," she said, glancing toward the fountain, "has already placed into the *cours superiéur.*"

Nicole tilted her head in polite surprise.

"She's that one there. With the long legs."

Below such short dresses, both pairs of legs seemed exceedingly long.

I could feel Nicole prodding me with her eyes to go over and meet them. She wanted me to have friends, dates, and soirées like Odile, but I'd stayed in every night since my arrival. I knew my place was at the fountain, but what was there to say?

"Is she Spanish?" I asked.

"Leyla? No, no. She's from Istanbul," Mme. Lallier said, fascinated by her own words.

Mme. d'Aubry murmured her approval. "And I thought I was exotic with a Dane."

The two *filles,* oblivious to this conversation and having finished their cigarette, now tested the water with their fingers. To reach it, they each had to lean way over; their long straight hair, blond and black, spilled over the side while their feet were lifted high off the ground. There was a small shriek and they straightened up laughing. One had splashed the other.

"They're beautiful girls, aren't they?" Nicole said, as if admiring figures in a painted scene. I was relieved I hadn't gone over and marred the spectacle.

"It's funny," Mme. d'Aubry said to her. "You can only hear your Provençal accent in a few words, can't you? I don't know why you try to disguise it."

Nicole scowled playfully as she denied the accusation, but she didn't manage to disguise her irritation at the comment.

"I don't hear it at all," Mme. Lallier said tactfully, then looked with relief as she saw the husbands coming with their cocktails.

The three women were handed drinks in slender glasses and took seats on the sloping edges of the wrought-iron chairs while the men moved to the garden's east boundary, where M. d'Aubry pointed out various buildings on the neighbor's property, barely distinguishable now in the dim light. Marc stood a good deal taller than the other men and hung his head like a drooping flower to listen.

The *filles* remained at the fountain and there was no place for me to go but toward them. Then I heard, miraculously, Lola calling my name from around front and hurried to her.

Five children stood in line at the edge of the driveway. Lola beckoned me over, but before I could inquire, Claude d'Aubry, who looked about Odile's age, came zigzagging toward them on his dirt bike with Guillaume on the seat behind him.

"I'm next! I'm next!" Lola shouted, and swung herself on. I told her it was a bad idea, but all three d'Aubry children insisted they did it every weekend they came out here.

When they came back, Lola's hair was blown to one side, her cheek pressed against Claude's shoulders, her arms locked tight around his waist. She didn't hesitate, but I could feel how she didn't want to get off so soon. Guillaume claimed it was his turn again and got on before the two little Lallier boys could stop him.

When they had gone, Lola tried to describe how it felt to ride the pitted trail through the woods across the street.

After a while, one of the boys said, "They've been gone twice the time anyone else has."

And a few minutes after that, the other said, "Now it's triple."

When they came back, Claude was walking the bike and Guillaume was crying beside him. He made no sound but his face was in the contortions that by this time I knew well. I didn't understand one word of Claude's explanation and waited for Lola to translate. They had skidded. It was nothing, but Guillaume had refused to get back on or be left to walk on his own. Claude, disgusted with the lot of them, wheeled his bike back to the barn.

We tried to stop Guillaume from running to his mother, but it was no use. As Lola and I came into the garden she was wiping his face with a cocktail napkin. She was livid. I braced myself.

But Nicole looked past me to Claude behind us.

"Do you have a license to drive a motorcycle?" she called.

"It's not a motorcycle, Maman," Lola said.

Nicole kept her eye fixed on Claude. "It *is* a motorcycle."

The men at the edge of the garden turned, and their pale faces began to float closer through the sudden darkness. Guillaume stood beside his mother's chair but no longer touched it, his eyes cast down.

Claude in fact never had to speak. His mother, M. Lallier, and several of the children all leapt in at once. But Nicole was not daunted by the opposition. I didn't need to understand the words to hear what was said. It was all done without raised voices or accusatory fingers. Drinks were refilled and the artichoke hearts passed around, but Nicole got the argument she wanted. Eventually, people began to listen to Marc, who had been muttering from the beginning, *Laissez tomber, laissez tomber,* and stopped responding to her. After Mme. d'Aubry had insisted that the dinner would be spoiled if they didn't come in that minute, Nicole made her last remark, very nearly under her breath as she put down her full glass. It was something about the raising of children, and it made the other adults recoil visibly.

At the table, Marc followed the conversation with belated glances at the speaker. His face reflected the reactions of others without having grasped the topic. I felt his detachment as if it were my own.

But for Nicole, the incident had been a purging, and she now entertained the table with a long story about the prime minister's sister. M. Lallier giggled through his nose, while M. d'Aubry chortled so deeply it caused him to cough; Mme. Lallier honked like a goose, and Mme. d'Aubry laughed in silent seizures with tears rolling down her cheeks. When they had all pulled themselves together they looked at Nicole fondly, less with forgiveness than in sheer gratitude. At the end of the night she was kissed warmly by the women and held a bit too long by the men. The flush of her face gave her skin a burnished luster and her dark blond hair gleamed its thousand shades beneath the single lamp in the hallway. By the time she was through with her good-byes and afterthoughts, Marc had already started the car. I sat alone in the back seat; the children lingered on the lawn with their friends until the last possible second.

The barrier of language closed down around me like bars. Until this moment I'd enjoyed the impossibility of communication. Without words, I was released from the basic obligations of courtesy and social interaction. At dinner, I'd overheard Guillaume telling the other *filles* that I didn't speak much French, thus setting me free from anything but occasional sympathetic smiles across the kids' end of the table. And Nicole would never know that I'd heard her speech in my defense at the beginning of the evening. In this way, life could be kept extraordinarily simple. But now, just for a few seconds, I would have liked to slip through the barricade in order to say something to Marc. I would have liked to see his head knocked back by a brief laugh, for when he laughed he looked like Lola and was full of the same delight and hope she carried, as if his adulthood were still ahead of him.

Nicole's shoes crunched in the gravel behind us. I remembered Mme. d'Aubry's comment about her southern accent. I wondered when she came to Paris. Clearly she had worked hard at becoming the kind of person who could tell a story about the prime minister's sister at a château just outside the city. Marc had mentioned his mother in Neuille, and his sister in Munich. But I had never heard Nicole speak of relatives anywhere, just as she had never heard me speak of mine.

Seeing their mother, the children leapt into the car, continuing an argument. Lola punched Guillaume and he punched back, shoving Lola into me. I shouted "Hey!" louder than I'd planned. The unexpected English made them stop and imitate me. "Hey!" "Hey!" they cried to each other. I could tell, though I didn't know exactly how, Marc was smiling. Perhaps it was his head, which gave a little toss, or his shoulders, which shook slightly. Perhaps it was nothing visible at all.

He reached over to switch on the radio.

"*S'il te plaît,*" Nicole said, and snapped it off.

He said something gently, beseechingly, and Nicole did not counter him when he turned it back on. He found a station playing "The Boxer" by Simon and Garfunkel. One whole summer, the summer after fourth grade, my sister and I listened to nothing else but this one album, lying on the floor of our room and memorizing all the words written on the back cover. I was relieved to hear that they were still only on the first verse. It was painful not to sing along. I almost wished Nicole had succeeded in shutting it off, though I enjoyed the sudden conspiracy with Paul and Art, whose lyrics only I could understand. I worried that Lola would ask, as she often did, what the song was about and I would have to speak in French and then it would be over. But Lola was too tired and soon fell asleep against me. Guillaume followed, sinking slowly into Lola's lap.

We swished on through curved roads toward the highway, through strands of mist that rose up over the windshield at the last moment. I mouthed the words to the song, grateful for the feel of them on my lips. In the silence that followed, I could hear in my head the next song on the record. Then they played it. They were playing the whole album.

Lola shifted position against me. "You have a beautiful voice," she muttered. I hadn't realized it was audible.

Up front, Nicole's head rocked from side to side until, as they turned onto the highway, it slid onto Marc's shoulder. He stroked her hair tentatively, then, sensing the depth of her sleep, with more confidence.

I sang them back to Paris.

La Sequana sat ringed in opals of swollen light. We moved through the watery haze in a small cluster, as if still confined to the car, and while we waited for Marc to unlock the door with the long black key that hung on a nail above it, the wet air fell on our bare hands and faces and traveled through our bodies as we breathed.

Lola leaned on me heavily. The night was absolute around us, so shrouded and close and damp that I saw in Lola's half dreams Claude riding toward her in the rain on an old bicycle.

"But I don't really love him," Lola murmured, and for once I was the only one to understand her.

Marcelle

LUCIE AND I HAVE SOUP AND BREAD, AN OVAL LOAF I BOUGHT THAT MORNING INSTEAD of the usual baguette, which has made her smile because yesterday she told me about the oval loaves her mother used to bake at this time of year, the end of spring. The day has stayed cold. Clouds we thought would burn off by noon have only bloated, squatting on their heavy haunches above us.

We planned to eat quickly and get back to the garden but her hands won't warm. She looks angrily out at the sky, then back down at her fingers. To straighten them causes her a pain she tries to conceal from me.

I get up to light the fire beneath the kettle and, when it boils, pour the water into a wide breakfast cup, which will soothe her hands when they hold it.

She has been nearly silent all day, but now the tea flushes her face and heals her hands and I know she wants to talk. I worry what she might ask and what I might tell her, so I quickly circumvent: I hold up a photograph I found in the drawer by my bed. It is a young woman alone, in a plain white dress, leaning against the door of a stone barn. At her side, in her left hand, are flowers hanging upside down. Her gaze is stubbornly averted from the lens. "Who is she?"

Lucie takes the picture from me and holds it a long time. "Nicole's mother, Marcelle. When she died Nicole came to live with me for many years. The room you're staying in was hers. This was taken on Marcelle's wedding day."

"What was she like?"

"Ah," she says, shaking her head. She looks down at her hands, trying to stretch the fingers.

I pour her another cup of tea and wait for her to continue.

* * *

Her name was Marcelle Maunier, and she married Octave Guerrin when she was seventeen. He was from the next farm over, and their fathers had been planning the union since the evening their wives sat side by side and heavy-bellied in the Guerrins' garden. The agreement was not made in words exactly, but it was understood that if one was born a girl and the other a boy, the farms would be consolidated in the next generation. The women smiled, followed the curve of their taut stomachs with a lazy but careful hand—and each prayed fervently to God that hers was the boy.

Marcelle grew up alone in her house, but right next door were Octave, then Xavier, and finally Max Guerrin. They all headed off to the same schoolhouse in the morning and were put to chores in the afternoon. The boys often worked over on the Mauniers' farm, and Marcelle was called regularly to the Guerrins' to help in the kitchen or with all the laundry the boys produced. It wasn't exactly an even exchange—three boys for one girl—but the parents had removed the stone wall in their minds, once Octave and Marcelle had been delivered to them safely.

On her sixteenth birthday, her parents took Marcelle to Limne for dinner. It was July and they were seated outside in a courtyard with white pebbles on the ground that flushed pink, then scarlet, as the sun slipped into the dip between two blue hills. Before they left the house her father had pinned a gardenia to her dress, and now its smell hung before her in the humid air. She felt uncomfortable with her parents, whom she'd rarely seen beyond the boundaries of the two farms and her grandfather's porch, where she was served tea that smelled like a chimney fire and the most delicious chocolate wafers that dissolved on her tongue. She wished they were on that porch now, though her grandfather had died and her parents had sold his house in Roussillon, the house where he would nod to the sky and announce the arrival of the mauve hour and put the kettle to boil.

The restaurant owner came for their order. Marcelle watched his contempt dissipate as her mother ordered for them all with confidence and relish. She had once, long ago, lived in Avignon. They ate cold salmon mousse and stuffed lamb shoulders and a hot lemon soufflé. They drank white wine with the first course, red with the second, and a sweet champagne with dessert. The sky turned violet and her parents' faces softened, becoming the faces she had known when she was very young.

Her father held up his glass. "My precious daughter, whom we twice almost lost to sickness and now have had for many full, beautiful years, we thank the Lord for you every day. And we shall do so even more frequently this year, our last year with our only child."

Marcelle looked quickly to her mother, whom she could count on to explain her father's stories, to trace the lines of his ellipses. But this time her mother offered nothing but tears.

Marcelle pulled her mother's hands from her face and pleaded with her to explain, all the while suppressing an unexpected blend of panic and joy she felt at the suspicion that they were sending her away as her mother had been sent, perhaps to her father's godmother in Toulouse or to her mother's older sister, Aunt Anne, in Paris.

Instead, they told her she would marry Octave this time the following year. She refused. They insisted. She refused again. Her voice grew loud, and just as the owner appeared in the archway her mother slapped her.

"All right," said her father. "You do not have to marry Octave." He took another sip of his sweet champagne and by the time his Adam's apple had risen and fallen, she guessed it was a ploy.

"You think that if you forbid me to marry him, I'll want to, is that it?" She had never spoken to her father like this. But the thought of marrying Octave—the predictability that would envelop her, the routine, the precise repetition of their parents' lives. She pictured his hands working a knot for hours instead of simply cutting the rope. He would never cut the rope, never act on impulse or frustration. He would contain each and every surge of emotion. There would never be anything the least unexpected. And soon enough she would be as predictable and bland as he. And what if they had children—she couldn't let herself think of it further.

"No," her father said, "that's not it. You will marry Octave or you will marry one of his brothers. It will be shameful for you to marry younger, but if you are so hard set against Octave, who is the best of them, who is good and kind and honest, it is our only option. Though you are beautiful to us, my child, it will come as no surprise—"

"Why are you saying these things? What have I—?" But she could not continue, for she understood now. The land was all they had to offer her. It was what their whole lives had been leading up to, this gift.

Now she could see the pain in her father's eyes; she could see how it hurt him to perform this way, to bully her. She could not look at her mother; she could not yet forgive the blow that stung beneath her eye.

"I have no choice, then. This has been decided all around."

"You have a choice among three brothers."

She considered Xavier, the wild one. He had shaped himself precisely contrary to Octave. Where Octave was cautious, he was reckless; where Octave was grim, he was gleeful. He had passion and curiosity and a devilish, thin-lipped smile. But he was not an even keel. Xavier was one to meet on a train, flirt wildly with at a dance. He would make you laugh as he made love to you. And then he would make someone else laugh just as hard. He was unable to resist wielding his power.

She considered Max. Though only thirteen, he was tall and broad, already by far the most handsome of the three. He was a gentle, dreamy combination of his older brothers, with Xavier's passions turned inward, Octave's patience made contemplative. He wrote things in a leather notebook he had made and sang sweet songs to his little cousins. There would perhaps be a wait to marry him—three, or even four years. But how could she live on like that, waiting for her husband to grow up? How could she continue in the Guerrins' kitchen while her betrothed darted through with urchin friends all soaked from a swim in the quarry? How could she marry a man whose diapers she'd changed and washed, a man she'd taught the alphabet to, a man who'd sobbed in her arms on slaughtering days?

At least with Octave, she told herself, it would be a placid existence. She wouldn't be betrayed; she wouldn't be expected to mother him. She wouldn't disappoint her parents, who'd been good to her, who'd never resented her for being the girl in this inevitable bargain or for somehow blocking the path for more children. Her parents had carefully swallowed their disappointments so that her life would seem as simple and effortless as the rising of the half moon behind them.

"Octave," she said firmly. They lifted their heads and beamed with pleasure for her, as if the choice among three had been all the choice in the world, as if she herself had chosen to marry and whom and when.

This infuriated her the most, the way it quickly and permanently became her decision, the way at the wedding a year later she overheard them telling guests how she simply announced on the night of her sixteenth birthday that she would marry Octave Guerrin. People loved this story. It seemed to revive their faith in the necessary conviction that love lies no farther than your own backyard. Couples danced closer that night than they had in years; teenage girls looked across to the same group of boys they had seen every day of their lives with nascent curiosity, and the boys looked back.

No one but her father sensed Marcelle's despair. Because they willed it so, they saw a pleasant-looking girl (not a beauty, not even as a bride) achieve her dream. If she looked a bit wan, it was only due to her nervousness about the night ahead and the years to follow, about how to please this man she'd finally caught. But her father heard in her voice at the altar a voice he'd nearly forgotten, which, years earlier, had calmly asked where the belt was when it was not hanging from the nail by the stove and, after it was over, had uttered promises that were never broken. Once she'd charted the boundaries of right and wrong, she never transgressed. He wept then, while the voice continued, as he remembered his obedient child and the earnest face she'd lifted up to him as she offered him his belt. He danced with her first and yearned to hold her close, closer than any woman he'd ever held in his life. And even if the guests hadn't been watching, he couldn't have done this, for her arms and body were adamant, her feet made of stone. He was dancing with a smoothed-faced, open-armed statue who spoke to him still in that child's voice that claimed to understand punishment.

Why were they given the girl? He would never feel such things if he were Octave's father, who was beaming as he delivered glasses of hard cider and received slaps and pats and kisses.

But he had married Marcelle's mother out of love, and where were they now? As far apart as two humans could be. Suffering the same griefs had not drawn them closer but thrust them apart. He looked at his wife now, dancing with her cousin René. Her changeable eyes matched today the pale green of her dress. Once those eyes had been liquid and her emotions had floated within, perfectly visible, like bright fish in a clear sea. Now they were as depthless and opaque as ice. He saw that she and

René were singing to the music. He no longer liked her singing. Perhaps it was better to begin without expectation and to end without disappointment. Comforted by that thought, he moved from his spot against the wall toward the cider keg to congratulate the father of the groom once more.

Marcelle and Octave produced children, three girls, in rapid succession. Then the news of the Germans in Poland traveled up their hill and, right behind it, the call that beckoned its men away.

She watched him leave from the front window. She told him it would be too upsetting to stand at the station with the other women. He knew he was giving her her freedom now, though he didn't know in what ways he'd stolen it from her. His presence in the house elicited a recklessness he'd never seen before in Marcelle Maunier. He knew her, had always known her. She was, he'd thought, a lot like him. She was quiet and careful and prudent. If he came home a bit early for lunch and if she were in a window slicing apples or weaving her thick braid, he could stand unseen and watch her deft fingers, her unabating concentration, the swift precision of her movement, just as he had seen her through the windows of their mothers' kitchens all his life. But once he stepped into the house, the scene vanished. She became awkward and rigid; she made every excuse to be out of any room he entered. Once she took the children to the quarry and didn't return for lunch or dinner, and when he found them there, they were chasing the light of the moon in the black water. Sexually, she would reject him for weeks, sometimes months, then come to him in the afternoon, insistent and flushed, to lead him to a spot deep in the cherry orchard on what used to be her father's land. But she didn't enjoy it, didn't even seem to feel it, and afterward she drifted off ahead of him, pale and rigid again.

Did she imagine herself the only one to have made a sacrifice? Did she think this marriage, this life, was what he had wanted? He wished now they had spoken of these things. On the train he cried, two small tears he caught with his thumb before they spilled. He did not feel at that moment afraid of war or death or never seeing this station again. But out the window whole families gathered to wave brave and hopeful good-byes; wives and mothers cried openly; brothers and sisters and children kept their hands raised and swaying in bewilderment. He was not afraid of death, but he was afraid of not being missed or remembered. Even his parents were not here to see him off. They had accompanied Xavier and Max to their ship in Marseille.

Marcelle had stood in the window of their house and felt Octave pull the world apart, pull it wide open, with each footstep away from her. She buried her face in her youngest daughter's neck and hoped the child could not feel her smile.

Her daughters worked sedulously under her direction. Before the war she had forbidden Octave to put them to labor. She couldn't bear the thought of another generation harnessed to this land, but now there was no choice.

Octave wrote regularly, first from the front, later from prison camps, though his letters often arrived all at once after months of delay, and they wrote back all together at the long dining room table, with Monique, the oldest, as secretary, for she had the best penmanship, careful to keep the tone cheerful, careful not to mention Xavier's death or Max's disappearance. Soon their father became like a benevolent but poor uncle who wished them gifts but could send nothing but warm regards. He often wrote of various children he saw and compared them to his daughters, and by the third year of his absence it was clear that he no longer remembered that Marie-Jo was the one with the dead tooth, or that Monique got hives when she was angry, or that Juliette had the small ear, permanently curled tight like the shell of a garden snail. He began not only to confuse them but endow them with characteristics they never had. They weren't bothered by his confusion. In their own separate minds each fantasized about her father's return, and how beautiful and womanly he would find her.

Marcelle knew she was not like the other young wives with whom she stood in lines clutching ration tickets. They were ashen and aimless; their children skirted around them unremembered. They waited only for the news of their husbands' return.

Marcelle waited for the slip of paper coming up the hill in the hands of some youth. She knew it would happen. Soldiers had to move quickly, make decisions in a split second, be sharp and cunning and impulsive.

She was surprised that Octave had survived a day, let alone six months of combat. But he would not come back alive from internment. He grew weak and feverish if he missed lunch. She thought of him there, relying solely on his patience to get him through. She thought of him trying to recall the faces of his children and scrambling them. He would know he was forgetting them, and that would cause him more pain than anything else the war could inflict upon him. She wanted to remember one thing she missed about him, one thing to make her prayers for him more sincere, but she could not.

The day the Germans came to the house the air was thick with wet heat, and the smell of gardenia struck her as she climbed back up from the dairy farm empty-handed. She thought of the lavender dress she'd worn, the tables set in white stones. *They held the sky at our feet, those stones. Blood red, they were, when my father raised his glass.* Nine years had passed, but the flowers always returned her there, to the restaurant in Limne on her sixteenth birthday.

The shape of a German—the sharp epaulets, the tightly cinched waist, the bulbous thighs, the narrow booted calves—was a shape recognizable at any distance. She thought, at the sight of him, she'd stopped dead in her path. She thought she'd frozen in terror, but she was moving, sprinting to the house to reach it before he did. But there was already another inside, interrogating the girls. He had them lined up in the kitchen and placed his fingers under their chins when he asked them with the few French words he had learned where the hidden ones were. Marie-Jo was crying; Juliette stood silent and blanched; Monique was the only one who spoke, repeating over and over her sincere bewilderment at the question. When their mother appeared in the doorway, they flocked to her. The soldier reached for his gun. The other, clearly his superior with his fancy flat-topped hat, slipped past Marcelle and told him in perfect French to put it down. The soldier maintained his position, oblivious to the words. The officer spoke again, harshly, in German, and the weapon was lowered. The officer turned to Marcelle, who was aproned in daughters. She wondered if her girls knew they were holding her upright. She managed to look straight at him.

He asked her a series of questions: where did their land begin and end, how many barns were there, what did they raise, did they have help, had they or were they now hosting strangers? He asked her these questions and she answered, but all the while she felt they were saying other things. She felt light-headed, as fear began slowly to drain out of her. Her children held her tighter.

Then he fired a command at the soldier, who straightened up, saluted, and moved rigidly off toward the back of the house. Caught on the heel of his boot was a little pink duckling that Juliette had made for the cat out of yarn. It bobbed wildly behind his stiff walk. They all saw it at the same time but the officer was the first to laugh, a strange short chortle that gave way to deep wheezes—a laugh that had been welling up for days, perhaps for the whole war. The soldier turned around, having reached for his gun instinctively. His officer, suddenly sober, barked at him, and he continued toward the back. At the sight of the duckling bobbing once more, the officer was plunged into another fit of convulsions and had to reach out to the kitchen counter for support. In the days that followed, while the girls re-created more and more terrifying versions of their interrogation by the Boches, it was the laughter in her house that Marcelle remembered most vividly.

They watched the Germans leave from the same window that had framed Octave's departure. Just before the bend in the path, the soldier looked down. He raised his leg but, before he could unfasten the yarn, he lost his balance and had to put his leg back down. After three attempts, the officer, who'd been waiting farther on, backtracked to help. They could see he was grinning still. While the soldier steadied himself with a hand on his back, the officer leaned down, gingerly removed the pink duckling, and put it in his breast pocket. Then they both straightened up and walked on out of sight.

After that, he was ubiquitous, that officer: on the terrace of the Café Plaire as she stood in line at the butcher's, in a car at the turn up her road as she made her way home, inspecting the dairy farm when she tried again for cheese and butter they'd already sold to the black market. She never saw him with that soldier again, or with anyone else. He was always alone. He never acknowledged her, never made the slightest intimation that they had met, that he had once laughed in her house. She wondered if the pink duckling was still in his left pocket.

She rapidly withdrew from contact with her neighbors. People had begun to denounce resisters. The Valois boy, whose clubfoot prevented him from going to war, had been reported as aiding the Maquis, the militant arm of the Resistance, and was taken off in the morning and delivered home at night with mayflies sewn in the empty sockets of his eyes. Many openly assisted the new government. The widow Dupin had let the Milice and the Waffen SS entertain in the unused portion of her house and less than a week later was found swinging from her kitchen ceiling, hanged either by informed Maquis or the Milice itself for fear that she had heard too much. Marcelle avoided her parents and in-laws as well, for they could not relinquish the image of Pétain as their hero. He had saved them in the last war; he knew what he was doing. Still, while she was careful to ignore the rest of the world, she could not help but hear about the Germans who occupied their town.

The officer was apparently a commander of sorts. He lived on the second floor of the Hôtel Pons. He did not drink alcohol. He read only French books. Could he have relieved Christian Valois of his eyeballs? Could he have kicked the chair from beneath widow Dupin's small feet? And the execution of the town's police force, of which her cousin Alphonse had been a part, could that have been his idea upon arrival? She wished she could see him committing these crimes. Instead, she saw him with a lemon water in the shade of an umbrella, reading Gide, or stroking the silky backs of the black cats that sidled up to him at the dairy.

She began to wish for her husband's return, but each time her silent prayers were shattered by the sound of laughter in her house.

She saw him standing at the announcement board. No one else was in the street, and she walked toward him. She told herself to stop and turn back around, but she could not. He was studying a schedule for the cinema in Alt and wearing what he always wore. But it was no longer the crisp, sinister uniform from the propaganda posters that were pasted on the old walls of their town. She willed that image back but it wouldn't come. She knew now that his slate-gray trousers were the color of his eyes.

She stood at his right, feigning interest in the marriage announcement of Lucie Peyraud to Émile Quenelle. Nobody had had the heart to take it down, though they'd only been married three weeks before Émile had gone off and been killed. Staring straight ahead, she asked, "Do you have that duckling in your pocket still? My cat is quite forlorn without it."

He turned to her, expecting a madwoman beside him. His face softened when he saw it was her. "A duckling?"

"You wouldn't be delivering anything into the hands of the enemy. Brigitte the cat is a dyed-in-the-wool Pétainiste."

She spoke quickly and his smile was delayed by the translation. When it came, her chest swelled and each strong pulse of her heart seemed to lift her briefly off the ground. She leaned against the board for balance.

"*Die klein Enterich.*" He chuckled, reaching for it. She watched his fingers fish gently in his breast pocket, and though she knew it was in the left, not the right, she dared not say so. *Die klein Enterich.* It didn't frighten her. Up close it was a quiet language, a kind language. He fixed his eyes on her as he fumbled in one wrong pocket, then another. He had long eyelashes and the beginnings of a beard that looked like it had been singed by the sun late in the day. She could feel the sound it would make against her palm. He was younger than she'd thought. She held his gaze, aware that she was not beautiful and that her profile was slightly more alluring but also aware that, with this man, she would never be able to behave with diffidence or insincerity. When he moved to search the fat left pocket, he said, "Please," indicating that he needed help in emptying it. She held out her hands, imagining bullets or small folding knives or vials of acid that might leak onto her skin. She became aware of the absence of footfall and chatter in the street. People were taking detours through town. No one would come to her rescue. "Don't worry," he said, "I don't have a corpse in here."

He pulled out an enormous wad of torn paper. At first she thought it was shredded lists, names now dealt with, but as she looked closer, she saw they were cinema stubs, perhaps a hundred of them, perhaps more. She giggled and the pile trembled in her hands. Some of the tiny pieces flipped to the ground.

At the bottom of the pocket was the duckling. He handed it to her with a stern face, but she could see him struggling against a grin. "Have you ever seen a film?"

"Yes, of course."

"But you would never want to see one accompanied by a German."

"No."

To take the toy she had to drop her handful and she walked away while he was still bent over, picking up his bits of paper, his hundred nights or more, off the ground.

When she got home, she locked herself in the bedroom to wait for the strange pain to subside. She sat on the chair by the wardrobe and felt the wetness. She lifted her skirt and pulled down her underclothes. It was not blood. For the first time in her life she reached down to where her mother had told her it was bitter luck to touch. It was swollen and soaked. She kept touching and the pain doubled. She jerked her hand away but something drew it back. Soon there was no pain, only an imperious need to keep touching. She could not stop. She heard a whacking sound, she heard her own breath, she felt her mouth open and remain open. She knew she should stop, but she could not keep her hand from its circular path. She marveled at the wetness, the tenderness, the fierce need of her whole body that she continue. She didn't know where it would end. Would she spurt like a man? She could feel something approaching from within, something that couldn't possibly escape. But it had to. It had to. She brought the other hand to her shirt and unbuttoned. She pushed her palm against each breast, then squeezed the nipples with her fingers. Slowly and all at once she felt herself unfold, a million dark petals uncurling on the ocean's floor.

It wasn't a week after the Liberation before they came for her. They had come for so many that there was no shock. Her children knew—Monique had suspected it from the very beginning, as soon as Brigitte's pink toy reappeared. It was only Octave who protested in earnest. He had arrived home three nights earlier, in time to watch his father be shot on his knees, tied to a post in the center of town. He had been accused of delivering a message, one sentence, once, to Alt. They placed the note, unmistakably written in his own hand, between his fingers before they tied him up: *Colonel Hemmer still awaiting your word.* Octave watched and felt he almost willed the shots himself, three shots, a perfect triangle over his father's heart, one for each of the sons he betrayed. And now his wife. But, he thought, a woman did not instinctively love her country like a man. Still, he struggled with the intruders, demanded to know the accusations, and received a swift blow to his jaw from the butt end of a Resistance rifle.

It was his daughter Juliette, the silent one, who told him. She fetched a warm cloth for his wound. "Maman was with a German." *Was with,* not *helped.* Not *the* Germans but *a* German.

Five weeks later she was led back the eleven miles from Alt. Prodded by men on horseback she walked in bare feet, an oversized pair of black shorts, and a white cloth wrapped several times around to cover her breasts. She was relieved her family was not in the last and largest crowd she had to pass through, the crowd that lined the streets of Plaire. The women touched their hair and their husbands held them tighter as she came close. *Just like a man,* she heard someone whisper. A boy reached out to touch the tar on her chest. Another sang the Vichy anthem, *"Maréchal nous voilà, Notre Sauveur,"* until his mother clamped his mouth. She wondered which one in the crowd had seen them, which one had uttered her name and why. She focused on every gluttonous face. They thought she had been beaten senseless. They thought she'd lost her mind like so many others and couldn't recognize a smile—all of their unconcealed, ecstatic smiles.

Schadenfreude. He'd taught her that word. Joy derived from the pain of another. She hadn't believed such a word could exist. Had he known how well she would learn it? Had he given her the word for protection? Schadenfreude. She held it up before the greedy eyes and moved past. But his memory was contained in that crowd, not in her. They would remember far longer and more clearly the sharp crests of his cheekbones, the angle of his hat upon his head, his gait up a hill, and the way he held a book, tipping it slightly toward the sun while he remained in the shade. They would remember because fear is the most tenacious of all emotions.

The three girls watched their mother proceed up the hill.

"She looks like a goat," Juliette said, and though the other two said nothing, they saw she was right.

Monique and Marie-Jo tried first to remove the swastika, but the process was arduous and slow. Despite the strong solution they had mixed up, the tar would not loosen without hard strokes with a rough cloth that tore open the skin. Finally it was Octave who had the endless patience for the task.

That evening they ate dinner at the big table which, for five years, had been used only for writing letters to their father. Juliette broke her vow of silence and spoke to her mother, offering to help make a raspberry torte. Octave came to the table in his best suit, his wedding suit, which was now two sizes too big. Monique filled a tall jar with irises, and Marie-Jo wrapped a bright scarf around her mother's bare head. Out the window the sun burnished the sky from below the earth, and as the purple dark rushed in, the world glowed eerily.

"The mauve hour," Marcelle said, laying aside her knife and fork. Her daughters followed her outside, and for the first time she spoke to them of her grandfather and of the thin wafers and smoky tea he served her on his porch. "I'm going to find some of that tea and we'll have our own mauve hour." She looked down at their tinged faces, and they tried to look bravely back and not remember their own slain grandfather or their dead uncles or the bruises beneath their mother's dress. Behind her they could see their father in the window, a silhouette through the lambent glass, lighting his pipe. *So this is how it is,* he was thinking, *to stay behind.*

Their last child came to them the following year, and they gave her the name Octave had wanted to give every daughter before her, his favorite name: Nicole, which means victory.

Le Dix

"ROSIE," NICOLE SAID, FROM THE DOORWAY OF MY ROOM LATE ONE NIGHT. SHE WORE a red hourglass dress and gold necklace that had been hammered flat. "I'm sorry to bother you, but this is not healthy."

Nicole expected me to have a social life as active as hers. Other au pairs lived for the night, she said. Paris is such an exciting city, especially when you're young.

"You're going to make yourself sick here." She waved her arm at me sitting at my desk with my French textbook in front of me. "You could learn so much more French at a club!"

"But I don't know anyone to go out with," I said truthfully.

A few days later I got a call from an American named Leslie who was a friend of the long-legged Leyla. Leslie, it turned out, worked for Lola's friend Francine. She apologized for not calling sooner, then asked if I'd like to get a drink.

"Tonight?" It was a Wednesday.

"Yeah. After you put the kids down."

I had no good excuse, and Nicole was beside me, whispering, "*Oui, oui!*" so at half past nine I headed out to meet her at a bar called Le Dix. In my head, to Leslie whom I did not yet know, I unlodged my English, describing the family, the barge, the raised tub in my bathroom. I looked forward to commiserating about the trials of miscommunication and the humiliations of indentured servitude.

Ahead, the café at the corner was lit up and bustling. A few customers sat outside in winter coats, their hands wrapped around hot drinks. One man sat alone, picking his nose.

Mais c'est dingue ça, I thought as I passed. I liked the word *dingue.*

The next block was dark and vacant, every shop secured by a metal grille and padlock. The space outside the *oisellerie* was empty too, though a few feathers were stuck to the pavement. I stepped closer to the shop and listened. There was scratching and chirping and rustling, and after a little while I could make out the low steady cooing of the doves. Lola always touched a dove's tail for good luck. I wanted to tell Leslie every little detail of this street.

The metro stop was unmarked, a sudden flight of stairs descending beneath the sidewalk. A monthly pass came with the job, and I had used mine twice. I slid the orange ticket through the meter in the turnstile and hurried down the hallway marked Gare d'Austerlitz. There was only one line at this stop, so the passageways were small and without vendors or musicians, though the walls were plastered with the same enormous advertisements: on the left was a poster for an Italian movie, one large breast held in a man's hand, and on the right a yogurt ad. They were repeated for the entire walk to the rails. *Spoon, lip, smirk, litter, wind, corridor, wrist, nipple, wind, sign, trench coat, slouch.* I let English flood inside me as I rounded the corner.

On my side of the tracks there was only one man, pacing, but on the other side the plastic seats were filled with teenagers. They spoke loudly, with great echoes, and their laughter rose and fell and rose again. I listened, uncomprehending, envious. I sat at the cracked edge of a chair and pushed my hands into the shallow pockets of the pea coat I had bought when the weather turned cold. I thought of my sister and how we used to squat in the kitchen after school, our heels pressed hard to our groins to keep from peeing, one of our father's girlfriends hovering above. There's no separating you two, one would always say. Another said, Sometimes I don't know where one of you ends and the other begins. Maybe I'd start laughing again tonight.

Le Dix was not hard to find. I could see, from where the escalator brought me aboveground, a cluster of people on the opposite sidewalk waiting to get in. In the cold, their chatter came out in brief white gusts. Cigarette breaths lasted longer, rising in great bulbs up to the second-story windows, from which women in sleeveless shirts and men with faces shiny with sweat leaned out and sent their own frosted smoke up higher. Behind them, bodies moved beneath colored lights, each to their own rhythm.

I realized I didn't know what Leslie looked like. I hadn't thought to ask, and the door was flanked by people clearly waiting for others. But as I crossed the street, scanning each person, there was only one American face: the mouth ajar, the cheeks fleshy and vulnerable, the eyes wide and alert but slightly unfocused. Leslie recognized mine as well.

"Rosie. Hi."

"Hi."

A few heads turned toward us. I hadn't spoken English in public before. *Américaines,* I heard someone say, and I felt myself being dropped into a small disposable bag.

Leslie seemed oblivious. She spoke loudly. "How's it going? The others are inside. We don't have to wait in line. I know the bouncer."

He was hardly a bouncer, thin as my arm and nodding immediately to Leslie even before she began speaking.

Leslie led me down to the basement, which was so densely packed with tables and chairs and bodies that the waiter in front of them deposited his large tray of drinks on the only table he could reach. The people there were responsible for passing them on.

"This place would be a total fire hazard in the States," Leslie said, letting the waiter squeeze back by her before we pushed our way into the room toward her friends, who were waving in the far corner. I was nervous they would holler out, or Leslie to them, then scolded myself for being so self-conscious. Nicole, I decided, was to blame. She had wanted me to go out, but she had made me ashamed of not being Parisian.

Tables were moved and chairs were tipped to let us pass. Amid the larger groups in the middle of the room, there was a couple sitting close together and speaking a language that was both familiar and entirely foreign. Ahead of me, Leslie had run into someone she knew, so I lingered beside the couple's table. Neither was French; she was Italian perhaps, he German or Dutch. Since I'd been in Paris, I'd heard so many different languages. There was a train station nearby and I'd taken to loitering there in the early afternoons, watching the departures, matching languages with destinations. I learned sounds quickly and soon could identify the nationality of most of the travelers. Sometimes, I tried to help people at the ticket counter if I saw them struggling with French. I liked being seen on the platforms without bags, being taken for a permanent resident waiting for a friend. But what I heard now at waist level was not a language I'd ever heard at the station, yet I almost knew what they were saying. Then I did know.

"They're speaking Latin," I said.

Leslie nodded without turning around.

Latin must have been the only language they had in common. I wondered what kind of relationship you'd have, speaking only Latin.

Eventually, we reached the other side of the room where the friends were waiting: a small frizzy-haired American and a lean well-dressed European.

"Rosie, this is Beth and Mariska."

We shook hands. I took a seat on the bench that lined the wall. Hot air from a vent in its base came up around my legs and into my face.

"Bertrand's here," Leslie said to Beth. "He's back with the cat woman."

"You're kidding. Where?"

"Outside."

"Did he see you?" Mariska asked. Her accent was neither American nor British, neither truly foreign nor truly native. Each word seemed like it came from a different English-speaking country.

"He pretended not to." Leslie smiled weakly, her tough face suddenly collapsed by this confession.

"Look," Beth said to her gently. "There's Cédéric."

"Oh, yeah," Leslie said, glancing up but not seeing.

I began to roll questions around in my head as I did in French, but before I could ask them the waiter waded halfway into the room and they yelled their orders to him. Leslie ordered sangria for the table, Beth asked for extra fruit in it, and Mariska passed him money for a pack of cigarettes.

"So where do you usually go, Rosie?" Leslie said, deliberately brightening up.

"When you go out, she means," Beth said.

"I stay mostly in my neighborhood. There are a couple of streets." I hoped I wouldn't be asked the names of bars and *boîtes*. I wasn't sure I knew what a *boîte* was.

"Rosie's mother is the most beautiful woman you've ever seen," Leslie said. "She looks like the woman in that movie we saw last week, you know, the love triangle one."

"All French films are about love triangles," Mariska said.

"My mother?" As soon as I said this I realized Leslie meant Nicole.

"Francine is petrified of her," Leslie said. "But that's because her mother is a jellyfish." She waved at a group of guys, very French in sports coats hung over one shoulder and gelled hair, the teeth marks from their combs still visible. One of them made a pistol with his finger and fired it several times at her. She pretended he got her, then turned back to the table. "I've often wondered how beautiful, I mean truly beautiful women live. Just day to day, you know? I mean, what it would feel like to wake up in the morning and not even have to think—"

"Of course they think about it," Beth said.

"Okay, think, but not worry."

"Yes, they do. They have more than we do to worry about. Can you imagine having this drop-dead gorgeous face and then having to watch it shrivel up?"

Mariska lit a cigarette and swung herself sideways in her chair, away from us. It was obvious she thought herself a beautiful woman.

"But what I really can't imagine," Leslie said, "is having a new *fille* come into your house every year and watch your husband pant around her."

"Leslie, that isn't happening to us all," Beth said.

"It's not even that I like him all that much. He's just so bleedin' French."

"Bleedin' French. Are you turning into a Brit now?"

"It's those Irish girls I went out with last night. They're contagious."

"Mine isn't French at all," I said. The sangria had arrived and, in combination with the warm air beneath me, it was beginning to relax me.

"Who?"

"The father in my family."

"What is he?"

"He's French, but he's not at all."

They seemed to understand each other when they spoke like this, but now they just looked at me blankly.

"I know what you mean," Mariska said, turning slightly back. "He's not confined to cultural characteristics."

"Oh, c'mon. You can't escape them," Leslie said. "But he certainly doesn't look French." Leslie turned to Beth. "Have you ever seen him?"

"Never. Only Lola."

"He's hilarious-looking," Leslie said. "Tall for a Frenchman. Kind of like Abraham Lincoln but not half as sexy."

"Abraham Lincoln is not sexy," Beth said.

"Abraham Lincoln is very sexy."

I wished we hadn't gotten off the subject of Marc, but I knew I'd blush if I mentioned him again.

Mariska got up to go to the bathroom.

Beth asked me, "Do you *tutoie* your parents?"

"No."

"And what do they say to you?"

I tried to hear Nicole, then Marc, in my head. "The mother says *tu* and he says *vous*. I think. He's not home all that much."

"My mother asked me the other day to *tutoie* her," Leslie said. "Just when I'm about to do her husband she wants to get all touchy-feely."

"It's probably nothing new for her," Beth said, and I could see she regretted it.

But Leslie wasn't hurt. "Probably not. The French have a totally different definition of marriage." She spread her arms way out and said loudly, "I love being just a number." Many heads turned briefly toward us. "Do you know what happened to me today?" she continued without a pause. "I was walking down Saint-Mich and some old man tells me to tie up my shoelaces. I told him I didn't feel like it. Can you believe the nerve of these people?"

"The gall of these Gauls," Beth said.

Mariska was squeezing her way back toward us. It was increasingly difficult to walk across the room, for groups were less separate now as more alcohol was delivered and bodies relaxed and spread, a leg stretched out here, an arm there, like bread dough in the hot hazy room. No man in the room wanted to make it easy for Mariska to pass by him too quickly. She smiled at each one patiently. Feet and elbows had to be removed from her chair in order to sit down.

The second pitcher of sangria arrived. "For the Americans," a woman with an aquiline nose and darkly outlined lips said as she passed it to them.

"I'm not American," Mariska said quickly. The woman didn't inquire further, though the man beside her in a yellow vest pestered her to do so.

Leslie watched a couple kissing on a bench in the opposite corner. Beth eavesdropped on a conversation beside her between a large German woman and a small Italian man whose shoulder and upper arm were pressed against Beth's. Mariska lit a cigarette. She was one of the few people in the room who had both a pack and a lighter. A few feet away a man hovered over a table of women while one slipped a cigarette from a leather case and another held up a slender onyx lighter. As he took the light, he looked not into the eyes of the woman who held the lighter but of the woman who had given him the cigarette. I supposed he thought this gaze appealing, but in fact his brow was furrowed like the skin of a shar-pei. Women held their long hair in a fist at their necks as they leaned down to accept the flame, or let their short hair spill over their eyes as their lips kissed the filter and the tip flared red.

Just as Mariska was putting out her cigarette, the yellow vest made his predictable move. She slipped a cigarette from her pack, then laughed at something he said. He called to his friends for his chair, which was then lifted over several heads. He nestled it beside her to take the light, his face less vulnerable now, smoothed over by the anticipation of conquest.

The third pitcher of sangria arrived. I sipped steadily in silence, Beth sucked on the purple wedges of lemon and orange, and Leslie talked. She spoke of Bertrand and how the cat woman stole him away, and of the father in her family, who rubbed his sweaty sock against her shin beneath the dinner table. While Beth nodded and sighed, Leslie told me about the impending visit of Beth's boyfriend and his sudden decision to bring along his best friend, with whom Beth was secretly in love. Occasionally some guy that Leslie knew would stop by the table, and her head would tip and her shoulders curl. Her face would lose its defiance and she would become nearly pretty, though it was such a tremendous effort that after they were gone her face would be shiny with sweat.

Beth ignored these approaches and departures and, while Leslie craned her neck up to the man looming over the table, told me about Mont-Saint-Michel, where they had just been last weekend. They had planned the trip in accordance with the full moon and an afternoon high tide, and had watched the sea rush in from a turret of the abbey. In the evening they had run out several miles on the wet sand but never caught the swiftly retreating sea. The week before that they had been wine-tasting in the Loire. For Toussaint, All Saints' Day, they had spent three days in Alsace, and at Christmas they were off to Dublin. They got student rates, stayed in hostels, and taught English on the side at a hundred francs an hour to pay for it.

"What about you, Rosie?" Beth asked.

Me. Swaddled in heat and alcohol, lulled by their talk, I'd nearly forgotten me. I thought of what I'd wanted to tell them, things about Nicole and her petty ways, Lola who made up for them, Marc and his sad sweetness, the street with the *oisellerie,* and the bathtub at the window that gave you the sensation of bathing in the Seine.

"What about me?" I felt drunk and miserable. Remembering the bathtub made me remember the hollowness of washing my belly and the yellow crust, despite the pills, that I had to scrub from my nipples. "I got pregnant in twelfth grade, and since I lived with my sister and she really wanted a kid, I gave it to her. I was supposed to go to college, but I came here instead." I regretted it immediately. Leslie would tell Francine, who would tell Lola, who would tell Marc, who would have to tell Nicole. Who would fire me. But I was angry. I wanted to punish them, make them feel guilty for their perfectly planned lives. And it felt good to tell the truth instead of the phony excuses about my passion for the French language and culture that I had been giving everyone since I arrived. I felt the laughter I'd been craving rise inside me.

"Oh, God, Rosie," Leslie said, seeing the change in my expression. "I almost believed you."

"Me too," Beth said, letting go a pent-up gasp.

"But Lola said you had a very weird sense of humor."

Beth stripped the last of the fruit with her teeth and dropped the rind in her glass. "Well, I've got that *examen* tomorrow."

We stood up into the layer of smoke that had been accumulating over our heads all night and said good-bye to Mariska and her man, who seemed pained by the interruption. There was no path in any direction to the stairs. I pressed hard through the piles of knees and ankles, the tangle of arms and chair backs. I gave people little warning. I heard Beth and Leslie behind me, apologizing, letting themselves get waylaid by the attention. I would reach the metro before they reached the stairs. I wanted to get far, far away from them. I wanted to be stepping on deck, lifting the black key from its nail, creeping quietly down the narrow stairs, pouring a tall glass of water, and watching the dark glinting river out the kitchen window, silent and alone.

Sweet Sister

IN THOSE FIRST FEW HOURS WE TOOK TURNS WITH HIM, EACH CAREFUL NOT TO HOLD him too long. A nurse set up a cot for her, but she crawled in beside me and we lay there together, passing him back and forth. "Your turn now, Rosie," she whispered, laying him heavy-headed on my chest, his purple lids sealed tight. After a while I lifted him back into her arms. It was that moment—when his skin was pulled from mine, when the weight of him was gone, when the inordinate amount of love no longer had a place to rest—that was the most painful. I watched him settle easily against my sister, and I lied. "This isn't as hard as I thought," I said.

Sarah had always wanted a big family. When we were little, she made me pretend we were two of seven children, or twelve, or fifteen. Sometimes she gave birth to all these other siblings. She'd walk around with a pillow strapped beneath her nightgown, then lie down without warning and holler like a lunatic until I pulled out the teddy bear or sneaker she'd lodged between her legs. The game petrified me, and I always begged to have fewer brothers and sisters. I hated the white creases in her red face as she screamed, and how quick and desperate her breathing became. Her death was something I'd been terrified of all my life.

My father never settled down with one woman again. He said he was picky, but my sister said he was scared. Sometimes it seemed he was too frightened to love either of us very much. He moved us from city to city without warning or explanation and, within a month or so, had found someone new to share his bed. He was erratic in his care for me—it depended on the girlfriend and her interest in children—but Sarah was constant. She got me up for school, packed me off with a sandwich, quizzed me before tests. I cried the day I found the short lifeline on her palm; I worried when she was in high school and drove around at night in unfamiliar cars; and I prayed shamelessly when, after nearly a week of listening to her complain of abdominal pain and fever, my father finally took her to the hospital. She came home five days later like a ghost: translucent, hollow-eyed—and infertile.

At twenty, she married Hank Mulvaney, who owned the restaurant in Cleveland where she worked. He'd waited a year to ask her out, then proposed after a month. He was thirty-three and said he was tired of restaurants. He wanted a farmhouse and a vegetable garden. She wanted to move somewhere and never leave. When they went to Lyme, New Hampshire, they offered to take me with them. I was fourteen and glad to go.

Before they were married, Hank had claimed he wanted to adopt kids—lots of them. But when, after two years in Lyme, my sister began to talk of it, he balked. He told her they couldn't afford it yet. He cut out articles about troubled adoptees. He suggested she go to the infertility clinic in Hanover. "I had a hysterectomy at sixteen, Hank," I heard her tell him. "There's nothing in there to work with."

Sarah worked in a coffee shop and studied at night for her teaching certificate, but I often found her folded in a tight ball in her desk chair, books pushed aside, her face drained of hope. I'd never once seen her cry, but she could disappear deep within herself in sadness. And if I tried to comfort her, she was the one who ended up doing the reassuring, insisting that Hank would come around, that he was processing, that infertility was much harder on men.

I asked him once, "What if you knew someone who was pregnant and she didn't want the baby?"

"What about it?" Hank said uncomfortably, wishing my sister wouldn't share her problems with me.

"Well, what if that person asked you to raise it? Would you do it?"

He looked at me closely. "I really don't want to hear that you've gotten yourself in some sort of trouble, Rosie."

I laughed. "The last time I kissed a boy was in seventh grade. But say I was. Just say."

"If that's how it was. If that's what you really wanted, then things might be different."

* * *

My sister was made to be a mother. You take one look at her and you see it. In her presence, you feel safe. Her hands seem larger and warmer than other women's, her laugh more sincere. You want to show her things; you want her to be proud of you; you want to never let her down. She gave to me all her life, and I wanted to give something back.

I chose Cal Cleary because he was tall like Hank and kind like my sister, and because he confessed to a friend that he had a crush on me. I chose him at the beginning of September, but it took nearly a month to get him to go out with me. I lingered near his locker between classes; I positioned myself in his line of vision during lunch; I began hanging out with the girls at the side of the playground after school, watching the guys play pickup basketball. "Silent Cal" our history teacher called him, after Calvin Coolidge. He always blushed when he saw me, but he never spoke.

I finally had to do it myself. "So, are you ever going to take me out on a date, Cal?"

He'd been reaching for something deep in his locker, and when he straightened up I saw small beads of sweat on his forehead. "A date? Is that some sort of midwestern ritual?" he said.

I'd been in New Hampshire almost four years now, the longest I'd ever lived anywhere, and still people thought of me as an outsider. Still, I had the upper hand here. He was the one who was nervous. When I turned to walk away, he said, "Friday night?" like the idea had been his all along.

Sarah nearly exploded when I told her. "You have a *date*? I thought they didn't do that here."

"It's not a big deal."

"Not a big deal! It's your first one!"

"I want to wear something really sexy."

"Not too sexy, though. You don't want to scare him off."

He came by at seven on Friday. I wore jeans and one of my sister's clingy striped tops. She'd bought me an underwire bra that kind of pushed things out a bit. I didn't want Sarah and Hank to meet him so I went out to the car the minute I saw him pull up.

Nothing happened in the movie theater. He kept his hands to himself and never reached for the popcorn at the same time I did. We had dinner at a Chinese restaurant around the corner. Silent Cal was no misnomer. The only time he said something that wasn't prompted by a question was when he stopped the car outside my house and said he'd had a good time. I leaned over and shut off the ignition, then the headlights. Our street was dark and still. I wasn't going to get out of that car until something was established between us. When I kissed him, he didn't separate his lips. I'd chosen badly. Instead of tall and kind, I should have looked for short and fast. I fell back to my side of the car, sighed, then opened the door.

"Wanna do something tomorrow night?" he said.

"Sure," I said. "Call me."

On our third date, I told Cal I was on the pill. We'd only kissed twice but I thought it might speed things up. It didn't. But he was definitely kind. He sent me roses once for no reason. He saved a seat for me at assemblies. He called me every night. He'd begun to talk a bit more, and I called him Chatty Cathy when he did, which he said was another of my midwestern expressions.

In November, Hank and Sarah went away for a weekend. I checked the chart I kept hidden in a shoe box with the thermometer. It was perfect timing. That Friday night, I gave Cal a few of Hank's beers and his hands became a little more exploratory, slipping beneath the underwire and tentatively touching my nipples. I reached down to the first button of his pants.

"Let's," I said, feigning breathlessness.

"Okay," he said, "let's." Then he shuddered hard against my hand on his still-fastened fly.

He started laughing. "I'm sorry. Just the thought put me over the edge." He reached down and started rubbing between my legs. "Your turn to go over," he said.

I rolled away from his hand. I didn't think it would be this complicated. I just wanted to do it and get it over with.

"I love you, Rosie."

It was the worst thing to do but I began to cry. I'd just wanted a one-night stand, the way it was on TV—a tumble in the hay, then a baby on the way. He kissed my neck, my ear, my temple, my mouth. He tasted my tears and told me he loved me again. He lay on top of me and I felt him grow hard. This is it, I thought, pulling down my pants, then his.

He came within seconds, before I could feel what sex was. When he called the next day, I told him I was coming down with the flu.

I prayed for it to work. Sarah and Hank had come back from their trip more morose than ever. They'd gone to stay at a lake house with two other couples, both of whom had children. According to Hank, Sarah did not say one word to an adult the entire time. According to Sarah, Hank became a nasty old man, swatting the children away like horseflies. By Thanksgiving I'd taken three different home pregnancy tests, each one with the same result.

I sat them down at the kitchen table. We'd had a big turkey dinner, but all the guests, single solitary people, had gone home. I knew Sarah was in a maudlin mood; she always was at holidays.

"I've got some news," I said. "I'm pregnant."

"Jesus H. Christ!" Hank said.

"Oh, God," Sarah said. "Are you sure?"

I nodded.

"It's all my fault," she said. "We had that talk, but I should have made you an appointment with Dr. Knott. I should have—"

I was impatient for them to understand. "I want you to keep it."

She looked at me as if she'd never seen me before.

"I want you to raise this child."

"What?"

"I do."

"Rosie, that's crazy. You're going to college. You're—"

"That's why I want you to keep it."

She looked at me, realizing for the first time what I was saying. A tremor passed through her. "Oh, God." She covered her mouth as her eyes began to fill. She turned to Hank when the tears spilled over her hands. He pulled her close and she began to sob, a sob that must have been inside for many years. Hank pressed his cheek to her hair and shut his eyes. Just when I thought he'd forgotten I was still there, he said, "Are you sure this is what you want, Rosie?"

"This is what I want."

Sarah came around to my side of the table and hugged me hard. "My sweet sister," she said. "My sweet sweet sweet sister."

* * *

I liked being pregnant. I liked the attention, the concern, the gratitude. Breaking up with Cal was the only unpleasant thing. I told him I'd met someone else and he walked away from me without a word. When I saw him after that, his face would flame up before he turned in another direction. I suppose I drifted away from my friends, too, but my sister and I needed the time together. Once I began to feel the baby move, she'd sit on the couch with her eyes closed and wait for it to tap against her palm.

I graduated pregnant and no one ever knew. At the reception afterward, I overheard someone joke about me gaining my freshman fifteen ahead of time. To me, the joke was on them. I was excited about the child. My sister and I were back in our world, only now I was the one who was going to lie down and holler. It was better this way; it was her death, not my own, that I was scared of.

The first week of July, I came into the house and found Cal sitting at the kitchen table. No one else was home. He'd grown some sort of patchy beard which only covered half his blush when he saw me. It was a hot afternoon and I was wearing an old workshirt of Hank's that barely stretched over my belly. I knew I didn't look just fat anymore; I looked unmistakably seven and a half months pregnant.

Cal was the oldest of five boys. His parents showed up together to all of his basketball games. Every other Saturday, all seven of them helped serve lunch at a homeless shelter. In August they rented a cottage on Lake Winnepesaukee. I hadn't wanted him to find out and for that reason stayed close to the house. But someone must have seen me out in the garden; someone must have told him.

"It's my sister's."

"What?"

"I'm giving the baby to my sister."

He pushed the salt shaker back and forth with the tips of his fingers to conceal how much they were shaking. He once told me how his littlest brother almost died, choking on a deflated balloon, and his hands had shaken then, too.

I knew what I needed to say to still them. "It's not yours, Cal."

He looked up at me, wanting to believe. "But in the fall. That's when we—"

I looked shamefully at my enormous belly. "I was sleeping with someone else." I created a guilty, reassuring face. He accepted it eagerly.

Through the front window, I watched him leave. His whole body swung into fluid motion. Out on the street, three kids whizzed by on bikes, one calling back, "Hey, Cal!" in a voice quickly thinned by the wind. He raised an arm, though all the riders had disappeared around the bend. Very soon he disappeared, too.

A friend of Sarah's recommended we see someone she knew, a social worker who counseled people on adoption. I told Sarah it was a waste of money. She reminded me that it wasn't my money, and we went.

Helen Gunther lived across town at the end of a cul-de-sac. Her house was part of a semicircle of new identical houses, each a different pale shade, each with a brick walkway and a small porch. On Helen Gunther's porch, beside the door, was a basket of strawberries and a note that read: *Picked these this morning out by Wilder's place. Thanks for everything! Love, Cammie.*

When she came to the door, my sister handed her the basket, and even though she read the card, she seemed unable to separate us from her appreciation. "I can't think of a better gift than strawberries. I really can't. And there was no need for a gift at all. Please come this way. My office is in the back."

Despite the heat, my sister and I had dressed up for the meeting, but Helen Gunther wore a faded denim shift. She was a large woman, over fifty, though from the looks of the kitchen and playroom we passed through, she seemed to have several young children. In the hallway, the walls were covered with drawings. On some there was writing. One said *I love you Ma* and another *Happy Mothas Day.* My sister lingered, touching the curled corners tenderly.

We sat at the far end of Helen's office, away from her desk, in comfortable armchairs around a coffee table layered with magazines and newsletters about adoption and single parenting and family planning.

"So," she began, eyeing the bulge that pushed apart my blazer, "Rosie's pregnant."

We nodded.

"And Sarah is going to raise the child."

We nodded again.

"Why?"

After a while, after I realized my sister was not going to answer, I said, "Because she can't have children."

"Lots of women can't bear children. I can't. Are you going to give your next one to me?"

"Rosie's off to college in the fall. It was an accident. The time isn't right for her to"—Sarah groped for words—"keep it."

"Forgive me. I'm going to play devil's advocate here." Helen turned back to me. "Women with babies go to college. Women with babies work, and go to the movies, and go on to lead challenging but pretty normal lives."

She didn't understand. "I don't want a baby, Mrs. Gunther. My sister does. I have never thought of it as mine."

"But that baby is yours, Rosie. No matter what you decide to do—"

"I have decided."

"No matter what you decide, that baby is yours and the whole process is going to be a lot harder for you if you don't accept that now." She turned to Sarah, who looked like a thin doll in her chair between Helen and me. "By law, Rosie has seventy-two hours after delivery to decide what she wants to do. It's crucial that you give her this time. Can you agree to that?"

My sister nodded, unable to trust her voice. She kept her eyes focused through the open office door to the hallway of pictures.

"Have you thought about what you will tell the child?" Mrs. Gunther asked her.

"The truth?" Sarah said, more as a question than a conviction. It occurred to me then that neither of us had imagined this child as any older than a few days.

"And what's the truth, as you see it?"

I'd never seen my sister so unnerved. "That Rosie . . . that she got pregnant too young, and I agreed to raise her child."

"Temporarily, until she's older? Or for the long haul?"

Sarah looked at me, bewildered.

"For the long haul," I said.

When the session was over, my sister left the room abruptly. To compensate, I stayed to get a closer look at the large black-and-white photograph on the wall of an alabaster statue. It was a figure of a young woman holding flowers, precariously set on the stone wall of a bridge.

"Has she fooled you too?" Helen asked.

I didn't know what she meant.

"It's a real woman. She's covered herself in some sort of plaster. And she stays perfectly still for hours."

"Why?"

"See that jar by her feet? People put money in it."

"Where is this? New York?"

"Paris. The Pont Neuf. Have you ever been there?"

"No. I took French, but I never thought of it as a real place."

"It's very real. One of the best cities on earth."

I heard Sarah open the screen door on the other side of the house.

"Rosie," Helen Gunther said. "It's not your fault your sister's infertile."

I acknowledged her without moving, taking my first lesson from the alabaster woman.

"Come back next week, even if Sarah won't. Relinquishing a baby is not easy, Rosie, not once you've given birth."

Sarah held him first. I'll never forgive her for that. Eight hours of labor and I didn't even get to hold my baby first. The doctor handed him to her. Later that night, when I accused her, she said she passed him to me. "I didn't hold him. I carried him to you. You held him." But I remember how it was. She held him first.

When we came home from the hospital, I held him in the car but she carried him in, Hank cooing beside her, doubts and statistics forgotten. I went upstairs, unable to block out their voices as they introduced him to the dog, then the two cats. In my absence, Hank had stacked milk crates outside my room. I was enrolled at the University of New Hampshire and freshman orientation began in three days. I dragged in the crates and began to empty my drawers into them. I could hear the baby begin to cry downstairs, and it soaked my bra. I shut my door but I could still hear him. I turned the radio on loud, and still I could hear him. I knew even in my dorm room in Durham I would hear him still.

She knocked. I shut the music off and let her in.

"He's sleeping now," she said. "He was just tired."

"You don't have to tell me every detail."

"Okay."

Nothing in my body felt right. It seemed to be ringing with pain but there was no part of me that I could point to and tell her, Here, here's where it hurts. I only knew that her presence made it worse. Helen Gunther had said that these would be the most challenging days for us, and that we should be honest but careful of each other's feelings. I saw now that it would be impossible to do both.

I pulled some clothes out of the closet.

"Don't do this now, Rosie. Rest. I'll help you tomorrow." She sat on my bed and patted the space beside her.

It felt strange to sit and have my body fold so easily now. I put the length of the bed between us. I didn't want her to touch me.

"He looks so much like you."

She wanted reassurance. She wanted to hear that this was still what I wanted.

I looked at the stuffed milk crates, and at the freshman face book on my desk. I stood up and began throwing the last of my things into a black suitcase. "I want to get this done," I said.

"Don't shut down." Her voice broke despite her efforts. "Please don't shut down on me." She cried like I did, as if she'd been doing it for years, her face all wrenched and soundless.

I hated watching it. I hated her honesty and her innocence of my schemes. I hated all her newly surfaced emotions and her sentimentality. I couldn't understand how we'd ever been close, how I'd come to live in her house, how I'd let myself be manipulated by her. I hated her. I hated myself. The only thing I loved was the touch and the smell of that little boy who was no longer mine. "You have no rights to me anymore."

That night, Hank tried to give me an envelope. I threw it back at him. "You can't pay me. You can't pay me for this. This isn't about money."

"You're going to need some cash when you get to school. Financial aid won't cover everything. You're going to want to go out and do things, like get a pizza at the Tin Palace or—"

"You don't know anything about what I'm going to want."

I watched him wrestle with his anger at me, weighing it carefully against the gratitude he should feel, knowing there were still twenty-four hours to go before I could sign the papers his lawyer had drawn up. "We'll talk about this later," he said, placing the envelope on the mantel.

My sister must have contacted Helen Gunther, because she called the next day.

"How are you holding up, Rosie?"

"Fine."

"Yeah?"

I didn't say anything.

"Are you really fine?"

"Yes."

"Would you like to come by and talk?"

"No, thanks."

"You had a boy?"

"Yes."

"What does he look like?"

She wanted me to crack. "Winston Churchill."

There was a long silence.

I hung up the phone gently, and she didn't call back. But I was glad I talked to her. She'd reminded me of the photograph of the statue, and of the city in the background. I headed toward the back porch, to apologize and to explain where I was going. But when I reached the doorway and saw the three of them in the wicker seat, I understood how little need there was for good-byes. I found the papers on Hank's desk. I signed them, dating each signature one day in advance. They didn't hear me as I dragged down my black suitcase, took the money off the mantel, and slipped out of their house.

II

I knew they weren't my children, but it was my job to care for them, to tend to them. I clipped fingernails, buttoned the backs of dresses, made snacks at homework hour. They were all I had in Paris, and even when I wasn't with them, I was watching them.

They told me their stories, but they underestimated my ability to understand them. They mistook the flatness of my gaze for lack of imagination, when all the while I was watching their worlds from the inside.

Guillaume

꽃

HE STOLE QUIETLY INTO HIS MOTHER'S ROOM TO TAKE A LONG PURPLE SCARF, WHICH he draped over the shoulders of the white bathrobe he wore. On the coffee table in the living room he spread a lace tablecloth and placed two candlesticks, a wineglass with a gold rim, and a cigarette box in the center. He lit the wicks with a match from the silver box, then closed all the shutters, so that the room, save for the two blades of yellow light and their twitching reflections, was quite dark for midmorning. He left, then reentered the room slowly, head down, one hand cradled in the other. He stood behind the table, raised his eyes, and spread out his arms to the empty room. His speech was inaudible except for an occasional *t* or hard *c*. After several minutes of this he darted out of the room and returned with a large book, which he placed open on the table and proceeded to read from, glancing up now and then at different parts of the room imploringly. When he was finished he closed the book gently and made a few more short speeches. From an imaginary decanter in his right hand he poured a few drops of air into the wineglass. He then raised the glass above his head, spoke, and brought it to his lips. From the box he gingerly extracted a pretend wafer and, with the same slow gestures, raised and lowered it into his mouth. He stepped to the side and, with the open cigarette box in one hand, continued to remove weightless, invisible disks, which he poised and dropped at precise intervals while his lips moved in the same configuration of shapes each time. When this was finished, he moved the glass to the left side of the table, placed the cigarette box beside it, lifted his terry-cloth arms again, and mouthed a few final words. He stood motionless as the room emptied out.

He liked to do this with real people, with Lola or his friend Arnaud, but he was more focused when practicing alone, he thought, returning the wineglass to its cabinet behind his father's seat in the dining room. And Lola was becoming less and less serious. He could feel how she didn't really pray, not even in church. He was worried about her; he prayed for her. He feared she had stopped believing in her own miracle.

Lola had saved his life with her faith.

He remembered fragments. He remembered the part of her hair as she prayed on her knees by his bed. She wore braids then, and her hair was separated perfectly from forehead to nape. He remembered that strip of scalp and how he'd long to scratch it, but by then they'd wrapped his hands. He couldn't understand why she didn't itch. When his exema spread and became infected, his fever was very high and he lost the sense of the parameters of his own body; he often felt the walls and mattress were in the same kind of pain, which wasn't pain exactly but a longing to be rubbed and clawed until the new scabs were between his fingernails and the wound was fresh and bloody again. In the hospital, Lola made an altar by the one window, on which she placed her largest piece of blue sea glass, his ivory elephant, and her locket with the cross on the outside and his picture inside. Once she sprinkled rose petals over it, though it couldn't have been Corpus Christi at the time. Once he woke up in the late afternoon and the window was open and a breeze grazed the skirt of his sister, who kneeled rigidly at her altar. Her legs were bare, and he longed to score bright red lines down them with the sharp unwrapped fingernails he no longer had.

Papa never prayed at his bedside, not once, and Odile and Maman were more discreet, closing their eyes in their chairs beside his bed only when they thought he was asleep. But Lola was fervent. There was always the rustle of onion-skin pages and the click of rosary beads. He could rely on the perpetual scurrying whisper of her Ave Marias. He knew he had lived solely because of her faith. Had she used it all up on him?

He heard the rattle of the back of his father's swivel chair from behind the closed door of his study. Soon he would be in the hallway. Guillaume hurried to blow out the candles, replace the cigarette box, and fold up the tablecloth. The scarf would have to wait until the path to the master bedroom was clear. It was Saturday morning, and they were the only two in the house. The study door opened and a wedge of light fell on the carpet. His father's shadow stepped into it. Guillaume stuffed the scarf into his pocket.

Papa was not a violent man. He wasn't angry all the time like Arnaud's father. He didn't insult or belittle very often. Still, Guillaume's heart raced as he fled down the other hallway to his room. Papa did not believe in God.

"Guillaume!"

"Yeah?" He didn't stop moving.

"What're you up to?"

"Nothing."

"Are you still in your robe?"

"Yeah."

"Did you close all these shutters?"

"Yeah."

A pause. He was noticing something, the smell of wax or fingerprints on the cigarette box. Then, "How about some breakfast?"

"All right."

"Get dressed first."

"I'm going to."

It was Maman who understood his vocation. She said he was blessed. He was her only son, and she often told him that the day he was born, she knew he was more than just an ordinary gift. She promised that some-day this fall they'd go visit an old friend of hers, Père Lafond, whom he could speak to about becoming a priest.

His exema had never returned, but sometimes when his mother came in at night and he felt her weight on the bed and listened to her voice above him in the dark, he felt in his heart an ache similar to the itching that once covered his body.

Papa sliced and grilled the bread left over from last night, or maybe even two nights ago. It was tough and chewy. Guillaume spread more marmalade on the second piece. Papa watched him eat with the same discouragement he wore when he watched Guillaume do anything.

Dear Christ our Savior, please help us to understand each other.

On the stove, white foam rose and sizzled down the side of the pan.

"I almost forgot. Hot chocolate?"

"Please."

Papa put a square of chocolate at the bottom of two breakfast bowls, then poured the milk over them. He brought them over, a spoon in each, and they sat stirring up chocolate swirls from the bottom until the milk was a deep brown.

"Mmmmm," Guillaume said.

"Mmm," Papa replied.

"Is today the twenty-fourth?" He knew it was.

"Yes."

He had hoped to make his father laugh, for when he first learned about days and dates, he used to ask about them incessantly. But Papa's yes was straight-faced and unremembering. Then, after a sip of hot chocolate, Papa said, "Of November. Saturday." He looked up at the clock. "Ten-thirteen and a quarter."

It wasn't funny. It came too late. But Guillaume laughed anyway. *Please, please, as you understand me.*

They sipped. Guillaume suspected he was drinking his too fast and put it down. Papa put his bowl down too. It was empty. He looked at all Guillaume had left.

"Don't you like it?"

"Yes, I'm just trying to drink it in moderation."

Papa laughed, not the kind of laugh Guillaume had tried to solicit before but the kind that involves an invisible shaking of the head. Sometimes he said, "You're your mother's son," but this time he didn't. A silence stretched between them instead, and Guillaume struggled for something to say.

Lola came bounding down the stairs.

"Ai-ya!" Lola said, crashing through the door, tennis racquet raised like a sword.

Papa's face bloomed. "Ai-ya!" he said back, and thrust out a butter knife. Guillaume felt the room relent, felt the walls ease back, the chairs sink, the window expand its view of the wrinkled water. They staged a duel with their weapons, lost in each other. There would be no understanding between him and Papa today.

Lola caught the butter knife between the strings of her racquet and twisted it out of her father's hand. Guillaume reached for the knife, which had fallen beneath his seat, and took it to the sink.

"You're not going to finish this?" Lola said, sitting down at his place.

"No, I am." But she was already swallowing, chugging the chocolate. It was gone.

"Lola!" His voice was louder than he had intended. "I was saving that! Papa made that for me!" He heard himself from some remote place. He was screeching. They were laughing. Papa said his head might pop off if he didn't calm down. Lola laughed harder.

She wouldn't get scolded. Maman wasn't home. To them, he was selfish. To them, he had no sense of humor.

Lola ducked to the side so quickly from his attempted swipe that two chair legs gave out and she fell to the floor. There was a loud crack.

"Get out," Papa told him as he bent down to her. "Get out and stay out!"

His father's voice was like acid in his ears. He turned and went. A slat of the chair had split, not Lola's skull. At the door he heard Lola. She was laughing.

In his room he knelt down on the patch of bare floor between the carpet and the closet.

Dearest Christ, please please. I am wicked and undeserving but only say the word and I please please I beg you to pardon my behavior and please help me in the future to respond appropriately to acts of ill will. Please help me to forgive as you forgive me.

He thought of Thérèse Lisieux at age five and her string of beads, one for every sacrifice, and how she smacked her sister and it was days before she could secure God's forgiveness.

I am not worthy.

He was still on his knees when Maman came in. He liked it when she found him praying.

He told himself he wouldn't cry when he saw her, but just her "Guillou?" behind him made a sob rise to the surface. She sat beside him and he fell into her, into her cashmere shoulder, her fragrant neck, her cold gold hoops.

"What happened? What happened?" she whispered.

He hugged her tighter but her embrace remained the same. He wished she'd hold him closer, closer.

"That hurts," she said, loosening his arms. "Tell me."

He knew he could stop crying now and speak but he didn't, wanting still to hold and be held, wanting so fiercely, and fearing the want would never end. He pressed his closed eye into her shoulder until it began to sparkle and great wheels of red turned gold and then the brilliant white of heaven.

"Tell me," Maman said again, unhooking his arms like a strand of pearls from around her neck. "Guillaume." Her voice was impatient. Her eyes were shallow, lighter than usual, the light green of a fountain basin, so shallow they might not forgive him.

"Please forgive me," he said softly.

"Did you try and hit her? Is that true?"

"I am evil. Please forgive me."

"Don't be absurd, Guillaume."

"I am, Maman. I am."

"Brothers are expected to hit their sisters."

"That doesn't mean it's right." He wished he could shed the child he was like another layer of bad skin.

"No, of course it's not right."

"It's a sin and I've sinned. I'm always sinning."

On the floor of the closet she spotted her purple scarf in the pocket of the discarded robe. She pulled it out and spread it over his shoulders. "You're not always sinning." She stroked the silk on his arms. "My little saint never sins."

Lola

THEY WERE FINALLY GOING. AFTER THEIR FIGHT OVER THE HOT CHOCOLATE, MAMAN had arranged for Guillaume to meet a priest up north that she knew from when she was a little girl. But they didn't go and they didn't go—this Père Lafond had a baptism one week, two weddings the next, Papa was away, Maman got the flu—but now they were finally going to have tea with a priest.

Maman was wearing white and beige. Papa was in a foul mood, having to drive so far on a bright Saturday, and would not compliment her.

"You look beautiful, Maman," Lola said, and it was true. She did look beautiful, particularly beautiful in this soft, weightless shirt that let through, where a gold cross pressed it close to her skin, the slightest bit of lace of her bra. She wore a hat, a simple beige hat, to match her skirt, and her hair peeked out perfectly as if it had been cut especially for the hat that morning. Her cheeks were rosy already, though she hadn't yet been out in the cold.

Guillaume appeared, his cheeks red too from Maman's powder puff that Lola had refused. He looked silly, all tucked up in a gray suit and a gray-and-red striped bow tie that was far too big beneath his small chin. Lola said nothing, knowing how important this day was to him and also knowing that one comment, one word, would set back their leaving for at least another hour.

They hovered over each other in the hall, Maman straightening Guillaume's tie, Papa finally putting on his own, a long thin blue and yellow one, complaining, demanding to know if five days a week in this getup wasn't enough. Lola knew Papa got to his office, took off his tie, and wore his doctor's coat all day long, but she didn't say anything to that, either.

At the last moment, Odile announced she wasn't going. Justine d'Eveille was having a lunch. She'd completely forgotten.

Lola didn't care that it was a lie. "Can Rosie come, then?" she asked. "There's enough room now."

"She's running some errands for me. Another time," Maman said.

They climbed the stairs, shocked to find such a cold bright day above. Lola waited for Guillaume, who was the last to emerge from the small door out onto the deck. He saw her but he turned toward the river, to its choppy green water and hard flints of sunlight.

"You're awfully quiet. Are you excited or nervous?" She reached to tousle his hair, but he ducked and blocked her arm with his own.

"Don't. Maman put stuff in it."

"Sorry." She tried to think of some way to tell him that if he didn't relax a bit he'd ruin this day that he'd been looking forward to for so long. She remembered the times she'd done that, ruined events with seriousness and expectations, but she also remembered that even after she'd learned this, after she'd warned herself, it still happened all over again. She knew warning Guillaume would be useless. It was something you had to learn slowly, going forward and backward and forward again.

Guillaume's hand trembled. She watched him try to lock the car door. It made her sad, how his fingers trembled.

Papa told them about the town they were headed for, how it was never discovered by the Germans as a central Resistance cantonment. He was born just before the war broke out, and Maman was born just after. This fact has always seemed significant to Lola, as if it somehow explained all the differences between them.

Guillaume gazed blankly at the seat back in front of him, his pallid face balanced above the big bow tie. Lola tried to imagine what he felt at this moment. Though he went to mass every week, he had never spoken to the priest, had only let his small hand be swallowed for a few seconds in the old man's soft flesh and white cuffs as they filed out of the church. Each Sunday, Guillaume planned to speak. Lola often caught him practicing his lines when they were stuck together in the tall wall of dark coats and shawls and scarves with frayed ends that itched her nose if she was pushed too close. As they stepped outside onto the stone steps and into the light, Guillaume was always defeated by the cool unfocused gaze of the priest, which was always one person ahead of the one whose hand he held in his.

That's Paris, Maman had said, reassuring him that they would go soon to see the priest she knew personally up north. It was perhaps the only time Lola had ever heard Maman apologize for Paris. She'd come up from the south at sixteen, and still she claimed that she'd never soak up enough of this city into her bones. Papa wanted to move away, they all knew, but it would never happen. Living on a boat is bad enough, Maman would say, but living in the country! The boat was her one concession to his desire for more rustic living.

Everyone but Lola seemed to have passion for a place: Papa for a little village in a foreign country, Maman for a wide sidewalk thick with shoppers, Odile for the open doorways of dinners and dances, Guillaume for a dark aisle and a high altar. And even if Lola had one, Maman would never indulge it as she indulged Guillaume. They wouldn't drive two hours to take her there.

When had Guillaume become so devout? Lola could believe in God in a crisis; she could feel him then. But Guillaume prayed all the time. He prayed to Christ. She'd heard him. Not to God but to Christ. He told her Christ was the same thing, one and the same, part and whole of the Trinity. Then why didn't he pray to God or the Holy Spirit? she asked. Because Christ suffered and died on the cross. Because he bled, he told her. He showed her, the next Sunday, an enormous painting on the side of the cathedral and the drops of blood that had seeped into the shroud that covered Christ's body as he lay in his mother's arms. I pray to him because he bled for my sins.

How was it that they were brother and sister? They had eaten the same foods, read the same books, gone to the same Sunday Mass (Lola, being three years older, to perhaps a hundred and fifty more), and yet he was the one who could explain to her in complete earnestness, I pray to him because he bled for my sins.

"He *believes* that," she told Papa in private. Like her, he felt nothing. He had only been to church a handful of times in his life.

"I know it."

"Does Maman?"

"I think so. That's why she goes."

"She goes to take us."

"Then you should ask her what she believes."

"I couldn't."

"Why?"

"Then she'd know I didn't."

"It's your right, Lola, to believe what you believe."

Of course she knew she had the right to doubt what she heard at mass, but didn't he understand how fragile her relationship was with Maman already? She wasn't pretty. She couldn't share what Odile shared with her, and she couldn't be her baby like Guillaume. It wasn't church exactly that bound them, but their alienation from Guillaume's intensity. In church he slipped away from them both. Odile hardly went anymore, for she got in so late every Saturday night that her mother permitted her to sleep in before starting her homework, so she and Maman were left alone together in the pew. The exchange of peace was perhaps their closest moment all week; Maman seemed to hold her tighter then, brush her hair away from her eyes with more tender concern. In that moment Lola was her only child, the child that mattered. No, she decided, she would definitely not mention it to Maman.

Maman was telling a story now, sitting sideways in her seat to see them all. Her lipstick was deep red against the white wool of her coat. What was beauty? What made the eye believe that this pattern was more beautiful than another? And yet if she stared hard at her mother she could separate the elements: the red lips an underwater creature in fluid motion, the eyes the soft center of something black and sharp-quilled, the nose delicate but growing great wings when she laughed.

And Papa, he wasn't beautiful at all. But men were different somehow. With them it was harder to separate their whole nature from their face. One didn't notice a terrible nose, if he was smart and funny. A woman with a terrible nose never became attractive, no matter how clever or hilarious she was. She just stayed the smart, funny woman with the unfortunate nose.

Guillaume had not spoken. It was so unlike him not to be whining, demanding that they stop talking about things that did not hold his interest. Maman was always the first to give in to him, apologizing, asking him to choose the topic. He was spoiled rotten, and Lola got in huge trouble for ever saying it. But today he sat still with his small Bible beneath his folded hands on his lap. His lips moved whenever he shut his eyes.

Finally they turned off the highway, and her mother read out the directions scribbled on the back of a dry cleaner's bill. Her tone now implied that a mistake would be made. She made Papa repeat them.

"A right at the inn, straight down into the center of town, a left at the town hall, and the church is the third building on the left. Easy," he said, but then they never came to an inn. They stopped at a corner to ask, and an old man leaned on the door with both his arms, looked into the car, and answered the question slowly. They had passed the inn. He lifted a finger crabbed like a ginger root and pointed behind him to the signless, ramshackle building. They spun around, took the turn, and went into the center of town. It was barren, empty of a fountain or open square, shop awnings, and people. There was no left, only a right at the town hall, and they had already passed three churches. Papa was getting irritated.

"Three churches!" he yelled. "A church for every person in this Godforsaken place."

Maman chided him. They were going to see a priest, after all.

They found it on their first try back out of town. "Well, maybe there is a God," her father said, when her mother nodded from the church steps.

Guillaume leapt out and cried to his mother, "Tell Papa he should stay in the car if he's going to talk like this!" They were the first words he had spoken in over an hour and a half.

Père Lafond appeared in the door in a black robe. Lola had hoped they'd catch him in a ratty sweater and mud-colored pants. But there were no surprises, she suspected, with priests.

His face was pale and cushiony and not unlike the face of the Paris priest, she thought, though this one was younger. When Maman introduced him, Guillaume stood there as mute and stupid as he did every Sunday on the cathedral steps. Sweat beaded above his lip. The priest took his hand briefly, then embraced their mother again.

"How is your family?" he asked her.

"They're right here. See for yourself." She laughed. "All except the oldest, Odile. This is my husband, Marc."

Papa gave him the handshake he used when they ran into one of his patients on the street: abrupt and one-handed. With friends he was warmer, often covering the greeting with his other hand. The priest took it impatiently. He had known Maman in Plaire, and it was *that* family he wanted to hear about.

"And this is Louise."

Lola winced at her name and told him the one she preferred.

But he didn't seem to hear her. "Marie-Jo," he said softly. Blotches of color rose instantly on his face and on the sides of his neck.

"Lola," she said again.

He turned back to Maman. "It's an incredible likeness, isn't it?"

"I don't see it," she said curtly.

"How is she, Nicole?" he implored.

Lola knew little about any of her aunts and listened carefully. Marie-Jo's husband was a fruit farmer, Maman said, and they had four children, all married. In the one picture Lola had ever seen, Marie-Jo was the tallest and most graceful-looking aunt.

"She's fine, Frederí," her mother said, looking past him to the door as a hint that he might let them in out of the cold wind.

But the priest was not satisfied. "Is she? Is she well?"

"I think she must be."

Unlike Maman, Père Lafond spoke with a thick southern accent. He clearly wanted to ask more, but Papa interrupted to ask about the grounds that sprawled behind the church in a great unkempt meadow. Soon the church would have to sell, the priest said. To whom? Lola wondered. Who would buy land in such a place?

The priest let them pass through the door. The pews of this chapel were mere slabs of wood placed at perpendicular angles. On the low altar stood a square table bereft of even a cloth, and behind it hung a simple pine cross—or what looked like a cross until you saw that the horizontal plank was missing and what remained was the light shadow of where it had once protected the wall from grime.

The priest's own quarters were plush. In his living room there were bright soft places for everyone. The priest sat in a red leather chair whose dents and puckers were molded to his large body. He smiled at Lola, pointing to a puffy chair beside him, but Maman steered her to the sofa along the far wall, and Guillaume sat in the chair beside the priest.

An elderly woman brought in a tray of tea and small chocolate cakes. "The tea," he said to the silver pot, as it came to rest on the table beside him. The woman disappeared back down the unlit hallway. No one spoke. The brief noises in the room became palpable: the purling of the tea into shallow teacups, the scrape of the clawed prongs as they seized the sugar cubes, the splat of milk before the cup was set on a saucer and passed off. When each lap held a cup and a cake, they came upon a more uncomfortable silence. Lola, feeling the priest's stare, kept her eyes cast down, moving from cup to bare knees to brown shoes and back. In the periphery, she could see Papa's hand stirring. He was wordlessly telling Maman, I take no responsibility for this disaster. He wanted the visit to be a failure and Guillaume to stop talking about becoming a priest.

Her mother searched frantically for conversation. She brought up the difficulty of finding work in the region, the needs of his parishioners, the charcoal clouds that loomed above the hills through the patio doors. And as if Maman were painstakingly lighting candles, this priest, with fat wetted fingers, went about snuffing out each flame.

"I have read about the unemployment, that here it is perhaps the worst in all of France," she said.

"This is a mistake they make, I think, to say what is bad and what is worse. Isn't bad bad enough?"

"Yes, of course it is." She waited for him to elaborate, and when he didn't she continued. "It must affect the lives of your parishioners a great deal."

The priest nodded, eyes shut.

Maman persisted. "It must be difficult to console them."

"Console?" he asked softly, and held his face up to her with a sweetly puzzled look, which he kept long after she nodded and they all waited for an answer that was never going to come.

About the clouds, he simply said, "Rain again," as if it were the beginning of a song. He stood up to pour more tea into empty cups, even into her father's, which was full and overflowed onto the saucer, then sat back down again, forgetting or refusing to refill milk and sugar.

Unlike all other men, the priest was not affected by her mother's beauty.

There was a strange snapping sound. Lola looked up and saw that the priest had a hand to his neck and was flicking the bottom of the stiff collar with his long thumbnail. His eyes bored into hers, and she looked quickly away.

Guillaume said, "I want to be a priest." His voice was shrill and impatient. The priest shifted his body beneath the robe to face Guillaume, who buckled slightly at the sudden attention, then said, "At least, I think it would interest me."

"Why?"

Guillaume studied the priest's face for motive: doubt, scorn, or ridicule? The flaccid mouth, the small eyes beneath doughy eyelids revealed nothing but an enormous capacity for waiting for a response to a blunt question. He lifted one leg over the other.

Lola instantly hated the bob of his foot and, when Guillaume didn't answer, she bought him some time. "He's always wanted to, ever since I can remember. He feels something—something powerful."

He nodded at Lola, then asked, leaning closer to her, "What does he feel?"

"I want to be a priest," Guillaume said, his confidence back but having heard nothing of the last exchange, "because I want to serve God as best I can while on this earth."

The priest turned reluctantly toward Guillaume. "Do you like this earth? Is it a good place?" He said the word *good* as if it were a word between them, a word only they could understand.

"It would be impossible for me to say if I truly liked it, as I know no other for comparison. As for it being a good or bad place, I think it is both."

Lola watched as Maman let her eyes drift toward Papa's bewildered expression. To her, it was no shock; Guillaume always spoke like that when he discussed religion.

"You have gone to a few masses, heard a few sermons—in *Paris* I'm sure they're quite stimulating—felt something, a shiver, a stirring in your soul, or maybe the cleanest, whitest silence that felt something like truth. It felt like—"

"Please, Frederi, he's only a—"

"No, Maman." Guillaume held out an untrembling hand to her. In that moment he seemed more her father than her son. "Let him finish."

The priest brought his chin to rest in his hand and spoke gently. "Guillaume, do you have any idea what you will sacrifice if you pursue this goal?"

"A lot."

"Yes, a lot." His pause was just long enough to exasperate Maman. She politely alluded to the time, with a hand on a watchless wrist, and suggested to Papa that they mustn't keep the priest from his duties.

Père Lafond, ignoring the exchange, said, "I entered the priesthood at sixteen. Do you know that since then I have rarely seen my family, never played soccer, never held the hand of a girl?" He looked beseechingly at Lola. An unfamiliar, mealy feeling clung to her skin. She glanced at her parents. They were watching Guillaume. No one had noticed the priest's attentions toward her.

"But it was God's will," Guillaume said.

"God's will," he snapped. "What does a sixteen-year-old boy know about God's will? What does God ever reveal about his will? You are a child, Guillaume. Remain a child. Let yourself be loved and indulged."

"God's love is the most powerful of all," Guillaume said.

"You're wrong," the priest said. His fat face had collapsed, and his gaze had fallen to Lola's left hand, resting on the arm of the sofa. "It took me thirty-four years as a priest to learn that it isn't." He turned back to Guillaume. "Don't waste that kind of time yourself."

Maman stood up and nudged Lola. Papa and Guillaume followed. The priest walked them to the door, and although Lola was first, he shook Papa's hand, then Guillaume's. She wanted to scoot by unnoticed, but he was waiting for her. She held her breath. As he leaned down to kiss her cheek, he whispered, "Looking at you, I can reach out and touch my past."

As Papa steered Guillaume swiftly away down the corridor, Lola lagged behind, trying to hear the exchange between Maman and the priest.

He was talking about her. "It's remarkable, isn't it? Even from the back I would swear it was her. Will you come again? Or perhaps I could come to Paris?"

"I don't know," Maman said. "Perhaps sometime." Then she appeared, stepped sideways over the threshold, but was jerked to a stop, one arm held fast in the lit room.

"Nicole, please, tell me a few more things about Marie-Jo. Anything. Tell me the names of her children."

Her mother shook her head.

"Why? Why can't you just tell me their names?"

"I'm sorry, Frederí. I don't know their names."

Her arm was released without another sound, and she turned toward Lola without seeing her in the dim hallway. For a moment, Lola saw pain on her mother's face as she walked unsteadily from the priest's room. But once she recognized Lola, her expression and her movements smoothed themselves over instantly.

Outside, the sun now bleached only the tips of the wild grasses in the church meadow, while below, closer to earth, remained dark and churning like sea reeds. Heavy clouds still clung to the hills.

Maman could not be comforted by a hug, at least not Lola's. Guillaume's might have been different, but even to him she did not show weakness or need, not like Francine's mother, who relied on her daughter's excessive affection on bad days. You could not hurt Maman and you could not relieve her. With Papa it was just the opposite. You could offend him by simply walking past him in a room; you could bolster him with the most absent hug.

Lola lingered on the stone steps, observing the world that lay before her: her father reaching in his coat pocket for the clump of keys he carried; Guillaume stamping in the cold, lifting the silver handle over and over yet knowing the car was still locked; and the whole depressed town beyond this street where there was no work and no words to soothe them.

She felt her mother's hand on her shoulder too late, just after she'd launched herself from the steps. She felt it, but it was too late and too cold to stop.

In the car they clenched every muscle and rubbed themselves warm. When the engine started up, cold air blasted through the vents and her mother slammed the heat off violently. Lola willed the silence to continue, needing room to think about all she had witnessed. But her father ruined it.

"Now there was a truly uplifting fellow. One of the chosen few—"

"Don't make things worse, Marc," her mother said. "Just drive us away from here."

Her father asked what the priest had said to her, but she just shook her head.

"Why did he want to know so much about Marie-Jo?" Lola said, hoping to help. "Did he love her?"

"Yes," her mother said.

"A lot?"

"Yes."

"And she didn't love him?"

"No."

"Who did she love?"

"The man she married."

"Did you know him?"

"A little."

"Do I really look like her?"

"No."

It was always like this, trying to find out about her past. It was nearly impossible to get any information. Maman didn't like to talk about things that had already happened, even recent events. Papa could think back fondly to a ham sandwich, but Maman only looked in one direction: straight ahead.

After a few minutes, Guillaume asked, "When can we visit again?"

No one answered him. When a blue sign for Paris appeared, Lola thought she heard her mother let out a whimper of relief.

"When, Maman?" he persisted. "When?" And though he stopped asking after that, his voice seemed to linger in the car.

Little bubbles of life cluttered the two lanes going south. Lola peered into the cars on the right as her father picked up speed. There were several families returning to the city. In one, the mother drove with one hand while everyone else slept. In another, the mother was leaning over into the back, trying to slap a child and missing, as her other children laughed. They passed a carload of teenagers smoking, then a man carefully picking his ear while a woman dozed on his shoulder, then an elderly couple staring straight ahead.

When Guillaume began to read aloud, first in a whisper, then, as he lost himself in the words, louder, she was forced back into her own bubble. He was reading from the Book of Job, a part toward the end when Job is pleading for an answer and is given only silence from God.

At the sound of the words, her father's hands clenched the wheels tighter. He was angry now, angry at the day, the priest, and Guillaume's relentless faith. But he was most angry, Lola guessed, at her mother, who had not been behind him when he marched to the car and who would not now answer him when he asked what had been said.

Guillaume carefully turned a thin gilt-edged page.

"Stop, Guillaume, please," her father said.

But he did not stop. He simply lowered his voice and read on doggedly, through God's remaining speeches, Job's repentance, and the part where he is given double what he had before and lives to see the birth of four generations of his family, to the end.

"'Then Job died,'" Guillaume said with satisfaction, "'old and full of years.'"

Lola vowed to remember this day, and every day that came after it. She would recall Guillaume's powdered cheeks and his stubborn voice. Years from now, she would tell him how it was through her eyes. And when her children asked about her childhood in Paris, she would have hours of detail for them, great reels of film to project onto their imaginations. She would remember everything about Maman, but she would not be like her: she would never bury a part of her life in a silent grave.

Odile

❦

ABOVE HER, THE SOUND OF ALEXANDRE'S SOLES ON THE DECK QUICKENED ODILE'S hands at her dressing table. *Do the shadow first,* Maman always told her, though all of Odile's friends and all the magazines advised doing it last. The bell rang, his two short jabs at the button, and her mother was in motion, feet sweeping across the kitchen, the coatroom, and up the stairs before Odile could put a sound to the breath she had caught to tell someone to answer it. There was an initial swell of greeting (they sounded, at this distance, in all their enthusiasm, like four or five old friends meeting haphazardly on the street), then the pair of voices and the two pairs of shoes spilled overlappingly back down the stairs and into the living room. She picked up the small baton and heard, as she always did with this gesture and this faint silvery smell, *shadow first.*

The voices were clearer now, separate, each waiting politely for its turn. They exchange words like money, she thought, with no further reflection. Instead, she berated herself for running late, for allowing these noises in the living room to occur without her.

When she had finished her eyes, she stood before the long mirror that hung on the inside of the closet door, and though there was no part of her that wasn't contained within its parameters, she had the sense that she couldn't see all of what others saw when she stood before them. Some essential thing was missing. She looked down at her shoes, then back up, but a true focus eluded her. She stepped closer. She had seen this face too much. It was neither pretty nor ugly. It did not exist as other faces existed. There was a cheek, an eye, a lip—but unintegrated, pulled apart, rearranged: one of Picasso's *Mesdamoiselles.* The familiar urge to smash the mirror seized, then released her. She took a deep breath, forced a polite smile, and shut the closet door.

She found them on the sofa, Maman sitting sideways with her legs curled beneath her and her shoes dropped on the carpet below, and Alexandre at the other end, an arm draped along the top edge, more comfortable than Papa ever seemed upon his own furniture.

"Alexandre was just telling me about Paul's accident. I can't believe it." What she meant was, I can't believe you haven't told me.

"Have you seen him today?" Odile asked Alexandre. They were both looking at her without full approval. The dress was unflattering. The square neck didn't suit her. Or perhaps it was the high waist. She waited for their insincere compliments.

"No. I'll go tomorrow morning." He felt guilty about this. He turned away from her, to his thumb on the seam of the cushion.

She stood hovering above them in the new dress, which now felt like a wooden barrel. Weren't they going to say anything at all? "Apparently his mind is not very clear yet," she said to her mother, unwilling to speak of Paul in his hospital room, clutching his sheets.

But Maman wouldn't ask for more detail. "How awful." She said this as she might say "How splendid" or "How peculiar," the potential tragedy of it glancing off her easily. "Do you cycle too, Alexandre?" She didn't want them to leave.

"I don't even own a bike." He lifted his hand off the couch in mock depravity. He was completely relaxed in her house, not tortured the way she was when talking to his parents. He enjoyed being around her mother's beauty, as if she were a vista or a shimmering body of water. She was beautiful, even now, curled up like a child in one of the long denim shirts she wore around the house. But the skin around the corners of her mouth had begun to sag, and her neck was ringed with three imprecise creases. The jewels of age, she had said once in a dressing room, tracing them in the mirror.

"That's just as well," Maman said.

The time had passed for compliments. "We should be off."

"You don't want to be the first to arrive."

"There'll be traffic." Odile shot Alexandre a look to pry him off the sofa.

He responded slowly, rising like an older man, shaking one pant leg and then the other from where they had caught on the rim of his socks.

Her mother walked them to the stairs and reached in the closet for a coat.

"The gray one, Maman."

"Not the white?"

"All right, the white."

The coat was handed to Alexandre, who opened it for her to step into. Maman smiled greedily at them. "You look beautiful," she said to Odile.

Too late, too late, Odile thought, to the rhythm of their feet going up the stairs.

In the car, Alexandre reached for his seat belt, careful to smooth down his lapel as he slid the strap over his chest.

"What are you doing?"

"I think we should wear these. Put yours on too." He didn't look at her as he fished around for her clasp, buried deep between their seats.

"Because of what happened to Paul?"

He gave no answer.

They had visited Paul the day before, and though he seemed to recognize them when they came in, the longer they stayed, the more confused he got, their identities shifting from friends to cousins to parents and back again. At one point he had grabbed at his bedsheets frantically, gathering one part, then another, convinced they were papers, papers at his father's law firm where he worked on Saturdays, that needed sorting. The impossible task had filled him with panic, and finally Odile took his hands and put them under the covers and smoothed the sheets back over his chest, assuring him that the papers were sorted and he could rest. Alexandre, through all of this, sat in a chair near the window. By the time they left, sweat had darkened his collar. But he wouldn't talk about it on the way home.

The dinner was across the city, near the Bastille. There was little traffic, and they arrived early. The Girards' apartment was on the fifth floor, and from across the street she could see, through the three balcony doors, the dining room and the tops of the tall chairs, the tips of flower petals and candlesticks, and the teardrops of the chandelier's cut glass, which held in thin spears the deep red of the dining room walls.

Alexandre took her hand as they crossed the street, and still she felt unsteady and conspicuous, as if she were arriving at this dinner alone.

The apartment was huge, the ceilings vaulted, the spaces between chairs and tables vast. Off to one side was a wide carpeted staircase. This was the kind of apartment Maman had always wanted, though she thought Mme. Girard tasteless. She had pastel slipcovers, striped and plaid in the same room. Beneath her chin tonight hung a heavy brooch in the shape of a cornucopia.

"You two look stunning as usual," she said, kissing them, ushering them in. "Micheline!" she called down the hall. "The royal couple is here!" They had been dubbed that by someone's parents. The perfect pair, the magnificent match. They had heard it all. "Micheline!"

Mme. Girard was exasperated by their early arrival and Micheline's absence, but Alexandre appeased her with lavish praise of the way she had decorated the apartment (they had moved in last summer) and, instantly mollified, she led them on a tour, forgetting she had already done so in September. When they came back down, the living room was half full of guests relinquishing coats and scarves to one maid or giving drink orders to another.

They all stood chatting amid the striped and the plaid furniture. Although she was aware of facing it during the long conversation with Jeanne and Christine, Odile only glanced once in the mirror that hung over the fireplace. When she did, she caught herself unawares and for a split second was able to see herself as she might see another: a pale, pretty face, a wide, perhaps inappropriate smile, and strong shoulders that held the posture and poise of her mother, which pleased her. The square neck was fine. She turned back and spoke with more confidence about the absurdity of the baccalauréat, which Christine's older sister had just failed for the third time.

When she was beckoned into a conversation behind her, she noticed the threshold to the dining room, the symmetry of the two long rows of chair backs, the stretch of table with all its leaves in place and covered by a white linen cloth bordered with navy satin. The first course sprawled in colorful porcelain platters along the length of the table. Some sort of cold fish, Odile guessed. On the sideboards were stacked the plates and bowls for the following courses. The dark green curtains rustled slightly at the edges of the balcony doors, nearly black in the dim chandelier light, a light that smoldered orange within those blood-red walls. At the center of the table, the unlit candles waited like willowy divas preparing to perform. Something must be done, Odile thought, with a scene like that.

Whenever she felt this urge to still and preserve a moment, every other scene within reach rushed toward her with the same kind of urgency: the kitchen, glimpsed briefly whenever the door was swung open, where Mme. Girard conducted her orchestra of hired help, and here in this living room where the boys and the girls had neatly divided, the girls near the hearth and the mirror and plaid, the boys among the stripes and the old foxed photograph of M. Girard's grandfather on the day of his appointment to the Académie Française. She wanted to paint these boys in their creased coats and shaved napes, these girls in their stiff sleeves and steep heels, the slopes of their shoulders and the poses of their hands more and more similar each Saturday night to their parents', which could be seen in some other living room in another huge apartment in Paris.

A clock struck eight. How would one paint this sound into this scene? How would one capture those plunging tones that were at once soothing and menacing, that began, each one, with the voice of an eager child and ended, no more than a second later, in a melancholy echo? The sounds, now six, now seven, seemed to accelerate the voices, the gestures, the hope of speaking and being understood. And then the last stroke, eight, tapering off like smoke above their heads. She wanted to capture that, bottle it: the effect of the stroke of eight on a roomful of people.

"Odile, you get prettier every time I turn around." M. Girard wrapped his large hands around her upper arms, lifting her slightly as they kissed.

"Thank you."

"You're catching up to your mother, though to surpass her would be quite a feat." He glanced at her friends Claire and Simone but found no words of reassurance, nothing to make them less resentful of her. Then he returned to Odile. "How is your father?"

"Fine. Busy as always." Papa was respected for his work but considered a freak, she was sure, at a party. He chose the most obscure topics or he repeated the puns Lola brought home from school. Either he rambled on or he sat alone, staring down into the one drink he never finished. While it embarrassed her to be with him, Odile envied his defiance of their codes. How she would have loved to go sit in a chair and study the scene instead of carrying out her half of this banal conversation about her family with M. Girard.

The bell rang shrilly at the threshold with none of the aplomb of the clock in the corner. It trembled frantically at the tips of Mme. Girard's fingers and would not be stilled until every head had lifted and turned, every smile had acknowledged that dinner was served.

Finally satisfied, Mme. Girard replaced the bell on its silver tray and returned to the kitchen.

Couples sought each other out for the move into the next room, where they would once again be separated. Alexandre gave her hand a long squeeze, an apology of some sort. Yes, she squeezed back, it's all right. What she was forgiving she was sure neither of them knew.

In front of them, Jeanne leaned to say something quietly to Luc and they laughed together, each reaching for the other's arm at the same time. Odile and Alexandre had introduced them almost a year ago. They were at a dance and there was a run in Jeanne's stocking and Luc gave her a piece of gum to stop it. They danced then, to several songs, and when they came back the run had traveled to her ankle and Luc had stepped on the gum, but something had happened. Their bodies no longer seemed cumbersome; their words weren't hesitant or polite. Something had happened—and so fast. Odile knew it had never happened to her.

"My sister, Isabelle, is here," Micheline Girard whispered to her, as she began to circle the dining room table, looking for her card. "And you've been placed next to her."

"Why?"

"Because she says you're more tolerable than my other friends."

"But why is she here? Why isn't she in Italy?"

"She showed up yesterday. She has a few days' vacation."

Odile didn't dare look down to the other end where Isabelle and her own place must be. It wasn't surprising that she had appeared at the table without suffering through any of the preliminaries in the living room. Most likely she had stayed in the kitchen, taking lessons from the hired chef. She was like that. She took either an intense interest or a profound dislike in things, and above all she abhorred these formal dinners.

When Odile took her seat, Isabelle was turned in the opposite direction, listening to Paul's girlfriend tell the whole story of the bike accident out in Vincennes.

Six places down on the other side, Alexandre was talking to Julie Silvan. Odile knew he was not thinking, as she often did, of how Julie's father died last spring on the train from Lyon after a massive heart attack just before the Tonnerre stop, how Julie's father had boarded a train one evening like so many other evenings and descended on a stretcher, had left Lyon alive and arrived in Paris dead. After Alexandre poured their wine, he leaned toward her and said something deliberately covert. Julie covered her mouth and began to shake. How did one learn to laugh again after death? Was it possible to forget, even for a few seconds at a time? Around Julie now, Odile never forgot death, and she always felt uncomfortable. Her words seemed frivolous, disrespectful. She wished she were more like Alexandre, who would never question or regret anything he said later.

She had been watching him too long. He would tease her about being jealous and she would tell him what she was thinking and he wouldn't believe her. To avoid such a conversation, she looked instead straight across to where Jean-Paul was telling the beginnings of a story to Marie-France.

"My appointment was at four-thirty and I arrived promptly." He never stopped talking about himself. Beside him, Marie-France was already flushed, not from the wine but from the pleasure and good luck of having been seated so close to J-P. She was already laughing; the mere tone of his voice, the way he said the word *promptly,* had gotten her going. She had been in love with him for years. Other eyes began to watch his face as he told stories that rendered them all slowly unconscious— unconscious of the long table, the courses yet to be served, Mme. Girard's sharp words to the servants when they tried to clear the plates too soon, the two bottles of wine M. Girard would drink by himself, the white cracks in the center candelabra where the polish had not been completely rinsed off, the dark green curtains that were too heavy for their rods, and the dolorous, solitary note as the clock in the living room struck the half hour.

Odile refused to be lulled.

J-P included her in his rounds of eye contact as he shepherded his audience, but she had never begun to listen. She used him to avoid

Isabelle, who had turned back from Paul's girlfriend and now ate with her head down. Odile could feel Isabelle's arm brush against her own as she lifted the fish bones with her knife; Isabelle was determined not to give J-P the slightest bit of what he got in abundance from everyone else. But Odile could not simply turn her attention to her plate for the evening. She wished she could, but it felt so rude even glancing down to secure a mouthful of fish on her fork. The most insulting thing she could manage was not to listen, though she compensated by affecting the face of a rapt listener.

Odile could smell her. It was not a perfume—Isabelle would never wear perfume—but a shampoo or rinse rising from still-damp hair. She had an impulse to turn and lift the long shank of hair from Isabelle's back so that it would not leave watermarks on the silk blouse.

They should have greeted each other already. She knew it was her duty, for though they were in Isabelle's house, they were on Odile's territory.

She had known Isabelle since they were five and seven. Seven going on twenty, twelve going on forty, Maman always said of Isabelle. She was intelligent—too intelligent, she had heard Papa once lament, as if intelligence were a great weight in one's head that might topple the whole body. Odile admired her intensity, and whenever she found in herself moments of pure focus, she attributed it to what she'd once observed in Isabelle. But despite all that promise (and this was an inevitable word in any discussion of Isabelle), she hadn't gone on to university. She was a sculptor's apprentice in Rome. Was it true she had asked to sit next to her? And now were they not ever going to speak? She waited until J-P paused for a sip of wine, then removed her attention from him altogether.

"Isabelle." She had aimed for some sort of tone of surprise but, upon hearing its first false syllable, continued in a soft voice that tried to imply an inability to break away sooner. "How are you?"

They kissed. Odile felt others watching: how rude not to have acknowledged the person beside you for an entire course. A servant's arm, clearing plates, came between them as they separated. Isabelle wore no makeup. It made Odile feel the absurdity of her own painted features. Isabelle's eyes were luminous and vulnerable, her lips full of natural color.

They were smiling sardonically. She would never answer a question like *How are you?*

Unnerved, Odile reached up to Isabelle's neck to touch a pendant that hung on a chain. "What's this?"

"Just a gift from some kids I tutor."

It was a tiny plastic key. Odile let it hang from one finger. She could feel the heat from Isabelle's neck across the back of her hand. "It's so green," she heard herself say.

Isabelle laughed, and the key fell back onto her chest. Odile withdrew her arm.

How is Italy? She didn't want to ask this. Surely there was a more interesting question to pose. She remembered the clock and wanted to ask her if she'd ever tried to sculpt sound. Perhaps the clock would strike again soon. She would ask her question then.

Neither of them picked up the next fork for the new course.

"How is Italy?" It couldn't be helped. The silence had to be filled, and Isabelle would not help. Silences amused her.

"Beautiful. Poor. Hot. Those are my standard adjectives, at least."

"And the nonstandard?"

Isabelle looked at her as if remembering her, Odile Tivot, for the first time. "Sensual is the first one that comes to mind. Not sexual, but they seem to pay close attention to all the senses separately." She shook her head. "I sound like a tour guide on a bus through Florence. But it's true." As she spoke, she fingered the key. Her hands were familiar to Odile; they were like coming across an old toy or a favorite picture book, the forgotten shape and color and texture suddenly so precious. How well she knew those hands, the long palms, the square, unfiled nails, the sharp, straight bones across the tall knuckles. "And you? Micheline says you're preparing for the sciences."

"I know," said Odile, responding to an unspoken reproach. She had long ago planned to do languages and art history. "I don't know what happened."

"You became practical."

"I guess," Odile said, feeling suddenly that if Isabelle hadn't gone she wouldn't be memorizing the formulas for magnesium sulfide or aluminum nitride. Perhaps every void in her life had been created by Isabelle's departure, though at the time it had seemed insignificant. She and Micheline had waved from their old balcony when M. Girard drove Isabelle to the train two years ago.

"Do you still paint?" Isabelle asked.

"Paint?"

"You made me that card, for my fifteenth birthday. I have it somewhere." She pointed upstairs toward her bedroom. The door had been shut when she and Alexandre were shown up there; she had barely thought of Isabelle then. Mme. Girard hadn't even mentioned she was home. Odile wondered now what was up there, what she treasured, what she kept in her drawers. Had she been home for the move to this new apartment? Had she chosen to keep Odile's card, or had all her belongings just been packed up and shipped across town without her? It was a watercolor of a lime tree, with fifteen limes on it.

"No, I don't paint."

"You did oils, too, didn't you? I know I remember one hanging somewhere."

"I did a few, but I don't think I have any of that stuff anymore. I don't know."

Isabelle's naked eyes bore into hers. *You should know,* they seemed to say. *You should.*

Odile was eager to get off the subject of herself. "Is it frustrating to be helping someone else with his work and not doing your own?" She was pleased with this question. It came out of nowhere.

"Sometimes." Isabelle's eyes drifted down as she gave the question more thought. What was it about her that made her seem more vital, more awake and alive, than anyone else in this room? There was an eruption of laughter on the other side of the table. J-P had reached the punch line of one of his stories. The girls laughed the longest, tinkling on like shattering glass. "It's actually quite good discipline to be kept away from it. It builds up all sorts of ideas and urges. Gioconda's work is conservative— well, I mean, she's not doing statues of generals or anything, but it's more reserved than mine—and I think that helps, too, to be bound and gagged all day."

"You work for a woman?"

"Yes, Giaconda di Niota."

"I pictured this old Rodin type."

She gave a weary nod and Odile wondered if her mind was capable of offering something Isabelle hadn't heard a dozen times since yesterday. "No," Isabelle said, "she's more of a Mme. Beauvais type."

Odile smiled in feigned comprehension. She knew she should know who Mme. Beauvais was, but no image or paragraph from her French civilization textbook came to her aid.

"Remember her? Down the hall at our old place? Tall and abrasive."

Odile was too embarrassed to laugh. The clock would strike nine soon. She would redeem herself then. "Do you have any time for your own stuff?" she asked, not wanting to veer too far from the subject of art.

"At night."

At night. An upstairs studio, street sounds coming through the high dark open windows in hot gusts, those hands focused and separate from her body—not separate, but laden, as if all of her self had been poured into them.

"Which is not as romantic as it sounds," Isabelle continued, and Odile wondered if she had said something aloud. "I drink a lot of coffee and have chronic back pain like an old woman." She reached behind her, arching and wincing, to rub the base of her spine. "Here, you can feel the knot." She turned it toward Odile, lifted her shirt, and pointed to a spot below the waist of her skirt. "You won't believe it. This huge bulb of pain. Feel it."

For a long time afterward, as more food appeared and plates were replaced by bigger and then eventually smaller ones, as they chatted on, and as the clock struck nine—nine perfect rings of sound encircling the two of them—the sensation of the tiny hairs, the moist skin, the springy rise at the base of the spine remained on Odile's fingertips. That one act of dipping down, touching, and withdrawing seemed permanent, as if somewhere, on another plane of existence of which she was only allowed partial consciousness, it was happening over and over again.

After coffee, plans were made to go to a nightclub across the river. The girls, all but Isabelle, gathered in Micheline's bathroom to reapply themselves.

"Poor Odile, stuck with the sullen sister all night," Marie-France said to her own reflection, which was still bright and beaming from dinner.

Before Odile could manage a polite denial, Micheline said, "She's not so bad anymore, is she?" Without waiting, she went on. "It's because she's all in love."

Odile recalled how when they were children Micheline used to accuse them of being in love and not loving her. It surprised her that Micheline remembered this now to tease her with. Though growing older had always frightened her, remembering the past was a pleasing sensation. She watched her own face in the mirror spread into a smile.

"With who?" Marie-France asked, lowering her lipstick in exaggerated curiosity.

"The son of that sculptor she works for."

"Giaconda di Niota."

"Is that her name?" Micheline said.

"Yes," Odile said, stroking on more blush to cover the rising natural one.

Watching her, Marie-France said, "God, I wish I had just one of your bones."

Alexandre was waiting at the foot of the stairs with her coat. He was a catch, Maman said. Clever, ambitious, handsome. He studied law, but in the summer he was an assistant director for his uncle's films, famous films. He went on location to places like Lima and Sydney. She had heard Alexandre's name a thousand times before she ever met him. All her friends had been and maybe were still in love with him; certainly Micheline was. She never knew why he picked her. Because you're so beautiful, Maman told her. Odile feared it was that simple.

Out on the sidewalk, Isabelle said, "Come with us," pointing to their father's Renault.

Not even to go to a nightclub had she put on a little makeup, and yet standing there between Micheline and Jeanne, she seemed more elegant and polished, as if the others were off to a masked ball. Her hair had dried in waves that caught thin crescents of light. She beckoned Odile to the car as though they were the oldest of friends. She glowed. She was in love with the sculptor's son.

Micheline explained that Odile had come with Alexandre, who then took Odile's hand and led her across the street, away from the rest.

In the car he encapsulated all his conversations for her, then teased her, as he always did, for talking to one person the entire meal. He imitated her, nodding, sipping. *"And then what? And then?* It's not talking, it's bloodsucking. You've got to learn how to spread yourself out in a room."

"Why?"

"Because it's a skill you're going to need all your life." He said this in a mock-parent tone, but he meant it.

When they reached the club, they circled around for a parking space for over a half hour. She knew not to speak while this was going on. He hated this part of any evening and yet behaved each time as if it were a wholly unexpected hitch, as if they didn't, every night they went out, comb some street for a parking spot. Tonight she used this time to examine his face. Was he handsome simply because of the absence of anything jarring: a nose like her father's, a hooked chin like M. Girard's, acne pocks like Luc's? His face was illuminated, then obscured, then lighted again as they moved beneath the lamplight of each street. In the dark he could have been any man; in the light his skin looked as glossy as wax. She looked at his lips. Had she really ever kissed them? They seemed unfamiliar to her. He wedged the car backward into a tiny spot.

"Finally," he said, cutting the engine and leaning back on the headrest. He tipped his head toward her. "You are really stunning tonight." With a finger he looped a bit of her hair over her ear. She hated the way it felt; it reminded her of being very young and playing in the sand. Don't do that, Maman said, lifting the hair free. It will make your ears stick out. But this was one of his tender gestures. Then he would kiss her. Once without tongue, then tongue, then without again. Not yet; now; not yet. She couldn't shake the impression that his lips were not flesh.

"I wish we didn't have to go in," he said, as he pulled away. It was a lie. There was nothing more predetermined than a night like this. If she had suggested they leave, he would have insisted on dropping in, just for a minute, just to see who was there.

Odile got out of the car and waited for him to join her on the sidewalk. He would jangle his keys after he put them in his pocket; he would lean on three fingers against the trunk of the car as he came around it. What had gotten into her? Why was she seeing him like this, at such a distance? At the beginning of the evening she had wanted to get out to the living room where he was with Maman; she had been jealous of their easy talk on the couch. And he was a kind, sensitive person. He always meant well. He had taken Paul's hand at the end of their visit to the hospital with the same firm shake he would have given him at the beginning of a party, as if to rouse him from his confusion. His collar had been soaking wet by then.

The club was packed with clusters of bodies shifting restlessly through its rooms. Luc, Jeanne, Micheline, and Isabelle were just inside the door. Alexandre leaned into the group and said something that made them all laugh. It was impossible to hear what it was, and if she asked he'd say it was stupid. He never laughed at what he said himself, and he never repeated a joke. He reached back for Odile's hand and Isabelle fell in behind her as they made their way to the bar.

The music grew louder and Isabelle put her mouth in Odile's hair, just behind her ear, to be heard. "Look at the tiles on the floor. They're gorgeous." And, a few seconds later, "There's a faucet over there. This must have been a bathhouse." Then: "Look at the ceiling!"

Odile had been to this club at least ten times. She had been here at the end of a long night when there were only a handful of people standing around, and she had never noticed what Isabelle somehow saw despite hundreds of human obstacles. Above them was a mosaic of tropical birds in flight, exactly as they would be seen from below. One bird had fuchsia talons, another a vermilion belly and long muscular wings. Despite the smoke and the flickering light, the scene was perfectly vivid.

"Isn't it spectacular!"

Odile kept her head craned toward the ceiling, which made her hair fall back and Isabelle's lips brush briefly against her earlobe. If she were the sculptor's son, Isabelle might have pressed her lips even closer, might have licked the lobe.

Ahead of her, Alexandre stopped. Into the other ear he said, so loudly it made her flinch, "Are you trying to break my fingers?" But he was smiling. At the bar he said more softly, "We really should've just gone home."

"Yes," she said. She had never been so uninterested in his waxy kisses. He handed her a rum and coke, and she took a long gulp. She rarely had more than two small sips of any drink. When they went to dance, her glass was empty. She set it on a table with embarrassment.

Usually she hated to dance in a crowd like this. There was no way to keep your own rhythm; you were always getting elbowed or stomped on by someone else's. In truth, Odile had always used the crowd as an excuse not to dance. She didn't enjoy dancing even when the floor emptied out. She never felt more like Maman than on the dance floor. Not that she'd ever seen her mother dance to rock music, but she knew if Maman ever did it would be identical. They shared an instinctive restraint, an inability to relinquish. Relinquish what? she asked herself, as she carefully shifted her weight from side to side, holding her arms as others around her held theirs, stepping small steps, trying to hear a beat that everyone else seemed to feel at their core. "Are you tired?" Alexandre had asked the first time they ever danced together. She thought of that question every time they danced now and could never see herself as anything but droopy on the dance floor. For some reason she had never thought before that alcohol might help. But the rum and coke seemed to clear a passage. After a few songs, she felt her arms leave her side in unexpected undulations; her feet, in brief intervals and in sheer imitation of the bald man beside her, nearly moon-walked. Alexandre gave her a cryptic look. Amusement? Disapproval? She didn't know. She didn't care. The next song had a quick staccato beat, and she found herself shuddering to it perfectly.

She had moved away from Isabelle, but now, feeling more confident, she peered between people to find her. Then she danced imperceptibly in her direction. As Odile got closer, she saw that Isabelle did not dance like anyone else. The song had a machine-gun beat, but Isabelle swayed in slow waves as if she heard some profound rhythm within the music. It was beautiful. She was lost in it. She had forgotten everyone in the room. What would it feel like to be wholly inside yourself, to give up that vigilant second self that believed it could know how others saw you?

Odile tried to fix her eyes on Alexandre, who reached for her with warm hands and an anticipatory grin, but, once released, her attention drifted back to Isabelle. She was dancing even more slowly now, her arms above her head. Had she had sex with the sculptor's son? Yes. The certainty overwhelmed her. Odile felt how feeble her own movements were, how expressive of her virginity.

Why was she still a virgin? Alexandre insisted that they should go at whatever pace she felt comfortable, but once he had told her he felt that she was trying to keep him in a tiny box and it was painful, physically painful, to be so cramped all the time. He told her that since she was a girl he didn't expect her to understand, but that was how he felt. Watching Isabelle, Odile realized she herself was also in a box. Perhaps tonight, she thought at the bar, gulping down another rum and coke. She would let him make love to her tonight.

On the way out they ran into Paul's sister. The passage was too narrow for three so Odile stood behind Alexandre, who spoke seriously and shook his head during the whole exchange.

"What did she say?" she asked, when they got outside.

"No improvement. Nothing."

"But they said in a couple of days he should be—"

"I know what they said, Odile, but they were wrong. He's not getting any better."

In the car, Alexandre sat with his hands on the wheel for several silent minutes before turning the key. Odile thought to reach out for his hand or stroke his hair, but she feared he might resent the attention drawn to his sadness and reject it. She wanted to withhold her touch until they got to her house. So she sat as silent and still as he, though the music in her head rang shrilly and the rum gave everything motion.

She hadn't noticed before that Micheline's car was parked across the street. She wished Alexandre would start the car; she didn't want to have to see the two sisters come around the corner. In two days, Isabelle would be dancing on Italian tiles, walking beneath an Italian moon. She hadn't said anything more to Odile than good-bye. Odile tilted her head to see if there was a moon above Paris. Roused by this slight movement, Alexandre turned the key.

He parked alongside her house, not one barge down as he would have if he were planning to stay.

Come in. It would have been easy to say. But she had never said anything like it. He decided whether he would come in or not; he decided when to slip his fingers into her bra and where to lead her hand. *Come in,* Odile practiced in her head, but she would never say it.

He hadn't cut the engine; he stared straight ahead, more ghoulish than ever in the mottled light from the street above and the river beside them.

Then the rigid surface cracked without warning. The stiff mouth gaped, the eyes crumpled, and the smooth cheeks bunched up around them.

"Alex." She touched his face. It was already wet. He turned from her, but she pulled him back. She leaned over and kissed him, but his lips could not conform.

He pushed her away and laid his forehead on the steering wheel. "I'm so scared for him, Odile."

"Let's make love." She heard the words with as much shock as he did.

He lifted his head and let out a sound that could have been a laugh or a sob.

"Let's." She took his hand.

"Not now. Not like this."

But no was not a possible answer. She had made her decision.

She brought his fingers to her mouth and began to suck them, the littlest finger first. She took her time. She let him cry. But when she got to the thumb he was moaning for her.

She reached down, lowered his seat all the way back, and climbed on top of him. She heard him say her name from a great distance, in both protest and pleasure. He was still crying softly and couldn't kiss, but his hands were full of another emotion as they grappled through her clothes and underclothes.

The alcohol sharpened her will but not her senses; it emboldened her movements, yet she felt as separate and numb as always when his mouth covered her breast, his fingers fumbled between her legs. But instead of stopping him here she let him continue. The car grew hot and moist with their breath. The city outside lost its definition and she felt drunk, newly drunk all over again. He kissed her now, a salty insatiable kiss. She could feel him grow harder beneath her as he spun his heavy tongue around in her mouth.

When he raised her again above him to reach her breast with his mouth, she saw instead small unpainted lips and she arched and shuddered and hollered to herself, *no*. She opened her eyes. Alexandre, she thought. But she felt the space between them swell and the only way to feel what he felt was to give in to the images in her head. She let the softer lips touch her breast; she let the thin hands with the sharp bones slip between her legs. She buried her face in damp wavy hair. She pressed herself hard against the body below her and everything but her own desire disappeared.

"Look at me, sweetheart," she heard, but didn't obey.

When he was inside her, she was inside Isabelle. She was the sculptor's son. Their cries were blunt and echoless against the clouded windows.

When it was over, he brushed the hair from her face. "Are you okay? Here, come here. Around like this." He made a place for her beside him and wrapped his arms around her. "That was beautiful. I felt so strange, so scared. This thing with Paul—"

"I know."

"It's so frightening that there might be permanent damage and that he might never . . . that he might just be gone, for good . . ."

She lay beside him with her back against his chest, which was moist with sweat and stuck to her every time he took a breath. As he spoke, his chin bobbed on her shoulder. She wanted to get out of the car, but he continued on about Paul.

The steamed windows seemed to be moving closer. She had thought about Isabelle while making love to Alexandre. Was she losing her mind? Of course not, a psychiatrist would say. You were scared and a little drunk. It was the first time. A person is bound to have odd, inappropriate thoughts the first time.

". . . and when you think of it, the brain is just this flow of fluids and electric impulses, and all it takes is a little jostling to throw it out of whack forever."

Her heart pounded harder and harder. There was something wrong, terribly wrong with her. *Breathe deeply, breathe slowly,* she told herself. With her fingers she wiped clear a patch of windshield and saw three figures beginning to make their way across the east bridge. One, ahead of the rest, walked swiftly backward. From this distance it was impossible to tell if they were male or female, young or old. The lights of the city were carried in pinpoints on the river, below them, and in big yellow smudges in the clouds above. She felt it rise soothingly inside her, that ache to preserve the scene, to forbid it to shed its frail layers—the walkers would reach the other side, the sky would whiten, the river would stir—and vanish in the churn of memory.

". . . and you were so wonderful, just pulling up the covers and telling him to quiet down. I wouldn't have lasted in there without you. I felt like throwing up. There's something about hospitals, those long corridors and knowing that behind each door is another person's tragedy. . . ."

And just then, as if she had willed it, a clock across the river rang out, one thin solitary stroke.

"How do you think, if you were a painter, you would paint a clock striking the hour into a picture?"

"What?"

Tomorrow she would search the closets for her paints. The easel was in the laundry room behind the ironing board. She would set it up right out here, on the river. She would remember these three figures. They were already stepping off the bridge now, the backward one facing forward again, hailing a cab with a gray sleeve. Nothing about them would be lost.

Alexandre held her tighter. In a little boy's voice, he said, "I don't think you're listening to me." Of course, he didn't believe it.

When he moved his hand toward the inside of her thigh, she resisted the instinct to clamp a hand on him as she had countless times in this car before, saying *not yet*. *Not yet* was gone forever.

And this time her mind would be pure. She would keep her eyes open and feel *his* lips, *his* body beneath hers. The first time was over, and now, the seal broken, she could return to herself, she thought, but her hands traveled down his spine to a soft lump and her eyes closed to find Isabelle patiently waiting.

III

Unfinished, Unsent

Oct. 3

Dear Sarah,

Please don't be angry. I know how worried you must've been but I needed this time. I'm better now. I've found a job on a houseboat taking care of three children.

How is everything there?

Oct. 12

Dear Sarah,

How are you? How are all of you? Sometimes it's so hard just to ask this.

Oct. 22

Dear Sar,

So much tugs at me sometimes. I want so much. I guess I always did. We all went to a concert last night. Just three instruments, piano, violin, and flute. What is it about music? In the car driving home so much seemed possible. I am still young. Sometimes I forget that completely.

Oct. 28

Dear S,

I'm sorry it's taken me so long to write. I've started a few letters but it's just hard to explain

Nov. 1

I remember so much. I am remembering all the time. Today I thought of the first time I realized you were not me. I was five and you were setting that red alarm clock and I watched you and I knew that you weren't having the same thoughts. That you wouldn't dream the same thing that night. And that we would die at different times. And that you might die first. It was the first time I ever felt alone. I feel that all the time now.

Nov. 3

I have insomnia these days. It's 3 a.m. and I'm in the kitchen and I feel like writing you the longest letter imaginable. I feel like writing you every little detail about my life here. Marc (the father in this family I live with) has insomnia too. I can hear him in his study. Every now and then his seat squeaks. It's not so bad having insomnia when someone else in the house has it too. We've only run into each other once. (I try to stay in my room but sometimes like tonight I have to move around.) We ate cookies and he told me his best way of falling asleep is to imagine untying this barge we live on and drifting downriver. I've tried it, but it doesn't work for me

It feels good to be sitting here writing you a letter, though I'll probably never send it. I've begun a lot of letters to you. There is this pressure I feel to account for things. I always think each time I'll circle around to the perfect explanation, but I never do. It was easy to describe everything to you before. I felt so good. I had a purpose. I felt important. I felt alive. The minute he was born, everything just flew out of my hands. I can't really describe it better than this. It's as if before I was the center of everything because he was inside me, and then suddenly I was just this sloughed-off thing. There was so much anger in me. I don't really expect

Nov. ?

One day is identical to the next, so it is impossible for me to know which one this is. I wake up. I make breakfast, lunch, and dinner. Mondays I go grocery shopping. I have no idea why I came here or what is to become of me

Nov. 17

My bathroom is on the Seine side and the tub is raised and when you sit in it you are level with the windows and the water. The light at dawn is miraculous. It makes you hope for things and believe you will get them

Nov. 22

Today I think is Thanksgiving. Is it the third Thursday in November or the last? I can't even remember. But today feels like Thanksgiving so I'll pretend it is, which means it's been exactly a year since the day everything was decided.

Nov. 29

You always wanted to know how it felt to be pregnant and I tried to answer you, though now that it's over I think I can describe it even better. It was like wanting and having all at the same time. It was like being perfectly full. And afterward you are emptier than you can ever imagine.

Dec. 15

It is late but I am so awake I know I won't fall asleep tonight. Finally I feel I am coming out of something and it feels good. Today was so glorious I probably shouldn't write a word. But if I describe it to no one, will it have existed? And who else to tell if not you? You are the only person I ever think of writing to. I try to write you letters, but I never manage to finish them. Maybe I'll throw them all in a big envelope and mail them to you tomorrow.

Saturday is Lola's thirteenth birthday, so at breakfast her mother asked if I would go with Marc to pick out a few things for her. We met at a metro stop at the top of the street at five-thirty, and my French just fell into place. It's strange how that happens, how one minute you can't put one sentence together and the next you speak in full paragraphs. More than anything it depends on who you're talking to. With Nicole my French is disgusting. Even when I'm not speaking to her directly, if she's just in the room, it's terrible. But with Lola or Marc it just flows. All right, maybe not flows but trickles steadily. It's strange. I'm a different person, or more of a person, with them. I just step into myself.

So Marc and I walked down this street just gabbing and laughing. I walk a lot in the afternoons, and it was wonderful to be one of those pairs of people I am always so envious of. There was suddenly so much to say. It was like being with you. How can I explain this? It's as if life rushes at you day after day and things happen but you never really think about them afterward until there's someone else there who brings it up and it all comes out in a kind of hilarious shape that you couldn't see before. There are some people who can pull things out of you that you didn't even know were there. I can hear what you're thinking but I'm *not* falling in love with him. And he would *never* fall for me. He's got a gorgeous wife, and the last thing he'd be interested in is an affair with the postpartum au pair!

Jan. 11

Today I taught Lola how to make chocolate chip cookies, and the taste of the batter and the smell as they cooked made me miss you terribly.

Jan. 25

Out on the deck at dawn, if it's calm and clear, the bridges' arches are long loops all the way across. The buildings, the iron railings, and the bare trees on the

opposite side all quiver slightly in the current, and sometimes I dream of that world in the water. I dream of the
people who inhabit it and

Feb. 4

In every dream I have I am still pregnant and always
protecting my belly, and when I wake up and remember
that I am empty it is like being drained of every drop of
blood

Feb. 7

I want to try and explain

Feb. 12

In Nicole's room there are chocolates in a silver box by
the bed and silk stockings pressed flat and laid in drawers
and a closetful of hourglass dresses. There is a carton of
letters, nearly all of them in yellow envelopes. She gets at
least one of these once a week. I haven't read them. They
come from the town she grew up in, Plaire (which is also
the verb *to please*), and when one arrives her mood changes.
She never opens it with the rest of her mail. She saves it to
read in her room. If she writes back she must mail it off in
secret. I haven't ever read one but I've studied the envelopes. They're addressed as if someone were in a great
hurry—or afraid of getting caught. And there's never any
return address—just the postmark to give it away. You need
to be here. You were always a better sleuth.

Feb. 15

I still don't sleep very well

Feb. 22

There are two parts of my routine here I love, making
dinner and Sunday mornings. Dinner is easy. It's just for the
three kids and they'll eat anything. At six, a radio mystery

show comes on, and I listen to it while pressing garlic or stuffing a chicken. You'd faint at what I've learned to do in the kitchen. Sunday mornings everyone goes to church but me and Marc. Sometimes Odile sleeps instead of going to mass but she won't get up until midafternoon. Nicole calls us *les infidèles,* and we have coffee (which I've learned to love) together while they're all gone. We exchange insomnia reports and it is comfortable between us somehow, despite my French, which is improving but not fast enough. Sometimes this feels like home, a real home, kind of the way the house in Lyme felt before

Feb. 27

I've been thinking about Cal today. When I think of him now he seems so young. I should have

March 2

I finally feel a part of this family. At Easter we're going on a big trip.

The Wide Room

❦

ON THE ROAD HOME, THE LATE-MORNING SUN IS HOT ON OUR BACKS. IN THE SAGE and mint and heather beside us, the clacking voices of insects diminish as our feet approach, then resume with a great swell in our wake.

We're returning from La Douille, the dairy farm on the other side of the hill. Lucie is in a playful mood, having teased the young farmer about the strange shapes of his roosters' wattles. He blushed, as if she'd said something tremendously personal, and she teased him about that. Despite his embarrassment, he seemed to enjoy the attention, and as we were leaving he handed us a thick slice of goat cheese.

"Before you arrived I hadn't been to La Douille for years," she tells me. "And not because of my health, either." Above all, she hates to be thought of as weakening.

"Then why not?"

"A number of reasons, I think." I can hear that she won't yield, and I know not to prod her. We walk in silence until she goes on. "But I enjoy going with you. You love all those calves, don't you?"

"They're like children." There is one, older than the other calves, with spindly hind legs that make her rear rise way up, giving her an ungainly walk and a look in her eye that seems to acknowledge her awkwardness. She reminds me of Lola.

"And the way you veer away from the sows. They're big but they won't hurt you, not if you stay away from their food. But what I like best is watching Jean-Baptiste watch you."

"I can't believe he didn't notice our clothes."

We'd headed out that morning and walked nearly a mile before realizing we were wearing the same thing: white shirts, black sweaters, and tan pants. It was the spark for her silly mood.

"Don't change the subject. I think he was quite distracted by you."

"I don't think so." These are Lola's words and tone when her father teases her. *J'crois pas, papa.*

"All I know is that I used to have to wait in that henhouse a full hour before he'd bring me a bottle of milk. Now he comes in a hurry, smoothing down his hair"—in her throat is a bubble of laughter she is trying to keep down—"tucking in his shirt."

I try to remain serious. "It's not true! I've never once seen him . . ." I can't recall how she said *tucking in.*

"You see, you're all flustered just talking about him."

"I'm not!"

We laugh hard and loud, coming over the crest of the hill that leads down to our driveway.

Henri Peyraud is heading toward us. Perfect timing, for going down the steeper slope isn't easy for her.

"What happy faces this path has brought to me," he says. Then he sees our clothes. "Is there a uniform on the hill now? Or have you joined an army?"

He smiles without teeth. Unlike Lucie, whose youth remains in her soft downy cheeks and childish heart-shaped grin, Henri has a crumpled face. Creases merge with deep cracks. His hair is white and stuck straight up, like Guillaume's *brosse.* But, as he is the first to tell you, he's still strong as a cart horse. He and Lucie have been friends for seventy-six years, since they were eleven and made to share a hymnal in confirmation class. They sang the verses backward—*faltered not has faith our, faith Our*—until they were given a switching on the backs of their knees and made to do a hundred and fifty Hail Marys on a bare kneeler.

He takes Lucie's other side. Her face soon furrows in concentration as the decline worsens and her shoes slip on loose gravel. She slows and steps sideways, then turns her toes inward as if learning to ski. Henri coaxes her down with soft words, spoken more gently than I could ever utter them: *Doucement, soigneusement, comme ça, ça y est, oui, oui, oui, oui.*

I concentrate on the ground as well, helping her in my mind to place each foot carefully. We pass without comment the driveway to Nicole's family's house, where the shutters are sealed and the ceramic roof tiles one by one slip and smash on the ground below. On the way up she pointed to the largest window, the only uncovered one, made up of several long rows of panes. Nicole, she said, had been the last to sleep in that room.

When the road flattens, her grip loosens and she becomes chatty again, telling Henri about the effects of Monday's storm on the Monbet farm, about the tree that fell on a pasture wall at La Douille and how all the cows are nibbling at it. "You'd have thought them giraffes! And how efficient Jean-Baptiste is becoming. Haven't you noticed, Henri?"

"I have noticed only that he works at the same snail's pace he inherited from his father."

"You should try taking Rosie with you." She glances over at me with a mischievous smirk. Her face is glistening from the strain of the slope.

"Please don't listen to her, Henri."

We stop at the mailbox and she hands me a letter without ceremony, as if it isn't the first letter I've ever received here. I drop it into the dairy bag, careful to avoid the handwriting, though the two stamps are unavoidably American flags. She has found me.

Henri leaves us there, saying he has to make it to the dairy farm before Jean-Baptiste takes his lunch.

"I don't think he'll be eating much today. Love ruins the appetite."

I smile distractedly, and when she takes my arm again her clutch seems tight and her pace too swift. Now that the land has leveled, her steps are sure and steady and force the rapid approach of the house. I want her to say what we'll do once the groceries are put away. I want a full day's schedule, busy hands and mind, with no time to sit in my room and wonder what to do with the letter in my lap. But she wants to rest and, handing the letter to me once again before hanging the straw bag back on its hook, tells me to go out onto the back porch and read it in peace.

Instead I go out the front door, tug open the woodbin, toss in the letter, and sit down on the stoop. From there I can see, for a few seconds at a time when the wind gusts the trees in certain directions, a corner of the long window on the second story of Nicole's house.

* * *

After Marie-Jo married Paco Paniagua with the bright red hair—the Spanish carrot, he was called, though he'd lived in Plaire all his life—Nicole was the only child who remained in the big house. As soon as her sister's belongings were boxed and carried out, Nicole, like Marie-Jo when Juliette had left and like Juliette when Monique had gone, moved into the wide room, the master bedroom with their grandmother's canopy, the enormous window, and its long pillowed seat. From that perch, she and her sisters had spent months of their lives peering through the myriad panes, whose glass warbled and warped the long leaves of cherry laurels, the luminescent skins of plums, and the rows and rows of vines, as if you were glimpsing the world beyond through a fat sheet of rain.

Now finally in full possession of the room she had coveted for so long, Nicole stretched herself across the whole window seat, arms above her head, seeing if she could touch one end with her hands and the other with her feet. Not quite yet, she told herself, knowing that she would grow and eventually be able not just to lie down and reach but to sit on the first cushion and cover the last with her legs. The room was finally hers, and unlike her sisters, who'd each only had it briefly, she would have it from now, age eight, until who knew when, maybe forever. She stretched herself with all her strength. Maybe her legs would be as long as her father's. Maybe she would never marry.

All alone on the seat, Nicole suddenly found the view less intriguing, and her gaze often drifted away from the patterns of purple and green and the haze strewn across the valley's floor into the room itself. As her eyes traveled from wall to wall, she remembered each sister and her reign here.

Monique, who was in it from age fourteen until her marriage at twenty, had been fanatically neat and clean, and more than once Nicole found her standing on the great bed, having removed the canopy so all that remained was a skeleton of wood. While the white lace soaked in a tub of bleach downstairs, Monique polished with lemon oil those walnut bones until they glistened and scented the whole room. She also slept immaculately, utterly still and in the exact same spot each night, so that Juliette, when she moved in, had to flip the mattress because of the impression Monique's body had made. Then Juliette could sleep as she liked best: in the middle of the bed, her arms spread straight out on either side.

Like Christ on the cross, Marie-Jo liked to say when they spied on her, though the expression on Juliette's face was pure unequivocal rapture, for she loved to sleep and slept deeply. Nicole could slip in and play in her room in the morning without waking her up. Marie-Jo, with all her impatience to acquire the wide room, was the one to spend the least time in it. She crept out the window nearly every night to meet up with friends at the quarry, and if she returned to find Nicole in her bed, she did not force her out, for fear that Nicole's revenge would be to reveal her nocturnal secrets at breakfast. So instead, without ever a word between them, Nicole moved dutifully over to the far side of the bed when her sister slipped in near dawn, smelling always of tobacco and whiskey, her hair wet from a dare. In the morning Marie-Jo would ask, "Was he here last night?" and Nicole would respond yes, for Frederí Lafond stood outside the window every night, waiting for Marie-Jo to accept him.

Whether he watched her comings and goings, they were never sure, but at some point on any given night a moon-shaped face was sure to appear below and would remain suspended, supported on bare knees in the courtyard dirt, for hours at a time. Whether he saw Nicole studying him was never clear either. When she came to the window his expression never changed; it continued to hold all the bitter hope of all the longing in the world. It was a pious, grave face, and she was not surprised when she heard, just after Marie-Jo's wedding, that Frederí had gone into a seminary up north.

Like this Nicole sat on the window seat, looking in and conjured up each sister as she had once been in this room. Being so much younger, Nicole had been exempted from the intense rivalries among the three elder girls and so did not really know her sisters as well or as devastatingly as they knew each other. But suddenly, with Marie-Jo gone and the house silent, their memory seemed sacred to her.

She didn't sleep nearly as well with Marie-Jo out of the bed, and her nightmare about a little boy and a stone came back again and again. Even Sundays with her father and evenings with her mother seemed different. As she headed out with her father for their usual long walk after church, Marcelle's figure in the window moved with desperate languor through rooms that seemed darker and emptier than ever, and as she sat with her mother in the kitchen at night, she became aware as never before of the slow scrape of Octave's newspaper across his leg while he sat alone in the next room. Suddenly every move Nicole made seemed to be a choice between her mother and her father, whereas before there was at least Marie-Jo to balance things out. But none of her sisters had spent the time that Nicole did with their mother. There was a certain devotion Marcelle lavished on her last child that she had withheld from the others, but none of them envied Nicole and what they saw as her suffocating burden. They had never truly forgiven their mother for what had happened during the war, and they no longer wished for her face so close to theirs; they couldn't imagine having things to say to Marcelle for hours after dinner.

Within a few years, Nicole wouldn't be able to imagine it either. She would strain to remember actual conversations, real words that were spoken, and would fail. All she could later recall was a certain game they had made up from the patterns of flecked color and shallow crevices on the surface of the stone table. It was a fortune-telling game, and when she remembered it she could feel how the windows slowly blackened, and how the oil lamp strained to reach the corners of the room, and how the objects before her eyes (the wooden back of a chair, a bearded iris in a jar, her mother's knuckles on the table) sharpened and seemed to inch closer and closer, and how this shift was always both soothing and frightening to her. It was at this time of day that she needed her mother most, though it was different from the need she had for her father, who coddled her, lifted her up, and held her, breathing his pipe breath in her ear. Her mother rarely touched her, save to brush her hair roughly from her eyes before school or to give her two weightless kisses good night.

Alone in the wide room, Nicole did not have to make choices—or so she thought until the afternoon in February, eight months after Marie-Jo had gone, when her mother appeared in the doorway with a letter in her hand.

"May I?" she asked.

"Of course." Nicole put down her book and sat up a bit straighter on the window seat. She couldn't recall ever seeing her mother in this room since she had vacated it years ago.

She came and stood at Nicole's feet.

"Is it for me?" Nicole asked.

Marcelle stretched out her empty hand flat before the windowpane. "I can feel the wind through the glass. This is probably the coldest spot in the house."

"Here." Nicole offered her the other end of her blanket.

Marcelle folded a leg beneath her and sat down exactly the way Monique did when she came to the window. The white envelope floated on top of the dark blue blanket she pulled over her. Nicole couldn't recognize the handwriting or make out the letters, though she could see that one side had already been torn open.

"Who is it from?"

In this light, a bright gray just after a noon rain, her mother's skin was coarse and bluish. The rims of her lower eyelids were a deep dry red. She looked at Nicole without the slightest idea that she had been asked a question. Instead she began to speak, in a slow, stilted, rehearsed way.

"I would like to ask you something, Nicole. It is something I've been turning over in my mind for a great long while. It is actually a dream of mine, and now finally seems a time when I might achieve it." She stopped to run a fingernail along one of the red rims, which then flared an even more brilliant color. When her arm fell back into her lap, she said, "I would like to go to Paris, and I would like you to come with me."

"For how long?"

But Nicole didn't need to ask, for in her mother's voice and in the unwavering underlined eyes was the defiant challenge: *I have never asked anything of you before this.*

"It's from Great-Aunt Anne, that letter?"

"Yes."

They looked down at the envelope, quivering between Marcelle's fingers.

"She has invited us. They have an apartment that's terribly big for them. She was never able to conceive."

"She couldn't have children?" Nicole asked, stalling, but her mother rushed on.

"There is so much for you there. Do you remember telling me once that you wanted to be a judge? You were only five or six. It was during the Bruno trial in Roussillon. You must have seen a picture in the paper." She had never seen her mother so agitated. Her eyes leapt from one place to another as she rocked toward and away from Nicole on the seat, her hands curled tight around the envelope as if it had become a rope. "And the dances and the dinners. And the Seine, Nicole."

Nicole could find nothing in her words to imagine. She couldn't remember seeing a picture of a judge. Was it a photograph or a drawing? Dinners and dances and the Seine? She couldn't see any of it. It meant nothing to her.

"We can't go without Papa," was all she could think to say, though she was also curious to know if she would have to wear a uniform to school and if she would have to take a train to get there. She loved taking trains.

"He would visit us. And we would come back to see him and the girls. Aunt Anne is very well connected. And she wants us there, Nicole. She has said as much right here." She clutched the rolled letter even tighter. "She married into a good family. She's able to give you opportunities. Opportunities to be someone, to be independent, to be a success. I think she's willing to do that for you."

What opportunities? Had her mother forgotten she was only eight and a girl? Judges weren't girls.

"There is life there. This"—she turned toward the window in disgust—"is not life. It is not the life I vowed to give you when you were born. You're not like the others. You know that."

Nicole didn't follow her mother's gaze outside but looked to the room instead, to the corner wall where Monique had taught her to stand on her head, to the rug where Marie-Jo had showed them all a naughty Brazilian dance their father later punished them for, to the closet where Juliette had sought refuge after her best friend Yvonne was struck and killed by lightning. This *was* life. It was all of their lives. It was all she knew. And her sisters, scattered now all over the valley, lived still in this room.

Her mother tried again to describe more vividly the flavors of Paris, the possibilities, all the worlds in that one city. She spoke of the variety of nationalities, of women as educated as men, of a certain painting she knew to be on the second floor of the Louvre. As she spoke, she became as flushed and alive as Marie-Jo when she whispered to Nicole in the mornings of her nights with Paco Paniagua, and as devout as the disk of Frederí Lafond's face tilted up to the long dark window. But her words of what could be fell somewhere between them, unheard by Nicole, who had filled her eyes and ears with what had been.

Even before Marcelle had ceased to speak, the bloom had faded from her face, replaced once again by the translucent blue pallor. She continued to rub first one rim of her eye, then the other, with an unfiled nail, and with each stroke Nicole feared she would draw blood. When she was finished, she said, "Tell me you'll come, Nicole. Say yes to me."

Downstairs she heard her father cough. He always coughed on the first puff of his pipe as he lit it. *Caught a bit of flame in the throat,* he'd say, or *Lungs still pink as a baby's.*

Her mother had drawn her knees to her chin, her arms tightly wrapped about her folded legs, the curled letter dangling between two fingers off to one side. She had become very small.

It must have been part of a fairy tale she heard when she was very young, though she was never able to find it in any storybook.

A boy is walking and walking, sometimes through the woods, sometimes in the desert, always with a huge heavy stone tied with strong twine to his ankle. He is looking for something: his home, his family, his town; Nicole is never sure. Parallel to his trail is a dark pit that weaves its way alongside him, the side on which the stone is tied. Sometimes his path narrows and the pit sidles up so close he must be very careful not to step in such a way that the stone slips over the edge, for he knows if the stone goes he will follow. Sometimes Nicole is the boy; sometimes she is just watching. Sometimes, lately, the boy is Frederí Lafond. The dreams in which the stone never falls have become just as terrifying to her as the ones when the boy is flung over the side and she wakes up.

She no longer went to her mother's small bed when she had the nightmares.

"Did you hear me last night, Maman?" she would ask the following morning. "I had one of those dreams. I called for you."

"Did you? I'm sorry," her mother would answer, smoothing Nicole's hair out of her eyes, sometimes even giving her a brief hug. Marcelle had become more and more affectionate since their talk in the wide room, but behind each touch was the sense that she was still waiting for an answer, and a tension had grown that could only be broken by Nicole's acquiescence. It became more comfortable to spend time with her father, whose eyes asked so much less of her.

Spring came late that year, delayed by rains and a scissorlike mistral from the northwest. The week after Nicole's ninth birthday was the first patch of steadily warm weather they'd had. On her way home from school that Friday, she noticed that the cherries were still small and black when usually by now they would have been picked and sold. There was a swift warm wind that stroked her bare arms and prodded fat clouds across the blue sky.

She had just checked out a biography of Danton from the library, which she was eager to take to her room and begin. If her mother was not in the kitchen she did not like to be sought out, Nicole knew, so she made her snack quietly and went up to her window seat. When the blue turned violet and the clouds massed in orange embers in the hollows of the hills, she got up to put on a light, trying not to feel uneasy about the onslaught of darkness and the emptiness of the house. Soon, her father returned and she heard him pause in the dark below before calling for her.

It was not particularly strange to them that her mother was not there, that dinner had not been started, and that there was no note or clue to her whereabouts. All those things had happened before.

But Marcelle never returned.

Their neighbor, Lucie Quenelle, came over each afternoon of the week that followed. She made bread and casseroles and stroked Nicole's hair until she fell asleep. But late in the night, after Lucie had gone home, Nicole could hear her father moving through the house, and when she could no longer hear him, she rose and watched him from the window as he walked out to the barns, to the creamery, and then across the fields. What she could not see was the vision before him of his wife, of her black shoes or her braided hair, so vivid sometimes he nearly tripped over them. She could not see how he trembled, pushed on through the dark only by the thought of his youngest daughter finding the body herself. And she could not know that he went as far as the quarry one night, or that he found the moon there, nestled in the black water like an eye rolled back.

But he could not look to the edges. Surely someone would have found her by now, he thought, and quickly turned away.

It was a ribbon that was found there. The magistrate brought it the next morning. Octave held it with two hands and nodded.

Nicole slipped past him in the doorway to get a better look.

"No, Papa. Maman didn't have any black ribbons." She looked carefully. She saw the crease in the middle and the smaller ones closer to the ends where the bow for her plait had been knotted. Yes, it had the length and the slanted ends of a ribbon of her mother's, but she had no black ribbons. Nicole was sure of that. Besides, her mother hadn't gone swimming. She'd gone to Paris. She'd told her father a thousand times. She would have taken all her ribbons.

Octave could not speak. He handed the ribbon to his child. She was shocked by its weight, how cool it felt in her hands. It was Marcelle's green ribbon, blackened by water.

They attempted to drag the quarry, but it was by no means a flat bottom. Crags and deep crevices, they explained indelicately, in front of the child. No body was ever found.

After her mother disappeared (she never stopped believing in the possibility of disappearance), Nicole never had the dream about the boy and the stone again. Or if she did, she did not remember it. Or perhaps it simply did not scare her. For what could possibly have terrified her more than the steady waking lie of her mother, not gone to Paris but lying beneath twenty meters of black water?

Times of Day

❦

A FOG HAD LAIN PRONE ALONG THE RIVER FOR THE MONTH OF FEBRUARY. MIDDAY it might separate briefly to allow a bright sheet of light to glint across the water, but mostly it stayed whole and motionless, receiving the incessant spit of rain silently on its back. After weeks of this, I began to feel permanently waterlogged and was often surprised to look at my fingertips and find them unwrinkled or to touch my hair and find it dry. My limbs were heavy, my skin raw, and my toes, no matter the pairs of socks, numb from the soggy chill.

"¿Tiene usted naranjas?"

"¿Tiene usted naranjas?" I repeated, stumbling a bit on the last word. I rewound and mimicked again.

Marc couldn't keep a secret. The trip was supposed to have been a surprise, but since the beginning of January he had been saying things like "Lola's eyes" (which were brown) "are the color of an Andalusian sky today," or quizzing Guillaume on his knowledge of the Moors, or asking Odile how many flamenco dresses she thought she had. At the end of a Sunday dinner two weeks ago he said, "So where do you think we'll be on Easter?" He tried then to assume a casual pose: he leaned way back in his chair, head cradled in laced fingers, as if he might have time for a nap. Even if this were a customary position, the curl of the smile he was fighting and the jiggle of his knee against the underside of the table would have given him away. "In Spain." The answer had slid easily out of every one of our mouths.

* * *

"Bueno. Déme por favor cuatro naranjas."

"Bueno. Déme por favor cuatro naranjas." My *r*'s were not good. I'd just mastered the French *r*, forcing it halfway down my throat, and now I had to bring it all the way up to the roof of my mouth. I stopped the tape and practiced: *"Rico, rojo, rosa. Rico, rojo, rosa."* Awful. An American speaking Spanish with a French accent. But the anticipation of a trip to Spain prodded me through each dank day, one after the other.

In the morning I still studied French, but during the afternoon in the kitchen, instead of my radio mysteries, I listened to the tapes Nicole had brought home and after two days abandoned. If she had finished all her homework, Lola would join me later as I did the dishes. She could trill *rico, rojo, rosa* effortlessly.

The tape fell silent; then a voice in French said to turn over for more *Español Ahora.*

"¡Español ahora!" I shouted with equal verve to the empty house.

I flipped the tape and returned to the cutting board.

"Y una cosa más. ¿Tiene usted manzanas?"

"Manzanas?" I glared at the machine but it carried on. *Pommes*, it said, in the booklet I kept on the counter.

I rewound a bit. *"Bueno. Pues, déme cinco por favor."*

"Bueno. Pues, déme cinco por favor."

There was a freedom in Spanish, or at least I felt free after the constraints of French. It was like unbuckling your belt after an enormous meal. Every word was pronounced the way it was spelled and each vowel had only one sound. I could speak what little the tapes had already taught me loudly and, except for the *r*, with a confidence that surprised me.

Everyone was out that afternoon: Odile at the library, Guillaume at fencing, Lola at Francine's house, Marc still at the hospital, and Nicole wherever she went during the day. She had appointments, committees, luncheons, meetings, but with whom or for what purpose I never knew. There was a detachment and a fatigue that pervaded Nicole's life as well as mine, which allowed us both to move in and out of the same spaces all week long without any sense of what the other was doing with her free hours.

"¿Algo más?"

"No, gracias."

I listened to several more scenes, one in a clothes shop, another in a line for a movie, while skinning chicken and chopping vegetables.

Across the water, streetlamps blinked on, then hung unsuspended and haloed pink in the fog. Grainy daylight drained out slowly through the long kitchen window. This was the start of the devastating time of day, when, if you turned on the overhead, the texture of the walls and the edges of objects became too vivid and you found yourself straining to remember one thing that had ever brought you any joy, but if you didn't and just let the window continue to blacken, sick and slow, it felt like being lowered into a grave. It was the moment when all pleasure of solitude vanished and you needed a body beside yours—or at least a voice calling your name.

"Es tres cientos veinte."

The recorded voices lost their echo. All interest in Spanish, in anything, was beginning to dwindle.

The first footsteps were the heaviest, and at the sound I realized I had been hoping for them more than any others.

"Aquí tiene."

"Aquí tiene," I repeated, not knowing anymore what I was saying, hearing the footfall, the briefcase dropped, the coat removed.

"Hasta mañana, Señor Perez."

"Hasta mañana, Señor Perez." My voice had lost its verve. The door cracked on its hinges.

"Hasta mañana," Marc said behind me.

He'd stopped in the doorway. Languages swam in my head. The cassette went on loudly to a scene in a crowed restaurant and I moved slightly to shut it off, then caught myself for fear of revealing my wish that he remain. Above the noise he asked how the Spanish was going, and though I meant to say *Ça va*, I said *Está bien* instead. Then he came all the way in the room and shut off the machine.

I thought of asking about the rain, which I could now hear slapping the river, but rejected that idea and struggled to think of something more engaging.

As if I'd said something, he raised his hand and leaned his head into it boyishly, wet curls flattening, then springing back. He was a man without vanity, a man who had never been given any indication by a woman that he was attractive.

"It's raining again?"

"In spears," he said.

Without Lola it always took us a few minutes to fall into sync. I looked back down at my work, still struggling for words. In my nervousness I'd chopped too many carrots. They covered the cutting board and overflowed onto the counter. There were enough carrot rounds to tile the kitchen walls.

"*Alors,*" he said, peering over my shoulder. "*Des carottes.*"

Who can explain why a few words in a particular tone can clear acres of sudden unfamiliarity? Could anyone else hear those words exactly as I did? Would that person look up and grin and find him grinning back, full of the sweet miraculous relief of having been perfectly received? He was not just mocking the ridiculous proportion of those carrots to the other ingredients on the counter. He was saying, If it's not carrots it's something else; he was saying, How futile life is, the slicing of carrots, the eating of meals; he was saying, How wonderful life is, to come home to the security of carrots in the kitchen; he was saying, Another day come to its devastating close. He was saying all this and I heard him because he was like me, entirely ambivalent about life. It was almost a question: Should I be full of joy or despair, Rosie? Joy, my face always replied to him, not because I felt sure that was the answer, but because I'd begun to want to make it his.

And so the idea of Spain lured me on through February and into March. The night before we were to leave, I slept deeply. I'd had a warm, pleasant dream, which I didn't remember until I'd pulled my suitcase out of the closet and begun packing. I hadn't been pregnant in the dream. A hand had slid up under my shirt and I'd felt both the heat of the fingers and the leaness of my own belly. That was all I could remember. I sat back down on my bed and felt again the warm touch. I hadn't been pregnant in the dream, and at first the relief of that absorbed any concern I might have had that the hand was Marc's.

I practiced my Spanish on the clothes: *un vestido azul, una camisa larga, dos zapatos negros.* Small waves of renewed anticipation rose and fell. The hand on my stomach brought strange, guiltless comfort. It was a harmless dream. With Marc there was no danger, no chance of a moist sock on my ankle at dinner. He was good and kind and could not keep the smallest secret. It was a safe crush. He was not a man who could have an affair.

My fingers, rapidly stuffing underwear into the side pockets of my suitcase, grazed against the comb. It's okay, I told myself, and pulled it out. It was even smaller and flimsier than I remembered, the blue plastic so thin at the edges it was translucent. The red hairs were still wrapped in the teeth.

Nicole gave me no warning, no sound in the hallway. She was simply there, leaning in through the door she had opened with no knock. "You haven't packed!" These were her favorite moments, when she found exactly what she was looking for, when someone did let her down precisely as she suspected they would. In this strong soprano voice, perfect in its fluidity even at 6 A.M., there was a note of joy.

"Of course I have," I said, zipping up the half-empty suitcase and pulling it off the bed and onto the floor. "I'll bring it out right now."

Nicole issued a punishing *très bien* and followed me down the hall lit only by the living room lights at the far end. All the children's doors were shut and the cracks between door and frame dark. She walked behind me impatiently; I could hear the air passing through her nose. I had a strange suspicion she was fantasizing about clubbing me to death; perhaps she'd prefer something cleaner, something that wouldn't stain the carpets: strangulation, maybe. When we emerged from the narrow passage she passed me immediately, dismissively, rushing toward her bedroom like a hurried commuter at a connecting metro stop. I almost laughed out loud at her sense of urgency.

I deposited my suitcase with the rest. Nicole and the children had matching suitcases of dark green leather and brass bolts, though Lola's and Guillaume's were slightly shorter. Beside these, Marc's tattered carrying case looked terrible, with its makeshift wire fastener to compensate for broken buckles and strips of tape so old even they were cracking apart.

It was so purely like him to have saved this case from childhood, from some first trip somewhere. Looking at this splintering contraption and all the efforts to preserve it, I could feel what it meant to him. I could feel his love of travel and the deep disappointment that somehow those dreams had been thwarted. I could feel his hands running over the surface of the suitcase as he pulled it out, all the urges and resentments and pressed-down yearnings rising up again. No doubt Nicole had pleaded with him to replace such an eyesore. I admired him for this small resistance.

I pulled the string for the overhead in the kitchen and began setting up for breakfast. I cut long slabs of butter, spooned out the English jam, warmed the remaining half of the baguette from the night before, and heated a large pot of milk. Every gesture was by rote: a straw at Guillaume's place for his apple-pear juice, a particular silver spoon, small and deep with a vein running down its center, for Lola's cornflakes. I saw myself from some other part of the kitchen as I slit a corner on a second box of milk and placed a banana beside a bowl for Marc. Was this why people went on trips, to feel this sort of impending departure from routine?

Marc appeared in the doorway, holding one of his books on Spain. "Rosie, what's this here?" He turned it around so I could read three words in italics just above his finger. He wasn't dressed in a tie for work; he didn't smell like the perfumed soap in the master bathroom.

"The Winter Palace."

"*Invierno* is winter? How do you know that?"

I pointed to the cassette player.

"You're pretty clever, aren't you?"

I was tired of his fatherly admiration. "It's just a tape. I listen and repeat. Like a parrot."

"I'm sorry. I hope you didn't think I was being condescending."

"Europeans always think Americans are stupid. I'm getting used to it." We were both surprised by the hostility in my voice. "I'm sorry." I looked down, pretending to arrange the condiments on the table.

"No, it's true. We're terrible snobs." The sound of his voice made me raise my head. I had hurt him. His mouth had caved in slightly, and he held the book on Spain closely to his chest. He didn't look like he'd slept as I had.

"I'm sorry," I said again, without meaning to. I hadn't meant to say anything else, for how could I explain the sight of him in his weekend pants and faded T-shirt, the way he'd held out the book, the way he hadn't issued a formal good morning but had just begun speaking, the way he looked up at me as if I were real and whole and good—how could I explain all that and the hand on my stomach and the strange new sensation snaking through and down, coiling heavily between my legs?

"Don't be. I'm an ass," he said, and left the room.

I went to the sink and leaned toward the wide window. Cold metallic air came through the glass. My groin brushed against the cabinet handle below, and I pressed hard against it.

Lola bolted toward me from around the corner. Guillaume was right behind, screaming at her to give them back. A pair of plastic goggles was placed in my hand, and just as Guillaume began to yell at me instead, Nicole came in.

"She won't give me them, Maman!" he hollered.

I gave them to him immediately, and Lola let out a great whelp of betrayal.

"You can't put me in the middle like that," I told her. Especially, I thought, when your mother is watching.

"But they're mine, Maman, they're mine!"

I slipped out of the kitchen then, hoping I wouldn't run into Marc, not now, and not ever again. I couldn't go to Spain with them. That much was clear.

Safely back in my room, I thought of my options. I could go into the kitchen and quit. I could get lost in the airport. I could jump out the window right now and swim away. Then I thought of the perfect solution. I could leave my passport here. I wouldn't be let on the plane at the last minute, and they would have to go on without me. It was perfect. I took it out of my purse and hid it under the mattress.

Two taxis arrived at eight-fifteen. Their exhaust matched the color of the sky all winter. A strong wind pierced through our sweaters and jackets as we waited to climb into the backs of the small white cars, but no one suggested fetching coats that would only have to be lugged around for ten days. I tried to imagine a clear blue sky, a windless day, a sun so hot it could change the color of skin. Dry heat, thin clothing, bare feet.

For a moment I let myself forget I wasn't going. I stood between Odile, whose face was badly painted and slightly swollen from sleep, and Guillaume, who was dangerously awake and restless, while Marc climbed down belowdeck with the drivers for the rest of the bags and Lola searched the house one last time, she promised her mother, for her favorite fountain pen. I stood between Odile and Guillaume so that the three of us could share a taxi, but once the trunks were closed and the doors unlocked, Nicole said, "You ride in that one, Rosie," and took my place. Go where you belong, she seemed to be saying, and so I squeezed in with Lola and Marc.

"Papa wants to ask you something but he's too embarrassed."

"Lola!" he said.

"He wants to know if you could fit this in your bag. I can't in mine." She leaned over her father to hand me the fat book on Spain. There was plenty of room for it in my knapsack. I'd just have to remember to give it back before he got on the plane.

It was warm in the taxi. The road was wet from the rain the night before and the tires sang as we rolled up the narrow ramp to the street. Ahead of us, the other taxi yielded to the stream of traffic from the left. Nicole sat forward between her children, her arms braced on the tops of the seats in front of her. Would she tell the driver, like she always told Marc, exactly when to go, and how fast, and, no, he shouldn't risk it just yet? She would be angry at herself for not asking me if I'd remembered my passport. I could see the look on her face perfectly. Their taxi lurched forward and we pulled up into the space.

Lola was making Marc promise he'd play cards with her on the beach.

"Only if Rosie promises too. Americans, they aren't very smart, but you should see how they shuffle a deck of cards." He turned and gave me a certain look I'd seen him give Nicole. It was more than an apology. It was a look that let down all guard, that did not attempt to hide vulnerability. In it there was not the slightest trace of self-protection. It was an intimate look and seemed to promise a lifetime of effort. When he gave it to Nicole, she hardened further. She couldn't return it.

I could. And after I did and we swung out onto the main road, I said what I knew I'd say from the moment I got into the back of the warm taxi beside him—"I forgot my passport"—and he had the driver turn right around.

* * *

At the airport, we checked our bags and hurried to the gate, only to be told that the flight was now delayed two hours. Odile and Guillaume went off to the duty-free shop while the rest of us had a snack at the cafeteria next door.

Nicole was in a miserable state. She'd given me some spending money for the trip, but instead of following Marc and Lola to the table, she waited for my total. I no longer had trouble with numbers. I didn't have to translate them first into English, then into numerals. I could see them as I heard them. But before I could count the change I'd fished from my pocket, Nicole reached over and plucked the correct amount from my hand.

I walked over to the booth Marc had chosen. When I put down my tray, he peered into my cup. "Hot chocolate. That's exactly what I should have gotten."

I swung into his side of the booth. I didn't care. Beside him, my irritation at Nicole melted into relief and gratitude and a soft longing that felt pleasant and manageable.

Halfway through her snack, Lola saw a boy come out of the duty-free shop with a long piece of black licorice. "I thought they only had alcohol and perfume in there," she said, and after securing a twenty-franc note from her mother, she left the three of us alone at the table.

There had been many times in the past months when, left alone with Marc and Nicole, I put on myself the burden of conversation. I would tell stupid stories simply to fill the spaces that made me, far more than it made them, so uncomfortable. Today I felt no such compunction. I wanted to be witness to the silence between them. But before it became too pronounced, Nicole got up and crossed the room to a cigarette machine.

"She smokes?" I asked, enjoying sitting so close to him in the booth and speaking of Nicole in the third person.

Marc shook his head and said she'd quit years ago. He started to say something else but stopped when he saw Nicole returning.

"I'm sorry," she said, peeling off the cellophane. She wasn't sorry at all.

"I know traveling makes you nervous"—Marc began, but she cut him off.

"It doesn't make me nervous. It makes me furious. This trip is already a full-scale disaster. No one knows why the plane isn't ready. I can't get an answer out of anyone. And if it does ever go and if we're lucky enough to get to Spain in one piece, the transportation system there will make today look easy."

"It *is* easy, Nicole. We're sitting here. We're drinking coffee and hot chocolate." He gave a glance toward my cup. I could feel his leg shift beneath the table. To press mine against his would have taken the slightest movement.

"I don't want to leave Paris," she said, as pouty as Guillaume. "And I know how I sound; I can hear myself. But I don't want to go." She caught a cigarette between two nails and drew it out of the pack. "I don't know how you got me to agree to this." She struck a matchstick on the side of its bright blue box, brought the flame up, sucked in, and with shut eyes blew it out with her first lungful of smoke. "It's a bad sign, this delay. But it gives us a chance to just go home." She pulled an ashtray toward her, then looked at Marc as softly as she could manage. "Please, let's just go."

He turned to me. "Nicole has never been on a plane before."

"That's not it, Marc."

"Then what is it?"

"It's everything. It's the whole absurdity of calling this a vacation when it is sheer work and worry and dragging bags around from one place to another."

I only dimly recognized the sentiment from the early morning. It was impossible to feel it here in the airport amid all the travelers and flight announcements and sounds of planes leaving or touching the ground. How could you want to turn around and go home now?

"We've already talked about all this. There will only be a few days of moving about and then we have over a week on the beach. No work. No worry. And we have Rosie." He presented me to his wife with an open palm, as if I were a large empty receptacle that by the trip's end would be full of all the trouble they'd averted. "Please," he said, and reached for Nicole's hand, which did not respond but remained flat on the table. He softly called her a name with several *u*'s that forced my eyes down to my tray. Within the periphery, his fingers fretted across her motionless knuckles. Her rings made it loud and embarrassing. "Please," he said again.

"All right." She pulled her hand away and hid it from him in her lap while the other brought the cigarette to her mouth again. When she stubbed it out and moved the ashtray to another table, she said to me, "Please don't tell the children. Especially Guillaume. He's frightened enough of my death."

With ferocious flaps of her hand in front of her, she waved off lingering traces of smoke.

"Yes, thank you," she said, accepting the mint I held out to her.

The plane climbed quickly into the green-gray clouds, which condensed and streaked on the window beside Lola. The small cabin grew dim. Then the clouds lightened and scattered and suddenly all there was was blue, a deep rich blue in every direction. As the plane leveled out, the sun glittered along its wings.

Across the aisle, Nicole let go of the cross around her neck and opened her eyes. The unexpected light forced them half shut again, and if I hadn't known her I might have glanced over at those tender eyes and the brown hollows below and the broad bone of her cheek and the spread of her lips and thought hers a warm face, an uncomplicated face, a face you would never dread or avoid. And yet I planned to avoid her the entire trip. I would be sure to sit the farthest from her at every meal, stand apart in every museum line, spread my towel away from hers on the beach.

I slept a little and woke up to the sun beating in on my hands in my lap. Lola had been waiting in the seat next to me and said immediately, "Look down."

Below us were mountains, deep dark jagged mountains capped with white.

"Don't they look like the most delicious chocolate dessert you could ever taste?"

"Yes," I said. It looked as if a few spoons had already dug in. *"Las Pyraneos."*

"Sí."

My eyes followed the earth to its rim, where it met the sky in a deep indigo curve. Everything seemed excruciatingly beautiful from up here.

Beside Nicole, Marc was reading about Cuenca, our first stop. I wanted him to look out his window and feel this pain as I felt it, the pain of the sight and of the overwhelming, breathless hope that can fill your chest when you are lifted far above the earth momentarily.

Leaving Lucie

❦

THE SUN IS DIRECTLY ABOVE ME AS I WALK BACK DOWN THE DRIVEWAY FROM THE mailbox. The silver birches out on the road shiver white in the strong breeze, as if they're laden with snow they can never shake off. Through the open door, I can hear slow steps on the stairs, then the kettle being filled at the sink. She's up from her nap; it's nearly time for lunch. Another letter has come. I slip it into the bin with the others and go inside.

We eat outside at the shady end of the picnic table: a cold lemon soup, sliced tomatoes, and a flat yeast bread called *fouace*. Lucie is groggy and distracted. She drags a piece of bread around the bottom of her soup bowl but doesn't bring it to her mouth. She's getting weaker. Her death swells up beside me, its back slick, its purpose unwavering, and the fear I feel only at night seizes me now in broad daylight.

A ladybug crawls onto her finger. "Have you ever heard Nicole sing this song to her children?" she asks. Then, taking in a deep breath, she lets out a series of high tremulous notes.

I want to lie and say I have, for how would she ever know? But deceit is too exhausting; it makes endless demands. "No. How does it go again?"

She sings more slowly this time. It is in Provençal, and though it has a lighthearted tune, it emerges dolorous from her tight, tired throat.

> *Parpaiolo, volo!*
> *Vai-t'en a l'escolo!*
> *Prene ti matino,*
> *Vai a la doutrino.*

When she stops, I imitate what I heard. It has been a long time since I've sung, and the pleasure of it breaks in great waves inside me. Lucie listens, territorially at first, then teaches me four more verses. We sit singing at the table, the shade lengthening but the afternoon growing hotter, the horseflies drinking up the vinaigrette left on the tomato plate, and the long leaves of the cherry trees clapping in the wind like soft-gloved hands at the music we make.

Later, in the cool of the kitchen, she tells me how Nicole left Plaire.

After her mother's disappearance, the land seemed to want to give something back. Black fat grapes, juicy plums, melons as wide as sun hats—never had the yield been better. Octave buried himself in the work, and Lucie Quenelle continued to come to their house in the evenings. On Saturdays, Nicole walked down to Lucie's for the day and after a few weeks started taking a small bag to spend the night. She preferred to be at Lucie's now. Her father no longer liked to talk in the evenings or take walks on Sundays. He'd stopped going to mass with her altogether. After the harvest, she asked her father if it would be better for her to move in with Lucie. She had hoped to provoke a response, to resuscitate his paternal claim on her, but he simply brushed a hand through the air and walked away.

She went to Lucie's because the house was warm and familiar. She went because Lucie put on a soft blue bathrobe at night and let Nicole lie against it while they read together in silence on Lucie's thin bed. She didn't know that her mother and Lucie had been friends, that her mother had come down the hill, just as Nicole had been doing on Saturdays all summer, for lunch several times a week. But Lucie had a pair of socks her mother had knitted for her, and jars of fruit with her mother's handwriting on the labels. And she had stories, lots of stories, about Marcelle, which she fed to Nicole like candy, one at a time. Nicole was happy there, and gave her thanks in prayers for Lucie, and hoped she was not betraying her mother, wherever she was, in doing so.

It was another cold day, the day the letter came seven years later, the same white writing paper with the same looped letters. It was sitting on the kitchen table this time, not floating on a blue blanket, not a rope in her

mother's hands. And this time it was addressed to her. She stood holding
the envelope for a long while, waiting for Lucie, whom she could hear
walking above her, to come down. It had been written with a fountain
pen with an extremely thick nib in a color she could not name, a dark
sinister blue. The fancy paper was so coarse the lines were mottled, and
she stared at them until they became snakes, twisting and halving themselves across a rough white plain.

It was from Aunt Anne, and it would have news of her mother's
reappearance.

She ripped open the expensive envelope, delighting in the extrava-
gance. She read quickly:

Dear Nicole,

    I am your Great-Aunt Anne. Do you remember me? I
saw you once when you were very small but very pretty.

    I live in Paris in a big apartment, too big for one
person and one small dog. We would like you to come live
with us. There will be lots of yummy things to eat and
beautiful dresses to wear.

    Come live with us so we are not so lonely anymore.

    With hugs and kisses,

                Your mother's Aunt Anne

"She thinks I'm four years old."

Lucie came down then with her own letter, which she handed to
Nicole.

Dear Mme. Quenelle,

    As I have received no word from you, I am now
planning to write the child directly. I trust you will not
impede such action but let my niece act with autonomy.
I live here in Paris, as I have said, in a large apartment in
the sixteenth, and alone, now that my husband has passed
on. The place is equipped with three servants and, upon
Nicole's arrival, a governess *à la anglaise*. Her life will
become a veritable Brontë novel.

Lucie, I have known you a long time, and while you yourself have refused many an opportunity, I am loath to believe you would let such a fate fall upon Nicole Guerrin. We must commence with her education now. It is what her mother, may she rest in peace, always wanted for her, and her wish alone ought to be respected. Please do not hinder it any longer than you already have.

With my best and most hopeful sentiments,

Anne d'Auvene

So Aunt Anne, too, believed she was dead. "What is a Brontë novel?" Nicole asked.

"I don't know," Lucie said. There were several words on the page she hadn't understood, and she hoped Nicole wouldn't find them all. "This is the third time she's written. I should have told you."

Nicole could see thin glossy streaks where tears had rolled through the powder on Lucie's face. She told her, "I'm not going. I don't want to go."

"You should think about it." She placed her hand on Nicole's arm. "There are many advantages she could provide. You would go to a fine school and learn an instrument and—"

"I know all about the advantages!" She shook herself of Lucie's clasp. "I don't care about the advantages! I want to stay here. This is where I live." She was hollering and it frightened her because she was yelling at her mother, who seemed to be gripping her now that Lucie had let go.

She would have kept on shouting if Lucie hadn't said, in a voice that cracked like a whip, "Stop it, Nicole," a voice her mother had never possessed. Then Lucie took her two hands in hers and told her, "You know what I want with all my heart. But you must never be afraid to do what *you* want."

"This," Nicole said, holding up the two letters and their torn envelopes, "is not what I want." She threw the papers in the fire and watched how slowly the thick paper took the flames and how all the writing seemed to slither to the far side of each page as the fire approached.

Lucie never spoke to Nicole as if she were a child, never put a fake lilt in her voice or told Nicole tall tales. Instead, she recounted stories from the newspaper or the gossip passed up the hill. She may have embellished a bit, but at the root was always a seed of truth. Nicole had loved her mother for her romantic nature, for her love of candles and storm clouds and hand-painted teacups, but she loved Lucie from the moment they met for her love of life exactly as it was.

In bed that night, however, two sensations accosted her mind. One was a voice—*It is what her mother always wanted for her*—the other a smell—the fluted vanilla candles her mother had read by in the evening. Thinking of the novel Aunt Anne had mentioned, Nicole wondered if she too read by scented candlelight in her apartment in Paris. *It is what your mother always wanted.* It was a sweet winter smell that always ribboned through her mother's small bedroom.

After a while, she led her mind to school, to the blond boy, Félix, who wanted to kiss her, and then to the trip she would soon take with Lucie to Avignon. She forced these thoughts to scud across the smooth surface of a certainty she would not acknowledge for several weeks: her mother was there, somewhere in Paris, and she could not refuse her again.

Every Sunday Nicole was picked up after mass and taken to one of her sisters' houses for lunch. No matter which house she went to, the afternoon always ended in the same way, with the sister making the obligatory offer that Nicole come live with her. But they each had large families and little money, and though she knew in their hearts they wished her to say yes, their fearful eyes begged her to decline. She knew too that it wasn't just the number of children and the insufficient income that made them hope for a *no* each Sunday. Her hair and her hands, the burgeoning shape of her body, and the way, if she weren't paying attention, she tended to tilt her head and look out the sides of her eyes when listening to a story— all these were the uncontrollable ways in which she was developing, in their minds, into a disconcerting incarnation of their mother. Once Juliette's twins had taken Nicole up to their playroom, and she had emerged wrapped from the waist up in white cheesecloth with all her hair piled up into a flesh-colored skullcap.

"Look, look, Maman! Aunt Nico is a mummy!"

Juliette blanched at the sight. "Get that stuff off her immediately!" But she rushed at Nicole before her sons knew what she had said, pulling at the cloth so fiercely it bruised Nicole's new and tender breasts, yanking along with the cap a great deal of hair. When Juliette was angry, blood rushed to her curled ear, and that day it throbbed a scarlet red, the blood swirling within like liquid through one of those knotted straws they sold at the Limne fair. Nicole watched, in utter confusion but without fear. Few things frightened her now, and these strange outbursts, usually caused in some inexplicable way by her own body, were something she had come to expect in her sisters.

The Sunday before she was to leave for Paris, Lucie invited them all to dinner. Octave came late, halfway through the meal, and barely spoke. He seemed not to understand the occasion. Oh, she was ready to go, to go and find her mother and never come back. She took a deep breath to contain a thick wave of anticipation. Then she saw Lucie at the other end of the table, talking to no one, chewing mechanically. This was their last Sunday together. Often in the evenings when she came home from one of her sisters', Lucie would tell her, "You're all wound up tonight." She'd fetch a sweater and her change purse and they would walk to town to drink lemonade on the terrace of the Café Plaire. If she spoke of her girlhood or her late brief marriage, Lucie's voice would crack. She never cried, or even let her eyes pool up, but her throat would tighten and words would creak out as if through an old door. Ever since Nicole told her of the decision, she noticed that Lucie's voice had begun to crack in the same way over things in the present or near future: the darning of Nicole's winter stockings, the purchase of their favorite chocolate, any mention of her trip to Avignon, which she now would make alone. Never, Nicole thought, had she caused someone so much pain, not even her mother. Her mother's pain, whatever it was, had come long before Nicole had refused her. No, it had not been her fault. She owed her mother nothing. She repeated this to herself: I owe my mother nothing.

But her bags were packed and everyone gathered to say good-bye and Aunt Anne had already transformed her late husband's study into a bedroom with fabrics Nicole chose from a book of swatches that arrived in the mail. And by the time she had convinced herself that none of this mattered if she could remain here with Lucie and her father and her sisters, who were hard at times and strange but loved her all the same, she could no longer remember why she owed her mother nothing. She had failed her once and she could not—even when, after everyone was gone, Lucie asked in a creaking voice if she'd like to walk up to the café—do so again.

The following Tuesday, they all clustered about her on the station platform. Nicole wore her best dress and her best hat, and though they had both been worn by at least two sisters before her, they felt new now beside the great green train with its wooden plaques by each door with the word PARIS printed in blue. To her sisters, too, the outfit was unfamiliar and each struggled not to say what Marie-Jo eventually blurted out: "You look just like Maman!" She knew they needed her to leave. Once she was in her seat and watching them through glass, their eyes brimmed and their mouths sank but their arms waved jubilantly, as if they were greeting a train and not seeing it off. Octave hadn't come. Nicole had seen the last of him that Sunday; he would die of a heart attack the next spring.

Lucie stood apart, closer to the door that was now shut and bolted. Nicole had said good-bye to her last, knowing that she would be revealing to her sisters whom she would miss the most, but doing it anyway because she needed Lucie to know. Lucie was old and would only get older. Already her long torso curled forward; already the first two fingers of her right hand had begun to stick together. The reasons for leaving and for staying swirled in her head until the platform and everyone on it began to pull away from the window and her sisters' sleeves flashed wildly in the sun and Lucie raised her bare arm, bent at the elbow and cradled in the other hand, and kept it there, heavy and motionless, until the train curved left and they were gone.

The Sights

❦

I STOOD AT THE OPEN WINDOW OF THE ROOM LOLA AND I WOULD SHARE THAT night. It was tall and narrow, protected by five wrought-iron bars that began flush to the building at the top before, halfway down, billowing out and then gathering themselves back in at the sill, as if to allow for a curious head—but no more—to peer down into the courtyard.

We were in Cuenca, a small medieval city southeast of Madrid. The hotel had once been a monastery and was set at one end of a high ridge famous for its *casas colgadas,* the gaunt run-down houses that hung over it, threatening to pitch into the river below. Marc had pointed to this row of houses excitedly from the road as we drove in from Madrid, but our interest in this sight was quickly diluted by the inundation of its image on T-shirts, store signs, and restaurant advertising. On every block were at least a dozen references to these *casas colgadas.* "A whole beautiful Spanish city reduced to two words," he'd said, but once past the *plaza mayor* with its shops and tourists, and up where the streets were not much wider than an arm's span and convex mirrors were nailed to the sides of corner houses and cars had to swerve up onto the sidewalks to pass each other, Marc regained his enthusiasm for Cuenca.

The monastery was not *colgada.* It stood safely back a way, allowing only the garden to meet the lip of the high ridge. The rest were down there now, watching the end of the sunset we'd seen from the car. It had been Guillaume's idea to race down once our bags had been delivered to our rooms. He'd seen a statue of Mary on the opposite cliff, where she'd been put at the top of a tall white pillar. "Doesn't the sky look like a golden cape held out for her?" he'd said. "No," Lola had snapped, but she agreed to go down to the garden with everyone else all the same. I thought it

❦ 153

was something a family should do together on their first night of vacation, and I was feeling much less a part of this family now that I was out of their kitchen with no space and no routine to claim my own. What and when and where we ate was now entirely out of my control.

"*¿Pues, que toman?*" the waiter said, after depositing shallow dishes of almonds and olives on the table. He was looking directly at Nicole. With her Mediterranean coloring and *madrileña* hauteur, she'd been taken for Spanish from the moment we'd arrived that afternoon. As she'd done at the car rental, the front desk, and just now at the door of the restuarant, she shook her head without apology and said in French that she was French. Undaunted, the waiter asked again in Spanish, throwing an imaginary drink down his throat with one hand.

I spoke up and ordered a Coke.

"*Dos,*" Lola said. She was wearing a dress she'd bought last week, a long-sleeved close-fitting dress with pale flowers on black. When she'd held it up, I'd thought it a preposterous choice; Lola wore jeans and loose shirts and enormous black shoes. There had been nothing compatible about the girl and the dress she held. But now at the table saying *Dos* with complete confidence while reaching for an almond, she was transformed. No one else seemed to notice how graceful her long neck had become or how her breasts had risen. She seemed ignorant of the change herself.

No one ventured to order anything other than Coke. When the waiter had gone, Nicole commented on the filth of the floor: greasy napkins, olive pits, frayed toothpicks. Odile admired the bright tiled scenes on the walls. Marc studied the menu.

"What's *atún*?" he asked in irritation, as if, despite all his research and planning, he'd forgotten that all of Spain would be in Spanish.

"Tuna," I said.

"And *aguacate*?" Guillaume asked.

"Avocado."

It went on like this. Most of it was so similar to French I didn't understand why they couldn't make the small adjustments, the rearrangement of a few vowels, the loss of a consonant here or there. It was a strange thing to witness the limitations of language in these people whose facility with words I'd coveted for so long. When they gave their orders to the waiter, they muttered or blushed. Their discomfort gave me a confidence I never would have had otherwise. I used the verbs I'd practiced. I spoke in full sentences. The waiter gathered up the menus and complimented my efforts. Marc beamed at me from across the table, and I had, for a few blissful seconds, the delusion that the trip had been for my sake alone.

An English couple was led to a table beside us. They began to argue almost immediately about the definition of *sepia*.

"I'm certain it's squid," the woman said.

"*Calamares* are squid."

"And *pulpo* is octopus. We read that in the Susset guide at break-fast." Her s's were piercing, and after a few more sibilant exchanges, I had to put an end to it. *Sepia* had been a popular dish in *Español Ahora.*

"Excuse me, but I think it's cuttlefish."

"You do," said the man. His eyes fell back to the menu. "I think you're quite right."

"Quite," said the woman, dropping her eyes as well.

I was ashamed of my intrusion. I was the typical American, lean-ing over and butting in. But a few minutes later the woman was hold-ing out her menu to me, pointing to several spots on the page to translate. She asked where I was from, told me they were from Cornwall, and dis-missed me once more. When it came time to take their order, the waiter used me to explain the three ways of serving *sepia:* grilled, in its own ink, or in a cold salad. The couple told me about the caves they'd seen in the Basque region and the pilgrimage to Santiago de Compostela they were about to make.

"We're just demi-pilgrims, really," said the woman.

"The real pilgrimage begins in France and goes all the way across," added the man.

I explained that we were off to Toledo tomorrow, then Granada, then Mallorca for a week.

"You and all the Germans. You know, they own nearly half the island."

"The east side," her husband added.

I searched for both a response to that information and a way to extricate myself from their sporadic attentions. Conversation had stopped not only at my table but at many of the other tables around them, as if everyone else in the room were straining to test their comprehension. But before I found a solution, the woman wondered if it wasn't the west side of the island, and they were off again.

"Four years of it, and I can barely understand a word," Odile said.

"But the American is so different," Nicole said.

I felt a bit belligerent myself now and told her where the couple was from.

When dinner arrived, no one else could recognize the names of what they'd ordered and I had to orchestrate their delivery. The waiter seemed to have a faith in our communication that Parisian shopkeepers had never shown me. He was a man of about Marc's age with a severe underbite and eyebrows that coiled out in all directions. He poked fun at anything that caught his attention: skinny Guillaume's enormous appetite, Lola's giggle, the ring of crumpled napkins around Marc's plate by the time he'd finished. The playful intrusions irked Nicole.

"Just because we're foreign, do we have to be mocked like children?"

She seemed more exasperated than I had ever seen her, and whereas at home exasperation gave her face a brightness, her words a pointed power, and her whole presence an increased authority, at this table in Cuenca she seemed to shrink in dimension and importance. Marc barely acknowledged that she'd spoken. Mortified that the waiter might have heard and understood, he compensated with extra appreciation when several bottles of liqueurs and four shot glasses were brought out, compliments of the house.

The streets had been nearly empty when we'd walked into town from the hotel, but now, on the way home, they were clogged with a slow-moving stream of traffic whose headlights and taillights flickered as the overflow from the packed sidewalks weaved carelessly in and out among the cars.

"Stay all together now," Marc called, but there was bound to be someone who let herself get pushed back by the bodies moving seductively to the music that spilled out of nightclub doors, by the loud cryptic sounds of speech, by fear and confusion and exhaustion.

Nicole wasn't with us when we turned onto the emptier street of the monastery.

Marc told me to take the children back. Guillaume was crying by the time we reached the lobby, convinced that his mother had been abducted by Spanish pirates. With more patience than I ever would have had, Odile explained that pirates needed boats and water for their crimes. Marc was being silly to turn this into such drama. Didn't Nicole know the name of the hotel or at least its location on the ridge? She'd probably found a shortcut and was already upstairs in bed. This was Nicole we were talking about, after all.

Once in our room, Lola and I were distracted by loud, inexplicable, disturbing noises coming through the open window. There were low rattling moans and rasping cries. There were great thuds and long hisses.

"What's out there?" she asked, pulling me with her across the room.

It was cats, clawing and biting and screeching at one another, the females in heat and the males hunting them down. We watched in silence through the curved bars. The chases were elaborate, the females finding temporary safety and the males pacing, their tails straight up, heavy-gaited like angry drunks. Lola looked on with a fascination so great she momentarily forgot her concern for her mother, until we heard steps outside in the hallway.

There were two pairs of feet but only one voice: Marc's, gentle and continuous. Lola shut off the light and cracked the door open. They passed by. They were not touching. It was eerie to peer out at them unnoticed as they moved through the slit of the open door. "Here we are. Here we are at the room," Marc said, before the wail of the cats behind us drowned him out.

Marc insisted on going to the synagogues first and repeated his insistence several times before the clustered hill of Toledo even came into view through the windows of the minivan we'd rented, though no one had expressed the slightest resistance to the plan. Still, at the end of lunch in a large plaza called Zocodover, where, according to Marc's book,

Castilian Spanish was spoken for the first time, he announced it again with even more defensive determination. When we rose obediently, he seemed perplexed by how quickly words could become action. He was unprepared.

"Where do we go?" he asked me, holding the map out to one side so I could look on.

Nicole rolled her eyes and sat back down. She hadn't said more than ten words all day.

I stepped up beside him and took a corner of the page. The sun was directly above, hot in my hair, bright on the paper. It spread across my shoulders, along my arms, down my spine. Marc's face drew closer to mine as we squinted at the map. I suggested a route and he looked up, all business. It would never occur to him, I was sure, to think about kissing me.

They were not easy to find, the synagogues, despite the brand-new map and the signs marked SINAGOGA posted along the street. The city wanted to give the impression that these temples were as important to its history as the cathedral and cloisters, but in truth the arrows were misplaced or they led you down an alley of eleven unmarked doors.

I hung back and waited at the end of the first block for the rest of the family, until Nicole waved me along, saying that Marc would walk us around in circles if I didn't help him. And so I quickly caught up with him, and as the others lagged farther and farther behind, swayed by black and gold damask in window cases on one side of the street and by bright blue and yellow pottery on the sidewalks of the other, it became easy to imagine that Marc and I were traveling alone together in Toledo. I could feel his love of travel. I could feel it as he peered over a wall down to the bright green river that encircled the city, poked his head into a shop that sold only suits of armor, gaped as an entire high school band from Ohio in matching windbreakers filed past, each with a triple scoop of ice cream in their cones. He spoke only to navigate; otherwise he simply gave me wide eyes and small grins and an occasional nudge in case I was missing something in another direction. He was happy, happier than I'd ever seen him, which made me happy too, except when I thought of how his mood would irk Nicole.

It did. She made one brisk lap through the single room of the synagogue, paid not one shred of attention to Marc's descriptions of Jewish
worship and its brutal eradication, and left. I stayed. I didn't understand
everything he said, but most of it. Since the Inquisition the building had
changed hands several times. In the middle of the sixteenth century it
had been a hostel for fallen women.

The room was unlit, bare of objects, even of seats. Until my eyes
adjusted, it seemed like a hoax, to pay five hundred pesetas each to stand
in a dark empty space. Then slowly I began to make out the walls. They
were bare white except for a thin strip along the top—psalms, Marc said—
that seemed not carved but scripted in gold with a large quill, the ends of
each unrecognizable letter tapering off to a perfect point. In this room
there were not the shrines, the gold flake, the frescoes, the pipe organs,
the velvet cushions, the floor plaques, the vaulted ceilings, or the mottled
colored shafts of light from the high windows of the cathedral we'd seen
in Cuenca that morning, which made the synagogue's beauty and tragedy all the more pronounced.

Nicole had left already, and the others were edging toward the door.
There was no reason, then, I couldn't drift a little closer to Marc.

He stood in an alcove, studying the carved underside of the arch
above. "The shape of this arch is what they call Mudejar style," he said,
without turning. "Round arches are Moorish, but these were done by
Moors laboring for their Christian rulers."

The whole length of his neck was visible, the muscles taut, the
Adam's apple sharp as a stone. "But," I said, focusing on the arch, "this
was built for the Jews."

"It was. One of King Pedro the First's ministers was Jewish, and he
had it built." He went on about how that king was murdered by his nobles
for giving too much power to the Jews, how Jews were massacred again
and again in this city, well before the slaughter of the Inquisition.

I watched his hands as they rose and fell. He had wide palms
and long lean fingers. He stopped talking and looked around the room.
"What people do to each other," he said quietly. He remained very
still. "You can feel them here, can't you? You can almost hear their
voices."

I could feel how it would be if he placed those hands on me, if he bent his long neck down. The yearning and the comfort of the dream and his touch came back to me. If I heard any voices at all, it was the voices of the fallen women. I wondered if, once fallen, you kept on falling, again and again, for the rest of your life.

The rest of the family was waiting across the street, faces cast up to the sun. Nicole gave the appearance of being thoroughly relaxed: her body slanted against a low wall, eyes shut, head back, lips stretched into an accidental smile. Men walking past seemed torn between her and Odile, attracted to Odile's youth and length and languor but distracted by Nicole's presence, as if she might be a film star they couldn't quite place. When Marc reached the other side, transforming them into wife and daughter, the gawking stopped.

"Now the cathedral, Papa," Guillaume said, pulling on Marc's arm with both hands.

"All right!" he said, trying to hoist Guillaume sideways onto his hip. But Guillaume squealed and kicked and Marc dropped him back on his feet impatiently. Then he took the map from his pocket and held it out for me. It was a straight shot this time. I had no real excuse to walk with Marc, so I stayed beside Lola and watched him from a few feet back. He had bad posture and splayed feet, but I loved the way he moved up the street. His waist was long and narrow; his old blue trousers hung low. When he reached behind to scratch his back, his shirt was lifted briefly and I saw a few pale knobs of his spine. Every now and then he'd call back to us: "Did you see the shape of that man's shoes?" or "Can you smell the paella coming from that apartment up there?" He crouched down to look through an open basement window and found a man with a light strapped to his forehead inlaying the gold on a black ring with a tiny needle. "Did you know," he said, when we'd caught up, "that every family in the business has their own damask pattern?"

The cathedral rose up before us like all cathedrals, gaudy and spired, as if dribbled from a finger like sand. And like all good tourists, we stood before it in its large plaza, absorbing its glistening magnificence against the plush cloudless sky.

A row of apostles stood on each side of the cavernous entrance, and above its arch sat more people. Despite all their finery, their exquisitely

cut robes and scepters and headpieces, they seemed a clumsy design compared to the simple grace of the synagogue.

"Why is it," Marc said, to no one in particular, "that Christians believed themselves to be such worthwhile decoration?"

"I was just thinking the same thing," I said.

Nicole turned in our direction, paused a moment, then suggested,
not unpleasantly, "Why don't the infidels stay outside in the sun?"

I was sure he agreed to this not to be alone with me but to let Nicole
reemerge. She had spoken for the first time in the voice of her old
Paris self.

But when we walked across the plaza to sit on a set of shallow steps
littered with knapsacks and orange peels and the people they belonged
to in rolled-up shirtsleeves who smelled of coconut lotion or the spinach
and garlic *bocadillos* they'd just eaten, Marc said, his knees rising nearly
to his shoulders, "So, rejected from the house of God," and then looked
at me with the same relentless curiosity he'd had in his eye since we landed
in Spain.

We wound down the mountains of La Mancha south toward Granada,
stopping for the night in a small village whose center was split in two by
a deep gorge. Three architects had died—one accident and two suicides—
before another was able to complete the 200-meter-high bridge that now
joined the two sides of town. Marc had chosen this place for the bridge
alone, and before dinner we all had to indulge him in an hour's examina-
tion of it from all angles.

It *was* spectacular. It rose up in one narrow arch made of a pale stone,
which now, with evening falling, had turned a soft lilac. From above, the
water flowing through seemed a thin trickle; from below it was a loud
rushing river. Houses were embedded along the walls of the long ravine,
half hidden by boughs and vines and moss. The bridge was even more
striking from below, and the walk down the steep narrow path smelled
of new grass and the dinners on the stoves of some of the crouching houses.

The next day the land flattened out. On either side of the car, young
green fields spread from the road to the edges of strange gold and plum
hills. It was these hills that captured my attention, again and again, try as

I did to avoid the sight. They rose and they fell. They writhed at the corners of my eyes, bare flesh- and bruise-colored curves. They undulated: buttocks, breast, belly, thigh. The hollow of his back. The ridge of my calf. The movement of the car aroused me further. I tried to sleep, to escape my body, but my eyes kept opening back up to the land beyond. I was soaked and swollen. I wanted to touch myself. We had been in the car for hours without a stop. I'd forgotten my French. I nodded to things I didn't understand. Marc found me in the rearview mirror and said, "You must be tired, Rosie," and I felt like sobbing at the sound of my name in his mouth. It became painful, and the pain crept into my lower back and down my legs.

Everyone else had begun to complain to him. Hadn't he said they'd be there by early afternoon? Why hadn't they flown? Were they lost? He said it would be beautiful but it was all the same. It was too hot; turn on the AC. It was too cold; open the sunroof. Everyone had to go to the bathroom at once.

We stopped at a gas station. Before filing off to the toilet with the others, Nicole gave me the task of paying and inquiring how far until Granada. I walked around to the other side of the van, where a woman was standing by the pump. She wore a bright pink visor and faded pink slippers, the backs of which had been crushed down like sandals, and between these her body was hidden entirely by a pale green shift. Unlike so many of the faces I'd seen in Spain, hers had not been shriveled by the sun. Her skin was soft and loose. She greeted me with the silent understanding between native and tourist that acknowledges both the tourist's money and the native's control over what they will get for it. "¿Lleno?" she asked, and, without waiting for an answer, filled the tank with their most expensive fuel.

At a table in the shade at the side of the garage sat a man waiting for her to return to a game of cards. Marc came around the corner then, peering over the man's shoulder as he passed. I leaned against the van, aware of his gaze but not returning it. Out of the car I felt better—good, even. Sexy. Had I ever felt sexy before? I looked down at my breasts and the edge of my T-shirt where it met the waist of my shorts. It was a woman's body now. I'd lost the extra weight, but my hips were wider, my breasts still plump. Had my body ever seemed this inviting, this warm and alive?

He came up beside me. He had on a white shirt, an old dress shirt thin from wear and sharply wrinkled from a day in the car. A corner of the breast pocket had begun to tear. I could feel how soft the cloth would be, how the heat from his chest would rise quickly through it.

"Double solitaire," he said.

"What?"

He nodded in the direction of the table.

I'd loved cards once, the long cracking like knuckles of the shuffle, the hope a new hand brought, and the feeling of sitting cross-legged opposite my sister on a Sunday afternoon with a bag of candy or one of the banana-chocolate-marshmallow-fluff concoctions we'd make in the blender. What was it about foreign places that made you remember and yearn for so many things all at once? I looked at Marc for an answer, but his eyes were fixed on the land ahead. I wondered what he ached for and if he too saw bodies in all those hills.

I remembered my other duty. I turned and asked, *"¿Está lejos, Granada?"*

The woman clucked a few times, a sound I'd come to learn meant no.

The nozzle clicked off. *"Tres mil quinientas,"* the woman fired out at me.

I translated the number for Marc, who handed the woman a fifty-thousand note and grinned at me for being so quick. He hadn't noticed that the figure was on the pump.

Nicole appeared from around the other side of the garage. She had brushed her hair and retucked her shirt. She walked with a spine of steel but kept her eyes half shut and two hands on her purse as if for balance. As she came closer, I saw how her thumb was rubbing the edge of the purse's clasp. I could feel Marc realigning his thoughts and his posture at her approach. Gravel grated beneath his shoes. Why was everything so vivid here?

"I'm in the mood to drive, all of a sudden," she said.

"Good, because I'm in the mood to nap," Marc said. Did he not notice how phony this mood of Nicole's was? Had he not seen her thumb stroking her purse with such nervous desperation?

Guillaume wanted to sit in front. Marc came back with Lola and me, while Odile kept her spot stretched out in the rear. Nicole draped her jacket over the back of her seat. Her arms in the sleeveless green shirt, which I remembered from shopping on my second day in Paris, already had a brown gleam to them. She rolled down her window, hung out an elbow, and started the car.

We pulled out onto the highway. No one else seemed bothered by the way she pumped the accelerator, changed lanes, or swerved into the shoulder every time she looked in the rear or side mirror. The road crossed a wide river. At any moment, Nicole could pitch us right over the edge.

Marc fell quickly asleep. I snuck glimpses of him across Lola, feigning sudden interest in the other side of the road, which was identical to my side: the pale fields, the heaving hills. I'd never seen him sleep before. He wore a crushingly sad expression, which cut my arousal with a more gentle urge to cradle such a face in my hands. My sister told me once that there were men who needed to take care of someone and men who needed to be taken care of. Cal, at eighteen, was definitely the first type; Marc, at forty-nine, was the other. Cal would have wanted to marry me, like in a fifties movie. He wanted things to be in order. He would have tied my shoelaces in double knots if I'd let him. If he knew the whole truth, he'd never forgive me for the decisions I'd made.

In the rearview mirror, Nicole's face was placid now. She had picked a lane and stayed in it; her foot on the gas was more constant. She had regained control. But was this what she really wanted? She seemed both to need and eventually resent the power she claimed. I cadged another glance at Marc. He was so much less complicated. With him it would be easy to remove the sadness: three kisses with a few reassuring words and it would be gone.

Rain spattered the glass of the hotel's breakfast nook the next morning. "*No es normal*," the proprietor, pointing a scolding finger at the sky, informed the guests one by one as they came downstairs loaded with tripods and fat lenses and room-by-room guidebooks for the trek up the hill to the Alhambra. "*Va a pasar. Va a mejorar.*"

I sat with my French family, who carried no gear—only an Instamatic and a pamphlet from the front desk. Dull-eyed and only half curious, they turned to me for translation. The words were nearly all the same in French, I wanted to tell them.

They were a groggy family in the morning. I observed them from an altered angle today, feeling separate in a different way.

I'd come down first and had a *cortado* and a package of dry cakes that was brought to me on a plate by the owner's daughter, a small child who hummed to herself as if alone in the room. Among the guests already there—three Spaniards, a German, and a young American couple—I felt entirely French, and when Lola joined me I began speaking greedily, knowing that every word would bloom out of my mouth exactly the way it should. As the others took their seats at the table I'd chosen, they opened their plastic wrapped cakes and complained that they tasted like dust. Meals were serious to them, even this scant breakfast that came with the price of a room. Nicole had me ask for orange juice and toast. My Spanish came out nearly as well as the French. I loved the whole different feel of it on my tongue. The little girl gave me a quick adult nod, both an acknowledgment of the request and a commendation of my unexpected proficiency, and darted off. It was not difficult to ask for juice or toast— *zumo de naranja; pan tostado;* it was a handful of sounds delivered in the proper sequence—but it gave me a connection to the place, the room, the humming child, the wet red flowers on the bush pressed up against the window, that the others were deprived of. In Paris, they were the connected ones. They knew the streets and the styles and the faces of the famous; they knew the songs and the subjunctive and the name of every bridge. They were the standard I was always straining and failing to achieve. But here they were still simply French and I was a chameleon. Today I was not separate from them; they were separate from me, from me and everything else.

As if they too knew this, on the way up to the palace in the rain, they hovered close to me: Marc with his map, the kids with their questions, Nicole pointing out anything written in English. At first the Alhambra was unimpressive: a long line to walk on dirt paths from one tower to another. We climbed to the top of the tallest and saw the city below, flat and dismal, as if wounded by the rain. In the first of an endless series of small packed buildings, I was moved through the rooms not by my own volition but by the unyielding currents of other people, people who smelled of wet hair and wet shoes and murmured different languages in the same tones. There was beauty—walls, columns, and arches dripping with relentless ornamentation—but more vivid was the swish of Marc's windbreaker behind me. I fought the impulse to stop short like a naughty child to feel him bump up against me. Nicole moved more swiftly than the rest of us. I liked it that for rooms at a time people might have thought, as Marc spoke quietly into my ear and Lola tugged at my sleeve, that this was my family.

Out in the courtyard the rain had stopped but the sky was still low and fragile, as if we had stepped inside the shell of an egg. The sixty seconds of my every minute were spent in wait, in patient suspension until Marc's attention fell briefly back on me. When it did, the change in me was instant and extraordinary. I hoped it was only noticeable from the inside, but Odile caught it and called me over to the brightly tiled wall for a picture because, she said, I looked so pretty.

"You really do, Rosie," she said, not bothering to hide her surprise. She passed the camera to Guillaume so she could go stand next to me. We put our arms loosely around each other. Beside me and without heels, Odile was shorter than I'd thought. We were probably close to the same height. Guillaume wanted to take another, so we leaned in closer. After all these months, I suspected Odile now wanted to be friends. Part of me recoiled. She had been so distant and dismissive up till now. But at the other end of the reflecting pool, Marc looked up at the future photo, and reflexively, as if I thought he could feel it somehow, I held Odile tighter. Odile squeezed back.

Nicole was already on the path to the next building. A redheaded teenager leaned in toward her, as if they were both standing still, to ask for a light. She shook her head and the boy dropped back reluctantly.

Lola squatted at the pool's edge to look down at her green reflection, showing her underpants to everyone on the other side.

Guillaume accidentally took a picture of his left sneaker and Odile snatched the camera away from him, accidentally snapping a shot of a kneecap of a man from Wisconsin.

Above us all, the sky grew stronger.

Inside the Winter Palace it was even more congested, and we shuffled through, pressed together, reaching out occasionally to the painted walls and carvings, brushing fingers as our hands fell back at our sides. Light began to pour in like thick cream through high windows and low latticed archways. One ceiling held the pocked texture of a honeycomb. Carvings curled and roiled endlessly from room to room. In one, an Australian guide spoke loudly about blood and beheadings. In another, cursive phrases from the Koran swam like fish across a wall. Some of the lettering looked like L's and Lola traced them, saying they were trying to spell her name. I barely heard her, so great was my effort to maintain a reasonable distance of a few inches but no more from Marc's side. I was certain he was aware of my struggle, perhaps even bemused by it, steering me this way and that with an arm that never actually touched.

As we were disgorged onto the Patio de los Leones, the sun pressed down on our necks and backs like a great hand. All around the fountain people were shedding layers. It seemed as if everyone peeling off clothes must have been thinking in some vague way about sex. Everyone except Nicole. It was impossible to think of Nicole caving in to an impulse. Even an unanticipated smile seemed to frustrate her.

We walked into a large round room where people stood with their ears pressed to the wall. Some were speaking, though their voices were inaudible.

"What are they doing?" Guillaume asked.

"Listening for the sea," Marc said.

"Really?" Lola went to an empty spot at the wall. Guillaume and Odile went to another. They listened, then looked above them in bewilderment.

Marc laughed and told Nicole to go to a certain place along the wall. He walked to a spot directly opposite her and they stood speaking to each other back to back, forty feet apart, Nicole's head cocked like a teenage girl on the phone and Marc with both arms braced against the wall, as if it were about to cave in. While their children moved from one spot to another and the other tourists we'd been traveling through the Alhambra with filed in and filed out, Marc and Nicole remained in place, carrying out the longest public conversation they'd had since we'd left Paris, observed only by me, their *fille,* who took anxious note of such things.

Unforgiven

❦

SOMETIMES STILL I WAKE UP IN THE DARK ROCKING, AND IF THERE'S A MOON UP IT WILL be swimming, swaying like the old trawler that anchored on the opposite bank in winter. I'll watch its light for as long as I can bear remembering, until I know that it's me rocking and all I have to do is stop.

Without a moon through the window, everything is sucked up and stolen, and even the small bellies of stone against my palm along the hallway are pure hallucination. Everything is gone in the hot dark of the house, until I reach Lucie's door. Then I sink to the cool slate floor and wait to hear her sleeping. The sound is less a snore than a whimper, less adult than small child. It can be almost an hour before she comes out with one, and always only one, as if she once shared a bed with a sister who slept lightly and elbowed her hard at the first sound. There is always only one because even now, over seventy years later and the sister maybe dead, maybe lost to her in some other awful way, she still feels the swift nudge at her side. I hope she had a sister and that they shared a room and a bed, and that sometimes years and years ago she'd wake up with her sister's toes squeezed tight around her own. But I also hope she's forgotten all that, that her toes never feel too loose or too cold in the mornings.

Lucie is sick. There is pain but she won't complain. She takes meals in bed now: soup dribbles on her nightgown; peas fall in the folds of the sheet. I eat beside her, neatly, on a fold-out table that lists hard to the left. After lunch I read to her. After dinner I wash her with a cool cloth. Four times a day I carry a pan to the toilet. Once there was blood.

Last week I overheard her telling Henri to find someone in town to take care of her. "This is no place for a child," she whispered.

On his way out, I stopped him and begged to stay.

"I'll be back in two days," he said, and when he returned he was alone.

Each night is hot and long. Sleep comes close to dawn, for an hour or two, never more, and only when I can prevent my mind from traveling too far. Behind me, there are only mistakes; ahead, there is nothing at all. Instead, I think again of Marie-Jo, whom we saw in town the last time Lucie was well enough to walk there with me.

She was on the terrace of the Cafe Plaire, dragging a canvas bag between the plastic chairs toward the back entrance.

"That's one of Nicole's sisters," Lucie told me, and we stopped to watch. She wore an unbelted cotton dress the mottled color of a coffee stain. Her hair was iron gray beneath the corner of a scarf. When she saw Lucie, she dropped the bag, wiped her brow with her hand and her hand on her dress, and wound her way back through the chairs out onto the sidewalk. She placed her cheek gingerly against the old face, as if it might bruise.

"You're so thin," Marie-Jo said, though it was clear she meant old. I felt responsible somehow for this decline. But Marie-Jo looked aged, too. It was hard to believe that she was born only eight years before Nicole. If there had once been a resemblance, nothing remained of it. Marie-Jo's nose had swelled, her chin had doubled and grown fuzzy, her ankles spilled over the sides of dusty white loafers.

"What are you doing with that bag?" Lucie asked.

She told us. She spoke with a thick accent in sentences strewn with Provençal words, but I understood that she and Paco had split up and she was moving into a room above the café. She explained at length what had led to the decision (something about his mother and a plum tree), how their grown children, four of them, had taken it (badly, dividing into sides), how perhaps it was only temporary (his mother, after all, would not live forever). She held on to Lucie's arm the whole time she spoke, sometimes squeezing, sometimes shaking her so hard I had to steady her from the other side. Marie-Jo's other arm was even wilder. She flung it up to the sky, dashed it to the ground. She wiped away tears and covered up loud laughs at herself. When she sneezed, she didn't pinch her nose, like Nicole. She just bent over and sent a sharp *chhh* to the pavement.

Though Marie-Jo left no room for introductions, she included me as if my round American face were perfectly familiar to her. I stood there mute but amused, enjoying her clamorous gesticulations. Marie-Jo was alive. She was part of the world, with her accent and honesty and brushed-away tears.

It was only as we were saying good-bye that Lucie managed to insert how I had come here. Marie-Jo nodded as if somehow she'd already known, as if she saw in my face, as I could not see in hers, some trace of Nicole.

And then she was gone, across the terrace, hoisting the bag and disappearing through the doorway in back.

"She didn't want to know about Nicole?"

"No. Nicole has never been forgiven."

For five years after she left, Nicole came back summer and Christmas to Plaire. She sat in her sisters' kitchens and endured their criticism of her cropped hair, her polished fingers, the strange fabrics of her dresses. Far more painful than being different and apart was being alone in the conviction that her mother was still alive. Her sisters spoke of Marcelle as they spoke of long-dead aunts and pets. They brought up her name carelessly, without emotion, often in mild insult to each other. "That was just like Maman," one would say. Or, "Maman would have thought so." When Nicole was there, they pointed to her and told their families, "Can you imagine? This is how Maman wanted us all to turn out."

They believed Nicole had gone to Paris for a fairy tale, to live like a princess with rich Aunt Anne. She never told them she'd gone in search of their mother. Lucie Quenelle was the only person who knew that within a year Nicole had been to every hotel and pension in the city with the only photograph of her mother she possessed. She visited parks and museums. She rode buses and trains to all the outskirts. A long braid, a sky blue cardigan, a desultory step would send her heart racing, but these things in the end were never attached to Marcelle.

In the meantime, between searches, she fell in love. He was the brother of her school friend, Pauline, who often invited her to their country house on weekends. If they were to go on Friday, by the Wednesday before, Nicole had stopped eating, her stomach cramping tighter and tighter as the minutes advanced. At night her quick pulse made the sheet tremble against her skin, and she slept badly. Delivered on Friday evening into his presence, her body relaxed and Pauline's parents joked about the enormous appetite of such a small girl. They had taken to calling her Kitty, for she was often found curled up on a window seat fast asleep in the middle of the day. Her place at the dinner table was beside his, and she bit her lip to keep from laughing too hard at the little things Stéphane said. Everything about him that irritated Pauline and her parents was sacred to her: the way he crashed up and down the stairs three at time or swung the unwilling dachshund upside down. Even the way his voice would rise to a piercing squeak when he was losing an argument with his father was endearing to her. His face, apparently ordinary to everyone else, was the perfect orb around which, Friday to Sunday, the whole of her attention surreptitiously circled. He was two years and two months older, and it took him nearly twice that amount of time before he came to regard her as anyone but Kitty, his little sister's feline shadow. Nicole tried to take an interest in other boys, but the only ones she noticed were those in whom she recognized the slightest aspect of Stéphane. There was one with the same sort of wave to his hair, another with a similar gait. There were some whose resemblance to Stéphane was less easily identifiable and she would have to dance with them all evening in order to narrow in on it. And then there was someone named Marc, who, from the back, was wholly indistinguishable from Stéphane but head on was an assault to his perfection. More than once she had approached this Marc from behind, tugged at his jacket, and, as he turned around, felt violated by the contrast. Whenever this happened, Marc smiled right through Nicole's disappointment, as if he had somehow done it all on purpose.

It was a humid evening in March when Stéphane finally kissed her. She had gone with him and Pauline to a matinée, and when they came out of the theater, a brief rain had wet the streets. The air was warm, and up from the pavement came the sweet coppery memory of a summer shower. Nicole barely spoke, stirred by thoughts of Plaire and the lingering anticipation she often felt after a film. Pauline, anxious to prepare herself for a date that evening, moved ahead of them on the sidewalk. When exactly Stéphane took her hand, Nicole was never certain. It was a moment she had imagined so often that she had trouble believing she was not inventing it again. Then he stopped, waited for Pauline to turn a corner, and kissed her.

She had loved him for so long. She tried to keep it in, let it trickle out slowly, at the same slow rate his feelings would seep out for her. But it was like trying to contain a hurricane inside her. And he was not prepared. She knew his past better than he knew it himself. She could remember four Novembers ago, the play he went to, the girl he took, and the shoes she wore. She called him by his stupid family nicknames. She knew the foods he would not swallow. She knew a child had fallen and died right beside him in the park when he was four. There was nothing for him to reveal—except love, for which she waited patiently and in vain. When he took a job in London the following year, there was no mention of her coming, not even to visit.

The fall that Stéphane left, when Nicole was twenty-one, they drained the quarry in Plaire. Lucie wrote to say that remains had been found. There was to be a private family burial. The Church had refused to recognize it. The letter gave the date and the time. Enclosed was a train ticket to Plaire. Nicole didn't use it. She did not go to the burial and she never wrote again. The following summer, the town clerk leaked the news that Nicole Guerrin had sent for a copy of her birth certificate: she was to marry a man named Marc Tivot on the first of August.

IV

Les Deux Femmes Morbides

❧

FORMENTOR, ON THE ISLAND OF MALLORCA, WAS MARC'S BEST-KEPT SECRET. HE had not prepared any of us for its narrow peninsula road, its terrifying drops, its stark sand below, or the color of its sea, which was a blue unlike any other. It was not an Atlantic navy or a Pacific cobalt or a Florida turquoise; it was not even the color of the Mediterranean I'd seen from the plane that brought us here. It was a pure, perfect blue that seemed lit from above and below, as if beneath the basin in which the water rocked stretched a long luminescence, a cool, diffused sheet of light like the moon's, which rose toward sharp spears of sun. Against this haunting luster, the bright afternoon sky was unremarkable. We all stared in silence out the windows of the hotel minibus at the spectacle. Though I was seated far from him in the rear beside their bags, I could feel Marc's relief. His mouth would be taut with suppression of it. There would be a hard knot in his throat. His greatest pleasure was to please, and this sight was a small miracle.

Once we had arrived at this beach resort, there were no excursions: no maps, no bridges, no cathedrals or palaces. The trip I had grown used to had come to an end, and in its place was a new trip, to which everyone else seemed to adjust immediately. Each day they rose with renewed vigor to spend the day flat out on a towel. Their bodies—all except Marc's—turned instantly brown, Nicole's by far the darkest and most even, as if she hadn't tanned but simply washed off a chalky layer of Paris that had clung to her skin all winter. She was the first one in the water in the morning and the last out in the evening. She took quick, efficient dips, dunking her body all at once and reemerging a few seconds later in a different spot. Her hair that week was always wet and shimmering. Each time she came back to her towel she reached into her bag for her comb, cut a perfect part, made three strokes around her head, and lay back down. She wore the same black bikini bottom I'd met her in. Odile also bared her breasts, but Lola, who had surveyed the beach the first day and found this was not obligatory, did not. Nor did I. I rarely lay on my towel at all, preferring to dig in the sand with Lola and Guillaume or chaperone their trips to the snack bar, where we ate olives stuffed with anchovies and listened to a radio station that played American music indiscriminately while waiting for our chips and frozen lemonades.

On the third day, Marc followed me and Lola up there, and while the bartender went up to the main building for more ice and Lola was in the bathroom at the back and the others were 127 steps below (Guillaume counted every time), he stood close, then closer. It was barely ten o'clock in the morning; the stools at the bar were empty and the plastic chairs were still stacked against the far wall. From the transistor radio on top of the refrigerator crackled the song "Slow Boat to China," and as I was wondering whether to translate it for him, and thinking how smooth the voices were back then and how gingerly expressed the sentiments, and remembering a photograph in my sister's house of our parents dancing in Louisiana on the night they met, Marc kissed me. I had always imagined our first kiss would be unwilling, a slow struggle as if against gravity. Or tentative. Or apologetic. But this kiss was hard like a punch, determined, as if it had been a dare. He tasted of anchovies and sunblock. With his mouth finally pressed against mine, the ache for him was gone but nothing filled its absence except a dread of its return. I clung on until we heard a flush, leaving just the right amount of distance for Lola to jump in and wrap an arm around each of our waists. I wondered how she was able to walk right into the space between us, sensing nothing, just as later, at lunch, when I got up to follow the children back down to the water, Nicole told me to stay. We could watch them from here, she said, touching my arm and urging me back into my seat beside Marc. I did stay, and Marc asked me to order another *jarro de rosado,* and we all three clinked our glasses and polished it off as if there were something to celebrate.

Nobody else seemed to notice that the world had begun spinning in the opposite direction, or that the air was thinner this way around, or that the sun felt like ice and the long moon below the sea had been extinguished. No one noticed any of these changes, not even Marc, who was exactly the same, offering Nicole his wary, eager-to-please face, ignored pats across the table, and the same sulks and rebounds within their briefest exchange.

This became routine: the three of us remaining, long after our lunch plates had been cleared, beneath the thatched canopy of this restaurant on the beach where waiters in shiny black shoes slogged through the white sand from table to table. What do they make of us? I wondered one afternoon when the *rosado* had taken a particular hold, convincing me that our table with the pale pink cloth and blue-lipped tumblers must be the center of their world. I was certain they knew I was not French, that I was the *jeune fille,* that yesterday when Nicole had gone up to their room for a dry towel Marc had followed me into the ladies' room, lifted my breasts out of my bathing suit, and sucked one, then the other, circling the nipples so gently with his tongue it brought tears to my eyes. But it had been his solemn face so close that had moved me, for still his touch brought only numbness. It wasn't until I was alone again in the dank bathroom that my whole body began to throb again in want of him. Surely our waiters knew all this, even if his wife did not.

Nicole became more beautiful. I couldn't explain this, but the more Marc and I began to touch, the more beautiful Nicole became. It was not simply the sun, though her skin was now the polished color of expensive wood and her teeth were whiter and her eyes greener against it. It was just as much the languor of movement, the way she would doze off on her towel with both arms above her head or rub her full belly after dinner. The mask of strained pleasure had dissolved, and beneath it lay a face that at certain moments seemed nearly content.

"Days pass deliciously slowly here, don't they?" Nicole said, after lunch on our fourth day at the beach.

I agreed, lying, for I was aware only of their flight. Three full days left.

"Why do you think," Nicole said, "life passes so very slowly when you are a child and so quickly when you are grown?"

"Nicole," Marc whined.

"I'm not trying to be morbid. I'm just wondering."

"I think," I began, without the slightest idea of what I'd say but wanting to balance Marc's irritation with interest, "I think it's because"—and I saw in my half-drunk, sun-sogged mind a small child surrounded by tall kitchen furniture and on the wall an enormous clock, its second hand in fluid movement around the two other hands that never changed—"it's because when you are young, everything is so much bigger. The tables, the chairs, the clocks."

I looked from one to the other. They were nodding gravely. Yes, that was the truth of it. Then Nicole let out a strange sputter and Marc leaned over the side of his chair as if something on the ground had caught his attention, and Nicole, seeing his body begin to shake, could hold back no longer and hung onto the table for support and soon they were both, then all three of us, shuddering in absolute and silent laughter. Marc, taking in a breath, stretched his arms way out and said, his mouth unable to wrap completely around the words, "Big chairs," sending us all into more painful paroxysms.

When we had recovered, Nicole said, "No, I'm serious," her voice still a bit wobbly. Mascara had stained the pink napkin she held. "I want to know why."

"I *was* being serious," I said, feigning outrage as Marc often did.

"I'm not sure it's true that—" he said.

"You think that since your father put you to work from the moment you could walk, time always . . ." Nicole made circles in the air to indicate the predictable rest.

Marc looked as if a bird had been snatched from his mouth.

"I disagree," Nicole went on, "because I bet those days seemed infinitely longer than they would now. I bet your childhood seemed as endless as ours. Endless work, but endless."

"It did," Marc said. I worried that he would feel resentful or belittled and that the warm wake of the laughter would be disturbed, but he seemed simply pleased that his difficult childhood was being sufficiently pitied.

"I remember once," Nicole began, as she pulled an empty chair toward her and draped her legs over its arm, "I remember standing outside a church. I couldn't have been more than five. It was this time of year, this kind of weather. It was Easter Sunday, and my father and I were waiting for my mother and sisters to come out. They had gotten way behind us somehow, so we went and sat by this tree and I'll never forget how long it took for that church to empty out. It took so long I forgot what my mother looked like. Really, I forgot her face. I didn't know who I was waiting for anymore. My father lit his pipe and I waited and waited." For a moment or two, she was not beautiful. Her features seemed to forget each other, lost in this memory. Then, wholly aware, she recomposed them. "I swear to you the time it took for my mother to emerge from that church was the equivalent of what would be a year to me now."

"This was in Plaire?" I asked, solely for the sake of pronouncing the town with such a lovely name. I'd heard of it only through the children. Nicole herself had never spoken of the place.

She nodded, unsurprised that people spoke of her in her absence. "But why *is* it?" she persisted, looking out at the wet sand where Lola and Guillaume were batting a blue ball back and forth. "Is it simply innocence?"

"The beginning of anything is like that," Marc said. "You—"

I cut him off. "It *is* an innocence, I think. An innocence of loss."

"—have a piece of pie in front of you, and the first half lasts forever and the second half is gone before you blink."

"That's it, isn't it, the innocence of loss. My mother died that year, a few months after that Easter. And nothing ever felt slow again." Nicole bored her eyes into mine, a sustained penetration. I held it, not wanting to appear cowardly or guilty, the two qualities Nicole's presence enhanced in me. She seemed to be asking something desperately of me, something entirely unrelated to Marc and my involvement with him. At the edges of my vision, in the small spaces where Nicole's face was not, sand and water flickered red, then yellow, then green. I wished I could unloosen a memory as a return offering. But I could not.

"*Les deux femmes morbides,*" Marc said, somewhere out of periphery. "It should be the title to something."

Nicole began to watch me. Blatantly, unapologetically, she kept a vigilant eye on me when I spoke to waiters or elevator operators or the young man at the front desk. She created unnecessary encounters just so she could watch them play out. Sizing me up, straining to understand why her husband would be attracted to such an awkward, average sort of person.

It was puzzling to me too. Beside Nicole on the beach I was splotched and plump. My hair dried badly, in tufts like crabgrass. Guillaume made fun of the matronly cut of my American swimsuit; Odile told me to be more careful when applying lotion and eventually took over the process herself. I was always finding food in my teeth, flakes of snot in my nose, dirt under my fingernails. What drew Marc to me remained a mystery.

Whenever I was left alone with Nicole, I braced myself for accusation. I stopped asking her to repeat herself when I didn't quite understand, fearful that in the brief tangle of sounds was a sharp insinuation. I imagined again and again packing my bags in shame, boarding a plane alone, answering another ad. The only hope I allowed myself was that somehow Lola would not find out.

Late in the afternoon, Nicole stood in the wet sand and called me out of the water where Marc and I were judging the children's handstands. In her voice was a terrible reluctance, as if someone else had put her up to the confrontation. I moved through the water slowly. With each step there was less water and more of my own weight to carry. In the chest-high depth beside Marc I'd felt light and delicate. Now, as the waves lapped at my calves, then my ankles, then only at the soles of my feet, my body felt, more than ever, an enormous unnecessary burden that could be packed off at any moment.

She asked me to walk up to the snack bar with her. I glanced at the long flight of steps and wondered on which one it would be spoken.

We headed across the sand in silence.

On step number fourteen, Nicole said, "What you get, is it a *granizado* or *granizada*?"

My lips were trembling. "*Granizado.*"

"*Granizado limón?*"

"Yes."

"Is it *quisiera? Quisiera un granizado limón?*"

"Yes."

"*Quisiera un granizado limón.*"

"Yes."

Nicole said nothing more.

In the hut, it was dark and cool. Only thin straws of light slipped through and fell on the ground. There was one table free. I imagined how she would sit and place her wrists at its edge, on their sides, hands in loose fists. Her voice would be deliberately soft. But she moved toward the bar. The bartender raised his eyebrows to me with familiarity, finished his sentence to the two men at the far side, and came over. He asked me how the water was today (I'd forgotten to grab a towel and in my trembling dripped slightly still) and if I'd found a boyfriend yet.

"*No, todavía no,*" I said.

He nodded obsequiously to Nicole, then asked me what we'd like. I turned to Nicole, "You order."

"I can't," she whispered.

"Yes, you can. And I'd like one too."

"*Quisiera dos granizados limón, por favor,*" she said, perfectly.

"*Vale,*" he said, and went to the back freezer where the vats of lemon ice were kept.

"*Vale?*" Nicole asked, her eyes wide and alert like Lola's.

"Okay."

"Ah."

As we waited, Nicole swung her head all around, popped three almonds in her mouth, made a design in the sand with her toe.

The bartender slid the cups across the counter. It was clear he wanted to say more to her but was at a loss. Nicole took them and said, "*Vale, gracias.*" She walked past the table and out the door. At the top of the steps, she handed me my twin *granizado.* "I was so nervous. You made me so nervous."

"*I* made *you* nervous," I shouted, overwhelmed by relief, by the sudden heat, by the disappearance of the trembling.

"I wasn't sure if it would be *dos granizados limones* or just *limón.*" And, like this, she chattered all the way back down the 127 steps.

That night after dinner, I stopped just inside the French doors that led to the terrace. The evening had cooled slightly and Nicole was lifting a white sweater over her shoulders. She had turned her chair out to face the oblong moon and its restless streak upon the water. Marc was still seated square with the table like an obedient schoolboy, though he swayed slightly to the salsa music that rose from the level below, where Odile,

her new friend Aimée, and Lola had gone dancing. Guillaume slept
soundly with his head where his plate had been.

I remembered stopping like this in the doorway to the back porch
of my sister's house, just before I left. They were on the wicker couch.
Sarah was holding the baby and Hank was singing. I stood there, wit-
nessing my own absence in a room. If I had stepped through, I would
have disturbed them all—an ungainly swell in placid, defined waters.

I wished in a way I could feel that now, the necessity of my own
disappearance. But tonight Nicole was in a good mood and Marc anxious
that he might ruin it. They sat waiting for me, needing me once again to
soften their edges.

A waiter brushed past me with a perfunctory *perdón,* and I followed
him through the doors. Marc lifted his head. He had only two ways of
looking at me now: one that acknowledged everything between us, and
another that forgot it all. He gave me the first kind, a prisoner's gaze that
admitted both guilt and indignation, that begged for help yet knew the
futility of the plea, that confessed his own errors yet railed against a greater
injustice. It both imposed and apologized for his feelings for me.

I didn't know what I gave back to him. I aimed for a mildly affectionate and bemused look, a detached appreciation, a full and nearly glib accep-
tance of the limitations of our situation. Perhaps from a distance this is what
I achieved. But as the table came closer and I saw a bent leg jut out from
beneath it, the sharp kneecap defined by thin cotton pants, I felt that all
that remained on my face was the effort and not the mask itself.

When I reached my chair, he said, "Ah, you're back," and Nicole
turned and his eyes went blank.

At dinner Lola had conducted a psychology test she'd learned from
a girl from Geneva she'd met on the beach. You had to cross a desert and
were given five animals: a cow, a lamb, a horse, a lion, and a monkey.
Then you had to rank the animals in order of their importance to you.
After we'd all made our lists, Lola revealed what each of them represented.
Nicole had put the horse first, Odile the cow, Guillaume the lion. Marc
and I had had identical lists: Monkey, lamb, horse, lion, cow. Lola translated it to children, love, work, power, money. At the end of the meal I
managed to slip our two lists from the table unnoticed. I'd begun to collect—in my head, in my pockets—this kind of proof.

I'd mentioned that I knew a similar test but then stopped myself, realizing that it wasn't appropriate for children. Nicole remembered that now. "What about that other little game, Rosie?"

"Yes," Marc said, "the X-rated one."

"It's not really X-rated."

"Forget it, then," Nicole said, batting the idea away. "We need something truly scandalous."

"No, let's do it," he said. His hand flinched; instinct had drawn it toward mine and reason jerked it back. Even so, his whole body had begun to curve toward mine in a nearly proprietary way. Could Nicole not see this? Did she not recognize that her own inexplicable contentment was allowing it?

I told them the situation. There are five people, A, B, C, D, and E, on a boat way out in the ocean. A storm comes up and the boat begins to sink. There are two islands nearby and A, B, and C swim to one, D and E to the other. C is the only woman in the group and she is madly in love with D. Desperate to find a way to get to D, C goes to B for advice. He says he has no idea how to get there; perhaps she should ask A. A says yes, he does know a way, but first she'll have to sleep with him. C agrees. A keeps his promise and she is reunited with D. But when C tells D how she got there, he is furious. He tells her he never wants to see her again. Eventually E takes her under his wing and they spend the rest of their lives together on the other end of the island.

I drew the scenario on a napkin.

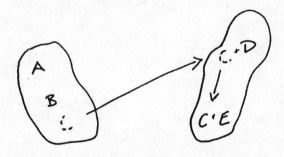

Then I took another napkin, ripped it, and slid a half to each of them. "So, now you have to rank these people from most admirable to most despicable."

Nicole picked up the pen and wrote hers out in a straight column without pausing. Marc wrote one letter and quickly covered it up. I laughed at him and Nicole joined me. I felt a warm pressure in my chest. I loved it when it was like this, when the connection between the two of them ran directly through me.

"Who's B again?" Marc asked me, his face empty of everything except the task at hand. There was no trace of recollection that he had kissed me now at least seven different times, touched my breasts, and before dinner in the elevator tonight told me that he was constantly imagining what it would be like to hold me afterward, after we'd made love.

I pointed to the arrow on the diagram in front of him.

"Okay, okay," he said, in my accent. But he didn't look up. He wrote his list.

"So," I said, "let's start at the bottom. Who's least admirable?"

"C," Nicole said.

Marc threw down the pen in mock outrage. "What? She's the *most* admirable!"

"Why?" I asked, secretly pleased by his choice.

"Because she makes this enormous sacrifice."

"For herself," Nicole said.

"For both of them," Marc said.

"She was entirely selfish."

"My God, Nicole. She was in love. And she was loved. She simply wanted to be with him for the rest of her life, her only life. She assumed he would want that too. Why is that not admirable, to have made a sacrifice for their union?"

Nicole had made a hard shell, thick as an oyster's, around her. "You know how I loathe your life-is-so-short speech."

"That's *not* what I'm saying."

I felt as if I were suddenly trapped beneath their bed, forced to listen to a conversation I could neither fully understand nor gracefully escape.

"I just don't see that making a sacrifice for love is so saintly. I'm sorry. Love is not a virtue, Marc. D sacrifices in the face of love, despite his love. He denies himself this pleasure because he has certain principles. That's admirable. Whether you agree with that system or not, it's admirable that he adheres to it even when it will only bring him pain. He has integrity. C does not. She doesn't waste any time making compromises. She is sexually manipulated but I don't find victims inherently admirable either. And if she loved D that much, she should have understood his terms and not simply behaved according to her own. She didn't have the first idea about love."

"That's absurd," Marc said. "You're missing the point, Nicole. You've missed the most essential point of it all."

Fight for it, Marc. Fight for that essential point, that warm irrational human element missing in Nicole that we have in abundance. Fight for a world built solely on love, whose first and last value is love, where people keep and cherish what they love, despite all systems. But he had retreated. He stared impotently at the black pen in his hand. Nicole stroked Guillaume's sunburnt forehead. He was still fast asleep. The white sweater had slipped off a shoulder and her taut skin seemed to glow in triumph.

We are at her mercy, I thought. She hangs us up the way it suits her: by the neck, by the foot, apart, squeezed together. Perhaps nothing we had ever said or done was not a part of her design. She had slipped her hands inside us and watched us dance for the simple satisfaction of what seemed to be her deepest belief: that people will always disappoint you. You can trust them for exactly nothing. What is it like, Nicole, to be a demigod? To lie on a silver cloud and watch us down below in the dirt, frantic to please and deceive you? What does it feel like to extend a painted finger, give a little nudge, and wait for the inevitable outcome? You beg to be betrayed, like any god begs, in order to condemn and be forever free from condemnation.

Nicole lifted Guillaume's sleeping torso and resettled it against his own chair. She stood up to peer over the ledge at her daughters dancing.

"She always wanted to be a lawyer," Marc said.

She turned. "I always wanted to be a judge."

Marc remained seated, tracing figure eights around his line of unanalyzed letters. "Who did you put as most admirable when you did this?" He looked up at me, and the blankness was gone.

At first I could not hold his gaze. I wanted Nicole back, Nicole laughing. I'd failed. I'd destroyed the connection. I wished I had the strength to lie to him, but I had lifted my eyes again and did not. "C," I said.

I started helping Nicole practice Spanish.

"*Estamos en la playa,*" I said.

"*Estamos en la playa,*" Nicole repeated. "We're on the beach."

"*Muy bien. Tengo hambre.*"

"*Tengo hambre.* I'm hungry."

"Look at the little girl watching Lola," Marc said.

I glanced toward the water, where Lola was creeping on her stomach along invisible hands through the shallows, her body swaying like a reed behind her. A small child watched from the shore, shadowing her progress down the beach, giggling when Lola's head dipped beneath the water and yelping when she shook it out at her.

"Isn't she adorable?" he said.

She was a pudgy child with dimples in her joints and thin hair that in the sun was clear as glass. Her skin, however, was brown like Nicole's. When Lola lifted herself out of the water, the little girl followed her back to her towel.

Marc had guessed German and I said Dutch, but the child was French.

"*Bonjour,*" she said to us, with a confidence that announced, unmistakably, *Here I am!*

In a bored, slightly condescending tone, a tone she used to use with me, Nicole asked her her name.

"Marni," the child answered, preparing her fingers for the next question.

"And how old are you?"

But Marni was already holding up her thumb and three fingers.

"Marni's a clever girl," Marc said. His voice, too, I recognized.

Marni looked over at two boys digging near a red umbrella. "They don't think so. They called me stupid."

"Are those your brothers?" I asked this quickly, hoping to be taken for one of the family.

"They're mean. I hate them."

"You don't really hate them," Marc said.

Up until this point, Marni had been directing all of her conversation at me and Nicole. Now she turned to Marc in the chair, meeting him full on with her small, heavy-lidded eyes. "I hate them all."

Under the red umbrella was a couple in plastic recliners. The man read a newspaper and the woman was waving at us. We were too far away to call out, but the woman called out anyway, saying we should send Marni back when she began to bug us. But she had used a word, *emmerder,* which wasn't just to bug but to bug the shit out of. It was a word Nicole forbid her children to say.

"You're not French," Marni said, turning back.

"No, I'm not," I answered, as swiftly as possible: *noshweepa.*

Marni, who was not particularly impressed, told me she used to teach her old *fille* to spell in the sand.

Before I could gracefully decline, Marc was on his feet, saying he'd teach Marni instead.

Lola trailed behind them but, because Marc never let her write or say the answers, she wandered back into the warm water.

"That's not a word!" Marni shouted again and again, her giggles rising up like slow bubbles out of a bottle.

From our towels, Nicole and I watched Marc, his long body folded in two, one hand writing and the other hopping along to keep up.

"Marc has a new playmate," Nicole, said, lying down flat again. "Tell me some more Spanish, Rosie."

"*Hace calor hoy.*"

"*Hace calor hoy.* It's hot today."

"*Marc tiene una amiga.*"

"*Marc tiene una amiga.* Marc has a friend."

"*Soy Nicole.*"

"*Soy Nicole.* I am Nicole."

Marni was tickling Marc's feet with a shell and he was howling, jerking his foot away, then coming back for more. Lola called to him to watch her somersaults, but he didn't hear her.

The woman beneath the red umbrella said "Marni!" sharply, not as a name but an accusation, and she went running. Marc came back up the beach.

"Marni's leaving tomorrow," he said, as despairingly as if he'd heard the sun wouldn't rise again.

"Papa, come swim!"

"Can't," he called. "Too exhausted." He fell into his beach chair. The nylon straps cracked and the tin legs sunk. He watched Marni peel the plastic wrap off a sandwich, hold it with two fat hands, and bite down. "She is such a clever kid."

This was the way it was with Marc. His heart had a narrow field of vision. I knew it held a great many things, but the aperture was small and I had to wait my turn to be rotated back around into the light where I would glow so brightly I'd be all he could see.

Nicole waited only for another Spanish phrase.

"*Soy Nicole.*"

"*Soy Nicole.* But you already said that one."

Like so many things, it happened around us. We did nothing to precipitate it.

The next day, Lola came running up to our spot on the beach with her friend from Geneva to plead for permission to go with her family for lunch at a nearby hotel that had a pool with two slides. Before jealous tears had time to collect in Guillaume's eyes, Nicole had secured him an invitation as well, and once they were packed off she announced that she, Odile, and Aimée would take a taxi into town for the afternoon. Magazines were flipped shut; towels were shaken and rolled; dark tanning oil was capped and wrapped in a plastic bag. Through all these motions of departure, Marc remained engrossed in his mystery novel. He raised his head once to answer a question about the room key. I sat up attentively, awaiting instructions. I might be sent up to wash out the children's dirty clothes from yesterday, which lay in a pile on their bathroom tiles, or correct the math packet Guillaume promised he was working on every evening before dinner. But just before turning away, Nicole simply told me the children would be back at the hotel at three.

In hopes that she could still see me out of the corner of her eye, I leapt to my feet and began to gather up all my things, as if I never would have chosen to remain on the beach beside Marc. As soon as they were safely up the steps and through the French doors, I put my bag back down in the sand and waited for Marc to receive this cue. He kept reading. He scratched the back of a calf. He turned a page. I knew he liked to stop reading at the end of a chapter and there was no break on these new pages. I didn't know whether to lie back down on my towel or shake it out and leave. I looked toward the water with false scrutiny, not seeing the sea at all. My eye was inward and miserable, wanting only Marc's elusive attention. Finally we could have more than a few minutes of privacy—how could he waste a precious second of it finishing a chapter? By now Odile and Nicole would be on the other side of the hotel waiting for a taxi. It took only fifteen minutes to get to town. What if all the stores were closed for siesta? Another fifteen minutes and they'd be back. I leaned down for my towel.

"You're not leaving me, are you?" The voice was much more comfortable and intimate than it had ever been before. For a moment I couldn't identify the change. It wasn't just the tone. Then I knew. He'd switched to *tu*.

"No."

I sat back down, the ploy of the packed bag in my lap. There was a gap between us, where Lola had been, and four small depressions that her restless fingers and toes had dug.

"I've got to get you closer than this," he said. I marveled at the difference from *vous*. It seemed as powerful as a confession of love in each sentence. "Do you want to take a walk?"

A walk. I looked to the water's edge where for five days I'd watched the slow stream of couples moving past. I couldn't have imagined something more thrilling, to be a couple walking on the beach.

Without discussion we headed down and away from the hotel, through the clear shallows, which made our feet paler and bigger than they normally were. Lola would have asked why the water did that, Odile would have stepped out, not liking the sight of her own feet, which she already thought too large, and Guillaume would have made fun of someone else's. I made a conscious effort to banish the children's voices. I was finally alone with Marc. I was going to enjoy it. But Marc didn't really seem to want to get me any closer after all. The distance between us as we walked grew so great that oncoming pairs, hand in hand or arm in arm, flowed through us. I thought of several things to say but hesitated to speak, unsure if I too should switch to *tu*. He felt like such a stranger now it would seem ludicrous. My fingers hung heat-bloated and sticky at my sides. I wanted him to stop and take hold of them.

A string of gray and black rock islands curved out from this end of the beach toward the horizon, the last of them only half visible, like apparitions caught in the glittery haze, where the blue of the water dissolved into the blue of the sky. So much of this trip had been spent gazing at spectacular sights, which always filled me, as this one did now, with an unexpected, agonizing frustration. Why couldn't I simply accept and enjoy beauty? What was it that stirred up this terrible discomfort? I imagined discussing it with Nicole. We would agree that it was the impermanence, the inability to possess, the reminder of death. And that was all true, but it was something else as well. I thought of the painting back in Paris of the three women in the white waves. I wanted to be able to paint or do something—write, sing, dance, I didn't know what—not just to possess but to express, to force it somehow through me.

We reached the end of the beach. Without acknowledging me, Marc stopped and turned toward the water. I stopped beside him. The silence between us had hardened, and all of the turmoil inside me rose and crashed against it. He was so rigid and remote, so full of inaccessible thoughts, that it felt like being with Nicole. I glanced back at our towels, the 127 steps, the long tasteful hotel where our rooms faced the other end of the beach. The scene was entirely indifferent to us. I was tired of my own passivity. All week I'd clung to the belief that I was less guilty because I was not acting but receiving. It was a lie. I took his hand.

He clasped back but kept his gaze on the sea. "I think the most painful thing about not believing in God is that there is no one to thank when you need to," he said.

I wasn't sure what he was thankful for, the sparkling islands or my hand in his.

"Grief I can handle on my own, but gratitude is less manageable. It requires something on the other end."

It was easy to blame it on the language barrier, to tell myself that my expression wasn't yet equal to my comprehension, but the truth was I would have been tongue-tied in any language. I felt young suddenly, holding this middle-aged doctor's hand, in a way I hadn't felt in a long time.

I wondered what would happen now with the hour and a half left to us. Nicole wasn't there to orchestrate us, and it seemed we might drown ourselves in our freedom to choose. I was aware of the cliff above us that at lunch we often spoke of climbing, and of the path that led up to it, just behind us now. Glancing at it, he said, "Should we explore a bit?"

I nodded, but something in my face must have revealed a hesitancy. He still felt far away. He was being so falsely nonchalant. Another surge of frustration came over me.

"I just want to do what you want to do," he said, lifting his hands defensively, and I could see in this gesture the years he'd suffered with a woman who did not love him, who rarely touched him, who was incapable of anything more than an occasional good mood, a woman who could receive even less easily than she could give.

I am not her, I wanted to say. Instead I took back his hand. "Let's go."

The sand on the sloped path was far hotter. Halfway up we had to step off onto a patch of scrub until the sting wore off. It was surprising to us that there were no other footprints, that no one had ventured up from the beach. At the top, the trail forked left out to the cliff and right toward a grove of trees. Another decision.

"It's your turn," I said, in the *tu* form, using an expression I'd only ever used when playing games with his children.

He led me inland. The path disappeared but we kept walking. All the sounds from the beach—hungry gulls, children splashing, gunned jet skis—fell away, replaced by closer bird and insect clamor. There were shaded patches, then wide-open areas of stiff fried grass. A path reappeared and wound us into a small overgrown courtyard formed by three sides of a low rounded wall that had the color and texture of soap. Olive trees hung over this wall, their leaves casting fluttery lime shadows. Once inside we saw it was a graveyard. Shriveled black olives stained the flat unmarked gravestones and crouched like withered beetles in the tall grasses between them. The odor of their baking clung to the hot air.

The white wall was cool on my back. When I put my arms around him, he let out a long breath and said, "You're so strong."

I tried to remember Nicole with compunction but all I could feel was a sadness for Marc, for I wasn't particularly strong; it was just that Nicole had never held him tightly. He was parched for affection in a way he hadn't revealed when stealing those quick kisses before. I kissed his neck and I thought he would faint in my arms. I moved toward his ear and he cried out. When we kissed, his mouth could only hold the shape of a moan. I envied his pleasure within the moment. He seemed to have drained his mind of memory and conscience, as if this early part of a Friday afternoon was for him a lifetime in itself, with no past and no consequences. I held him tighter, then tighter still, but he wasn't close enough. I could not wrap my arms around the afternoon. My desire for him, so pure and powerful when he was near but not touching, shattered now into terrible fragments of other emotions, all of which made me yearn for him still, though none was satisfied by his actual touch. I was at both ends of the moment, full of the anticipation of its beginning and the awful loss of its passing. *Feel*, I commanded myself. *Feel him here now.* His hands and mouth began to travel across my body. *Feel.* We sank into the grass and olives. *Feel him.*

He whispered all kinds of things, words I'd never heard or words I knew but couldn't make sense of. I wanted to tell him not to speak but found myself speaking back instead, in English. Finally I could feel him. Each time I spoke he swelled and filled more of me. I forced him in farther. With his first tremors, I gripped him hard, blood and life safe inside me. But he pushed against my clutch, extracting himself in one determined motion.

It is a subtle violence, the violence of absence. No one can see it; no one can be accused. Things rushed in to fill it—uselessly, grotesquely. Slick with sweat, he slid along to plant fat loud kisses on my stomach and shoulders. His skin felt like wet rubber. He told me I was beautiful, warm, fresh. He asked, "How do you feel?" stroking the damp hair from my forehead as if I were sick with fever.

I wondered how to say gutted.

"You have brought me to life," he said, when I did not answer, and settled his head on my breastbone.

Through the narrow leaves the sky seemed too dark a blue. There was only one cloud, compact, with sharp edges and thick shadows.

Though it floated in place high above us, it looked heavy, as if filled with mercury.

I remembered my mother. I never thought of her—I only abruptly remembered her. She was a simple, faceless fact that I was capable of forgetting for months at a time. All my life I'd felt lucky that I didn't miss her like my sister did; I'd felt stronger in that way, though I knew it was no feat, for I'd lost her before I could remember her. Unlike my sister, I'd never imagined my mother anywhere, never believed she was watching me, loving or disapproving of me. But at this moment I felt she was some part of that fat cloud that sat motionless in the dark blue sky, and I turned my face away.

My sudden sobs made me heave against him unwillingly, a parody of what we had just done. He did not raise his head but held my shudders tightly to him. I could smell his scalp. It smelled old. I ached for the smell of birth.

When it passed, he cleaned my face with his shirt. "It's all right," he cooed and stroked. "It was beautiful. I could taste it. I could taste your inexperience. It was like an orange, a tart and just slightly unripe orange."

He thought I was laughing at his bad poetry, and laughed with me.

I could smell myself on him. An evening and a morning had already passed, but now with the sun directly above again, I could smell myself baking in his hair, on his fingers, beneath his shorts, and the smell rose up stronger than the squid or roasted garlic or any of the other half-eaten plates that remained on the table. Even when the coffee, three doubles, strong and black, arrived, I smelled it still.

I could not look at him. I tried but his lips were so suddenly red and full and spread contentedly that my eyes recoiled without warning from his happiness.

Nicole drank her coffee in two neat sips. It was easier to watch her. It was easier because now it was done; everything had been pushed to its limit. I was certain Nicole knew. What exactly had Leslie meant when she said the French had a totally different definition for the word *marriage*? There seemed a camaraderie between them today. I don't care, I thought stubbornly, searching for a place inside myself to retreat. I found it in Lola, for we were going to make necklaces before dinner with dental floss and the small pink opaline shells we'd been collecting.

"Why did you choose France?" Nicole asked me. It was the first personal question she'd asked since my arrival in September.

I blushed deeper than my sunburn. "I don't know," I said, battling with a sudden inappropriate urge to tell the whole truth. "It was cheaper than China."

"So you were running from, instead of running toward?"

"Yes."

"Most of my decisions have been made that way." Nicole seemed to be studying me for unexpected traces of herself. "It's not a good way to shape your life."

"It's really another world here, isn't it?" Marc murmured, looking off toward the cliff.

He could do that, look at that end of the beach and not see the two of us climbing the path. He could only see what was there: the sand, the jut of the cliff face, the chain of rock islands glimmering out toward the horizon. He spread his satisfied lips wider. He no longer seemed bothered by whom to thank.

"It's spectacular," Nicole said.

"You're happy we came after all?" he said.

I winced. Why did he have to fish?

But Nicole surprised me. She gave him a slow guilty smile and nodded. "Let's go up there."

"Up there?" he said, as if it were the first time he'd ever contemplated the climb.

When they asked me to come, I pointed to Guillaume and Lola, who were playing cards on their towels with Odile and Aimée. Nicole said they still had another three quarters of an hour before they'd be allowed back in the water. So I said I didn't have shoes.

"None of us do."

Was she trying to trip me up, make me confess knowledge of the scalding path or the stained gravestones?

We walked close together, with me in the middle, discussing bullfighting. Marc wanted to get tickets for the one on Sunday, our last day.

He insisted that going to Spain and not seeing a bullfight was like going to Paris and avoiding the Eiffel tower. "It's silly. It's ugly. It's a poorly chosen symbol of French culture, but you have to see it. You have to define it for yourself."

"But you don't have to watch it bleed," Nicole said. "The children are too young to be exposed to such violence."

"They've been exposed to violence all their lives."

"And you're the one who shuts off the TV at the first glimpse of a gun. I can't believe you're arguing with me about this."

"I know. I'm surprising myself."

It was like a pretend argument. They seemed amused. They spoke across me but included me, as if I were actively participating, as if I had said clever things in support of each of their positions.

Eventually Marc mentioned Hemingway, and Nicole groaned. He ignored her. "Bullfighting is the meeting of life and art. It is real—it involves risk and death, but it is also a ritualized performance."

"Oh, yes," Nicole said, in a deep, haughty voice. "And it's man versus nature and logic versus physical strength. It's all rigged, Marc. The bull is weakened. He's practically dead before the fight begins."

"Not true. He's provoked and angered. A good fight is when he's at the peak of his force."

"If you believe that . . ." Nicole said, but she wasn't even riled enough to finish.

The path was just as hot and we stopped in the same patches. We moaned at how our feet stung and made fun of each other's moaning. Nicole looked like a little girl, lifting one foot, then the other. Marc could glance from me to Nicole and back again. Once more, I envied his amnesia. I felt vaguely nauseated by the scorching sand, the brittle scrub, and the leaf at my foot, blown off an olive tree in winter and now curled into a thin brown finger. There had been hundreds of these yesterday, cracking beneath us. I felt again that the land was punishing me. A horsefly bit me hard, and I thwacked it into juice on my leg.

"Bravo," Nicole said.

At the fork at the top, Marc said, "Which way?" His eyes tried to slide toward mine casually. They couldn't. He was rattled. He'd forgotten why they'd come. Nicole pointed left, then nudged me and shook her head at her husband's sense of direction. I forced a smile back, complicitous with her, complicitous with him.

I walked behind them on the path. Next to Nicole, Marc seemed half-hewn, as if his torso had been set down temporarily and precariously atop his long legs, as if the sculptor meant to get back to the project later. His arms swung and his head bobbed in no particular rhythm. The wind picked up as we came around to the cliff.

Nicole walked straight to the edge. Her hair was whipped into a lopsided funnel she didn't try to control. Marc and I hung behind and apart.

Without changing her position, Nicole looked back at me briefly. "Are you afraid of heights too?"

"Yes," I said, though I'd never been afraid before.

Nicole raised her arms high above her head. It was impossible not to think of pushing her. A few more knots and the wind could have knocked her over. At exactly the same time, Marc and I took a step closer, then, sensing movement, shot each other the same look, not our regular looks of affection or guilt, apology or promise, but of warning. In that split second, I saw we each half believed the other capable of a quick shove at the small of Nicole's back. After that, neither of us moved. We waited for Nicole to come back to us. When she did, she had hair in her mouth. Marc lifted it out for her.

Walking back, he kept his arm tight around his wife. His eyes met mine only once, then darted away. I watched the guilt spread across his face like oil, just as it had on my sister's that night when I'd stood in the doorway of the porch, when my sister had looked up from the wicker couch and been caught enjoying what was hers.

The Bullfight

ON SUNDAY, OUR LAST DAY IN SPAIN, NICOLE TOOK THE CHILDREN TO EASTER MASS. I stayed in bed, following them in my mind as they descended in the elevator and crossed the lobby. I watched the taxi pull up, the kids pile in the back, and Nicole, careful not to wrinkle the back of her dress, tuck herself easily into the front seat. I lay there and wondered whether Marc, too, was tracing their departure in his mind. We had not been given any time alone since that afternoon on the cliff.

Just as I was following them to the steps of the church, there was a soft knock at my door. It was the kind of knock you could ignore; later you could say you were still asleep, in the shower, or any number of things. But I rose and let him in.

"Morning," he said sheepishly, as if he couldn't help his appearance here in my room.

His wife was walking through the doors of a church with their children. It was nine o'clock in the morning. The familiar need to touch him battled with the knowledge that it wasn't right, and it would never be enough.

We sat opposite each other on the twin beds. He seemed to be fighting a tangle of emotions, too, and looked at me helplessly, but I had nothing to say, not in any language. Finally, he held out his hands, palms up. "I've never—" He stopped himself with a strange laugh. "I mean, this isn't something I've done before." He paused again, and when he continued his voice was louder and higher. "You would have thought that at the very least I could have chosen someone more—"

"Marc."

"Something less—" He was laughing now, half worried, half hopeful that I might take offense.

He left soon after that, and I didn't go down to breakfast. I saw him out the window a little later, walking toward the water, but I didn't look long enough to see if he went swimming or just sat on his towel the way he always did, his arms wrapped around his bent knees.

In the afternoon, I was sent to the bullfight. Nicole had refused to go.

Walking through the crowded corridors of the stadium, I tried to stay behind, away from Marc. But he looked back every few steps, and the confusion in his eyes attracted me still.

Once in our section, we pushed past dozens of legs, popcorn boxes, and lit cigarettes to our places on the bench. I ended up in the middle: Guillaume, then Odile on one side; Lola, then Marc on the other. It felt right that they should fan out from me, separate me from Marc. Three rows down, Americans were pushing their way through, boys in backwards baseball caps and T-shirts advertising universities or pubs in other countries. They were boys with wide shoulders and loud laughs, boys oblivious to their foreignness, their wealth, and their freedoms. I felt a sudden compassionate, maternal contempt for them.

Music crackled through the loudspeakers, and the crowd began clapping to it on the second note. I lifted my hands but couldn't find the rhythm quick enough. A door at the far end of the ring was opened, releasing the first bull and men on horseback carrying long poles. The smooth tawny dirt was stirred by hooves. The bull shot directly across the ring, then bent gracefully along its maroon curve back to where he came from. But the door had been closed. The long poles had spikes at their tips, and as the bull charged, ramming his horns against the horses' canvas covering, the riders stabbed with swayed aim as their frightened horses struggled to keep their balance against the blows. Beside me, Guillaume lowered his eyes to his feet and kept them there. On the other side, Lola was transfixed. The horses were ridden out of the ring and replaced by three men on foot armed with pink capes and shorter spikes, which were driven in pairs into the bull's flesh. Roars of approval erupted from the crowd. The bull's neck, back, and rump became littered with spikes. A woman in front of us passed out enormous sandwiches wrapped in tinfoil to her family. They peeled back the foil halfway and began to eat as the bull stood in one place, shaking and twisting and rippling his skin. Nothing he could do would loosen the spears. I could feel Marc's eyes shifting from the ring to me and back again. I did not look at him, not once.

The matador entered to a frenzy of applause. It would be over soon. The bull would be dead, and we could go back to the hotel where Nicole was waiting. The matador lured him with several languorous, calculated swirls of the cape. A sword was handed to him at the edge of the ring. A few more passes with the cloth, then the sword was raised high above the shoulders and sunk.

A violent thunder of voices and applause accompanied the crumpling of the bull. We sat within the raised walls of spectators. None of us stood to cheer this death.

In one motion the crowd sat again. The bull's legs were folded delicately beneath him. A team of horses was whipped in by men in black on foot behind them. Bells attached to their canvas coats jingled as they trotted. Pulled to a stop before the bull, the horses waited while the men looped quick hard knots around the bull's horns. Then they were turned and lashed back across the ring, dragging the body of the bull behind them. The men in black hollered and struck their backs violently, and the laden horses hurled themselves as fast as they could toward the open door. I stood to leave, and the children followed my lead.

"Should we go?" Marc asked me.

"Isn't it over?"

He showed me the program. There were more bulls to come.

"We can leave now. I think we've seen enough," he said, wanting to please me, but another bull was released into the ring and someone behind us asked us to sit down. So we sat to watch again. I could feel the children, so close to me in these packed stands. I could feel them breathing and shifting in their seats. I felt them so I wouldn't feel Marc, who was watching and waiting for me.

Guillaume knew his father thought him a coward, having watched his feet instead of the bull. This time, he thought, fixing his eyes on the horses and, after the horses were gone, the men with pink capes, he was determined to watch till the end. The new bull was fiercer. He shook off all but one of the spikes. Guillaume watched him, thinking, This bull will be dead soon. But right now he believes he will live forever. He thinks he will win, but soon we'll watch them tie up his horns, watch the dust swirl around his corpse as he's dragged off. He will see only blackness from then on forever. He will feel nothing, no wind, no heat, no pain ever again. It's like walking home from school and thinking, Now I am at the beginning of the block and the fish restaurant is at the end but soon I will be past it and I will think back to now when it was still ahead and how I will never have that time before the fish restaurant back again. And just like that, the bull is alive now and the sun has not slipped below the stadium wall and I can think *This is now this is now,* but all the while it is dwindling and soon the bull will be dead. And so will I, someday.

The matador entered, with a swayed back like a shoe horn. He pranced around the bull. A whole stadium full of people had come to watch life become death. Guillaume thought of the fallen Christ in Mary's arms he'd seen carried through the streets, this morning after church, and of all the bloody Christs he'd seen celebrated in his life. A cool sensation moved through him. He was thinking too much, his mother would tell him. He tried to pray but couldn't. Another wave of cold panic. The matador took the sword offered over the wall. He must not die, Guillaume said loudly in his head. He must not. Please do not let this bull die. With two hands the sword was sunk, but the bull kept moving, only the gold handle showing between his shoulders. He trotted around the edge of the ring in victory. Guillaume was equally as fervent in his gratitude. Then the bull came back around to the cape held out to him once again. He paused before it, as if remembering something. His hind legs gave way first, and he sat slowly, like an old obedient dog, then fell forward onto the small feet of the matador. Guillaume hollered out *No!* but it went unheard, swallowed by the backs that rose up in front of him and the terrible cheering that filled the stadium. Amid the snap of whips, the jangle of bells, the scrape of a body along the ground, a thought surfaced and would not be submerged. It bobbed two or three times before Guillaume acknowledged its arrival: *Perhaps there is no God.* The rest of his mind retreated quickly—he had never, ever, doubted before—but the brain is small and there was no place to hide.

* * *

To Odile, the ring seemed to have shrunk. The painted line along the maroon sidewall whitened. All the straw hats in the stands twinkled, even in the shade. Everything is more vivid now, she thought, after death. She watched the dark straight line cut in the dust across the center of the ring by the body of the bull, thinking of Aimée heading northeast on a train. When she wakes tomorrow morning, she will be passing through France.

The dirt was raked smooth, and the second bull bolted out. She will pass through France and see something of my face in the face of a girl who stands waiting on the platform of a commuter station. The train will rush on without stopping. Will it be then that she gets out her notebook? *Dear Odile, Passing through Cordes just now I saw a face. . . .* And will I in four days sit in my house with a page of her words in my hand?

Odile's eyes followed the movement of the bull, the spears in his flesh, and the stagger of the horses' legs, but what she saw was a lined page of black script she knew only from the scrap in her pocket that read *11 rue du Poids, 1032 Geneve.* Aimée wanted to be a writer. Perhaps it would be a long and beautiful letter. She imagined sitting on her bed with a sheaf of pages to savor. Then she felt her mother's shadow on the paper and jerked to, as if she'd been asleep. Two of the smaller spikes had been driven into the bull's neck. He flailed wildly and they flopped from one side to the other but remained caught in his flesh. All letters from Aimée would have to be destroyed. Her mother would misunderstand. *It's not true,* she pleaded. *It's not true.*

Beside her, Guillaume asked if she was okay. She was clenching her fists, her jaw, her knees. She snapped at him that she was fine. *I do not— I am not,* she thought, fixing her eyes absently on the thick spine of the woman in the backless dress in front of her who had risen for the matador entering the ring. There was a large pimple on one of her shoulder blades. *I am not.* The bull was heavy and angry and glistening; the matador was weightless and graceful and sparkling. His cape was the color of fresh blood. His suit was midnight blue. The sun had begun to ease itself down, sharpening everything. She was ashamed that it was the beauty and not the impending murder that moved her. She would write—no, she would not write. But she couldn't stop the words from forming. In the matador's hands the cape appeared sculpted like stone but was as fluid as a wave, taking shape after shape, each one solid and permanent, each one flowing into the next. When he reached for his sword, Odile remembered kissing Alexandre. He never kissed just to kiss, without design, without one hand launching other plans. Kissing was for her alone, while he waited in the distance for her to catch up and agree to do what he wanted, which always happened quickly and then he was off in the distance again, a different farther distance she could never hope to reach. She let herself, as if it were oxygen, take in a breath of memory of Aimée's kiss good-bye. Her stomach did a slow back flip. Girls experiment at first, the rational psychiatrist in her head was telling her. *The worst thing you can do to yourself,* Aimée had whispered to her then, *is deny it.*

It was time for the kill. The matador aimed, bending his knees and curling his back. He kept on his face a smirk that absorbed his fear. Only half of the sword went in, but still the bull collapsed sideways. Dust billowed up into the matador as he took his bows. Above them all, the sun had fallen between the wrought-iron configurations at the top of the stadium, and lace shadows lay on an unused crescent of the ring. But it was the bulls and the men in black she had to capture, and the perfect ocher line the slaughtered body dug across the dirt as the lashed horses lurched faster and faster toward the opening at the far end of the ring. Yes, she would write Aimée, for she promised she would, but only once and only about this bullfight.

The first stab made Lola wince for the poor bull. He was puffed up, slamming his body, horns first, against the canvas-covered horses. Her hands rose instinctively to her face as the tips of the long spears disappeared into his skin. By the time the men with pink capes arrived, the bull was inflamed with violent frustration. He wheeled round and round and received, with each furious charge, another wound. His spine sharpened to a long blade; his flanks hardened; his body grew heavier as it pounded through the dust. His coat was slick with a thick mix of sweat and blood. The matador made his entrance and stood directly below, his back to her, his hind muscles as tight as the bull's. Yet his movements were delicate. He was strangely gentle with the bull, and Lola, forgetting the sword he would soon carry, forgetting the inevitability of the slaughter, was lulled by their rhythm. He let the bull pass so close that blood was smeared on his flat stomach. The audience groaned with nervous pleasure, for this bull was smart and seemed to be aiming for him.

For the first time, Lola felt danger for the matador. The bull's horns were wide and sharp. There were black drops of blood on the ground. The matador's face was wet and pale. Beneath her own arms it was slick with sweat. The man and the bull were no longer separate. They seemed part of one inexplicable thing as their bodies anticipated each other, drawing closer, then separating, then coming back together. Lola watched them with a feeling rising and rising that she could not name. The matador's steps became less delicate. There was blood on the inside of his thigh. A few rows below her, a shirtless man pulled his girlfriend close for a long kiss, and Lola could see their red wet tongues tumbling over each other. She found herself wishing the matador would go for the sword and then was horrified by the wish. But he did exactly that, hiding it behind the cape for several more passes, receiving the bull backhand, then so close to his stomach that he had to curl his upper body over the beast to miss the wide horns passing through, which flooded her body with that same unfamiliar feeling she'd felt since the beginning of the fight. It was not the bull or the matador or the rolling tongues or the arms around her or the blood in the ring or her own slippery sweat, but it was all these things together. She felt like standing up and walking a long, long way; she felt like bursting into tears.

The sword was unsheathed now, and when the bull charged, he seemed to know, to expect, to nearly want the blow. He received the sword straight down to its base, carried it for two unsteady steps, then fell splay-legged and it was over. The feeling throbbed stronger inside her. Her father asked if she was all right. When she shook her head, he brought her closer to him and she gave in to the protection of his arms.

The music started up, tinny circus music that promised clowns and gags, not the slaying of animals, one after the other. Marc, holding Lola, tried to meet my gaze. I looked away. Why had he brought us here to this blood-bath? I was angry now, angry and sickened by Spain and all that had happened under its empty sky. I watched the horses instead of Marc, watched how with every nerve they wanted to bolt from the bull and how their riders with their reins and spurs and crops kept them in place, how training had overcome desire, how they obeyed decorum before their own instinct. I kept my eyes on these horses, for they had everything to teach me.

The matador wasn't in the ring for more than a minute before the next bull lunged and tossed him into the air. He was flung high, up and over the bull's body. Everyone rose to see. He landed on his back and lay flat on the ground, while the bull began to poke and prod. His shrieks were audible above the din of the crowd and the shouting of the other fighters, who had run out to distract the bull.

The children gripped me on either side. Guillaume's cheek was pressed to my upper arm and Lola clutched my leg. They trusted my body; touching it would keep them safer. They trusted that no one in the stands would want to see the matador die. And they trusted he would not, for their father had brought them here and they trusted him too. The bull was quickly pulled off and José Ramón lifted onto a stretcher and carried out waving. The bull was killed swiftly by another sword, without drama or flourish. But I could feel the terrible restlessness in the stands as the horses with their sleigh bells were trotted out past the rumpled spot with the human blood to the dead bull, a restless dissatisfaction, as if the wrong death had occurred. For people wanted more. People—all of us—want more and more. I glanced over at Marc. His face held all the hope and sadness in the world. He turned to me and, over Lola's head, said silently, "I miss you." I saw his hand fall from Lola's shoulder and slip under the folds of her sweater behind her.

When my hand met his, he clasped it tight, then stroked each finger individually. His touch was so familiar to me, now, that through it I could hear his voice, see his lips, taste his kiss.

The last bull shot out directly across the center of the ring.

Pleated shadows fanned out from the feet of the horses. Odile glanced up to see that the ring lights had been lit. *Wasn't there,* she would write, *something nearly comforting about the certainty of death?*

Guillaume was ashamed at having tried to test God. *I'm sorry,* he offered up. *I'm sorry,* he pleaded again, but he couldn't get through.

Lola could not shake the sight of the injured matador, writhing on the horn of the bull like a bug on the point of a pin.

Odile studied how the light fell on the glittering arm that held the sword. Did love, she wondered, include this desperate yearning to present the world as truly beautiful to someone else?

A spray of blood streamed out from the bull's nose, but Guillaume did not pray. He did not try to conjure up God in a place he'd clearly abandoned.

As the matador sank the sword, the woman in front of Lola put down her second sandwich to cry out, "*Sí, señor!*" The feeling returned, and the sweat that clung to Lola's body began to chill and make her shiver.

The matador sighted the bull with his sword, and Guillaume felt the agony of the animal, whose breathing was now a steady stream of blood, whose legs no longer moved in relation to each other, and whose eyes had become human with an expression of stunned betrayal. He remembered Christ's doubt on the cross, asking his Father why he had forsaken him. He bowed his head for the bull and for an end to its pain and felt finally that he was being heard.

The matador sighted the bull with the sword, and Odile imagined telling Alexandre about this day. He would only want to hear how the matador was gored by the bull. She wondered if there was enough paper in Paris for all her letters to Aimée.

The matador sighted the bull with the sword, and Lola trembled with the chills until she remembered her sweater behind her. She turned around and lifted it. Our two hands lay one on top of the other, frozen in place like two bodies found under ice. She waited for them to jerk apart, but they remained still. She waited for our voices to begin explaining, but we were silent. Then the crowd rose, for the bull had fallen with the fourth sword. On either side of her we applauded. "Don't clap!" Guillaume said seriously, but we ignored him, beating our hands together throughout the whole finale as the bull was brained and the matador, hoisted up onto the shoulders of the men in black, held up the salmon-pink ears. On either side of Lola, her father and I clapped and clapped, as if we might never have had to stop.

* * *

When we got back to the hotel, Lola insisted on going up alone to get her mother. "Alone," she said, shoving Guillaume away.

"We can just call her from here." Marc pointed at the lobby phone, and only the unbent fingers revealed his desperation.

"No." She punched the green elevator button until the doors wobbled open.

I knew it hurt her to be so rude to her father, whose face looked like a crumpled paper bag. Because the other children had witnessed this impudence, he said her name with disapproval but couldn't carry out further admonishment.

Guillaume and Odile went to sit on one of the couches in the middle of the lobby. Marc and I trailed behind, choosing seats at opposite ends. I followed the ascent and descent of both elevators by the illumination of digits above the sealed doorways. When the left doors parted again, Nicole stepped out in a canary yellow dress. Lola had changed her sweater.

Guillaume flew into his mother's arms, and though they'd been apart no more than three hours, the gesture didn't seem an exaggeration. Nicole was a half-forgotten, wonderfully familiar sight, and we all greeted her with kisses. I felt so overwhelmed by Nicole's presence—her bright dress, her thick smells, her moisturized skin—that I did not at that moment think of what Lola might have told her or how, watching the embrace, she would be realizing the extent of my deception. Even now, even with a witness, it did not feel wholly like deception. It still seemed impossible to deceive Nicole, who was saying to us, "You all look utterly green. I can't even say who looks the worst."

This wasn't a reproach aimed at Marc, for she examined him the longest with a gentle eye, as if she'd known he'd come back from what he insisted on doing having enjoyed it the least.

"Yes, I can," she said and nearly touched him.

Lola hovered near her mother, as if she wanted to hold her hand or take her arm but had lost courage before making contact. Beside Nicole, she was stiff, angular, and ungainly. Her knees were like door knockers, her neck, which had seemed so beautiful in Cuenca, a veined stalk. She tried to be the first one to describe the bullfight, but each time she'd secured her mother's focus, she was unable to remember what she planned to say. When Guillaume mentioned that one of the matadors had been gored, Lola pleaded for her mother's attention, but when she got it the incident seemed to dissolve before her eyes and she had to let Guillaume tell exactly where he'd been seized and how he'd been flung.

Carmen, the hostess, greeted us at the door of the retaurant and led us to a table in the center of the room. Odile remained standing beside her mother's chair, describing each matador and his outfit perfectly. Using herself as a mannequin, she re-created the jacket and pants, cuffs and lapels with such detail that at the end of every description it seemed she was wearing the suit herself. Guillaume interrupted her to tell about each death. When he got to the last one with the four swords, Lola jumped in shrilly, impaling a piece of bread with her knife. Her piercing voice made heads at several tables turn in irritation. Nicole scolded her. Marc flattened himself against the back of his chair, Guillaume took back possession of his story, Odile prepared her next suit, and Lola, out of habit, out of a desperate desire not to cry at the table, looked to me, but I could not receive her and turned my attention instead to the approaching waiter.

He was the one with the square jaw and closely cut gray hair who Nicole said belonged in an American detective movie. He knew to communicate through me. After he had taken our orders, he asked if it were true that we were leaving tomorrow. I said it was and he told me that the staff had enjoyed us, that we were good people, and hoped we had a pleasant trip back to Paris. I thanked him and he went back to the kitchen.

"He wished us a good trip back." I couldn't bring myself to translate *buena gente,* though I knew Lola had understood because it had been an expression on cassette four. I thought now of those cold wet afternoons listening to the Spanish tapes in the kitchen with Lola, waiting only for the sound of Marc's shoes. And I thought of how once in the fall we'd sat, the three of us, on the couch watching a movie, our three pairs of bare feet lined up in front of us on the coffee table. Noticing the length of Marc's toes, I'd said, "Look at your—" I hadn't known the word then and, instead of interrupting myself to ask, continued, "those little things at the end of your feet." I remembered how we were slouched on the couch, how much chocolate we'd eaten, and how our laughter seemed to shake the whole boat.

"You don't look like you've recovered yet," Nicole said to me, after our plates had been cleared.

"I'm all right." I brushed imaginary crumbs off the cloth. I did not want the attention. I wanted to slip away, to be again who I'd been on that couch, an American girl who spoke a handful of French phrases. I could say too much now. I could be expected to explain myself.

"Was it really awful?"

Lola, who'd received only sharp reprimands from her mother since they'd sat down, looked on in misery. I wanted to explain to her that Nicole couldn't always give what was asked of her, not to Marc, not to her children. But the chance for that kind of talk was gone forever. Lola would never, should never, forgive me.

"No, it wasn't so bad." I knew I should volunteer more, but faltered.

Marc rallied. He sat up in his chair and asked Nicole what she'd been doing, whether she'd finished her book, who she'd seen on the beach. He turned to Odile and asked her if she was sad because her friend had gone. Odile's eyes welled and he reached out to pat her arm, laughing sympathetically, saying something about the brief intensity of holiday friendships. Odile shook her head, but the brimming tears choked whatever she wanted to say.

To me, Marc said, "Your boyfriend's working tonight."

"He's been looking over here," Lola added reluctantly, as if she were breaking a vow.

"No, he hasn't!" I smiled—the three of us smiled—in terrible momentary relief.

As if he sensed his sudden importance, the young waiter, the one with the broken front tooth and the inch-long pinky nail, came and squatted by me. He had been our regular waiter at lunch. He too had heard we were leaving tomorrow. He asked, pulling out a paper bar napkin from his pocket, if he could give me his address. I felt my face redden. The whole table was watching this exchange. I knew I should offer mine but didn't. I took the napkin and thanked him. I didn't know how to tell him I'd keep in touch but he helped me. He asked, "*¿Me escribirás?*" and I said, "*Te escribiré.*" For a moment I forgot my blushing and my audience and felt only the strange simplicity of four words. Later, in the hotel room, after Lola had fallen asleep, I went over them. *¿Me escribirás? Te escribiré.* It was all I ever wanted to remember of Spain.

Windows and Trains

❧

LOLA WAS TRYING HARD TO FORGIVE ME. IN OUR HOTEL ROOM THE LAST NIGHT IN Formentor, on the plane the next day, in the taxi back home to the barge, she gave virtuoso performances. Her banter, laughter, and affection were so convincing that at times I caught myself believing the incident had not only been forgiven but forgotten. But then I'd catch her offguard with a hardness in her eye like the hardness of the river when we saw it again after Spain, when on that raw afternoon it refused to carry any reflection. Losing Lola was like losing gravity. I didn't realize how much I'd depended on the weight of her love until it was gone.

Her relationship with her mother seemed to suffer the most. Instead of swallowing her frustrations and opinions, she lashed out now and snapped back. Nicole punished her impertinence each time more severely, so that by the end of the first week of the spring term, all of Lola's young pleasures—candy, TV, telephone, and overnights—had been taken away.

On the Monday morning of the children's second week back at school, after I had made Guillaume's favorite breakfast (banana pancakes and German sausages), quizzed Odile on more science formulas, and fixed a strap on Lola's knapsack, I sat down in the emptied-out kitchen amid the dirty dishes. Nicole never emerged before ten, and Marc had gone off early to a meeting before the kids had risen. I'd heard him leave, though he avoided the kitchen now.

I thought of Lola hurrying to school, taking the quai steps two at a time. On the rue Greuze, she'd have to take her math book out of her bag and carry it in her arms because it was so heavy. At the entrance to the lycée, Francine and Charlotte would be waiting. She hadn't told either of them much about the trip. They were too envious: Francine of the money the Tivots had to go to Spain and Charlotte of the family itself. On holidays, Charlotte always had to go stay with her father in Rouen while her two brothers came to Paris to visit their mother. Lola would wait for them to finish their cigarettes (she herself hated the taste, but she liked the smell of other people smoking), wondering, as they ground them out on the stone wall, if she would ever tell them what had happened on her last day in Spain. Then the final bell would ring, and they would be carried in a great wave into the building and down the high-ceilinged hallways to class.

I looked around the room. Another week of making messes and cleaning them up. The milk and juices sat, lids off, on the counter. Butter, jam, syrup, and cereals were wedged between the half-eaten plates on the table. On the stove, fat congealed in one frying pan, butter in another. A big bowl of batter dripped between them. Glasses and mugs were scattered about. The coffeepot still gave out a dry gasp now and then. I felt foreign and unwelcome in this room that was once my sanctuary. My suntanned hands made the cutlery unfamiliar. The stone table I had set and cleared and wiped a thousand times refused to acknowledge me. The shiny appliances threw back an unrecognizable face. Only the window remained the same.

It was not a porthole or a series of small panes that you might expect on a boat, but a wide expanse of glass that cast the room in one of the infinite combinations of light the sky and the river schemed. It had been mine for months. I'd never seen any of them stand at the sink for more time than it took to drop down a plate or glass, or take more than a glance out of it to check for rain. But I knew that window intimately. I knew the temperature outside by how much cold it let in through its cracks. I knew when the phases of the moon appeared in its frame: the crescent came at dawn, the sallow half in the midafternoon, and the full moon at midnight, its light pooling in silver puddles at my feet. I knew its smell, its scratches, and the sound of wind across its belly.

Then Nicole came in and stole it from me.

She seemed oblivious to the mess as she reached behind a dirty frying pan for the kettle. While she waited for the water to boil, she stood at the sink and stared out the window.

I couldn't understand why she was up so early until I saw that the clock read ten-thirty. I'd been sitting at the table for nearly three hours. I moved to clean up but she was blocking the sink so I sat back down, relieved. It was Monday, shopping day, and there was laundry and ironing, and Guillaume had a dentist appointment at three, but the thought of carrying out any of these tasks turned my limbs to stone.

"Sometimes it looks like the window of a train, don't you think?" she said. "Sometimes I feel like I'm on a train. Or maybe I just want to be."

I stacked dishes and brought them over to the counter. Her eyes struggled over the pattern of buildings and passageways on the opposite bank that mine could follow effortlessly. It had never seemed like a train window to me.

The kettle screeched to a boil. I reached for it, eager for her to make tea and be on her way. But she lingered at the window, letting the steam from her teacup thread its way up into her face. She stepped closer, into the space between the sink and counter, then pressed her forehead against the pane. She let her skull roll hard to one side, then back, and I could hear the bone bump and the glass rattle in its casing.

I wondered if something had been revealed in their bedroom the night before, if they'd had a fight, if Marc had spoken in his sleep, if Lola had crept in and told her, and if now Nicole was creating this moment for my confession. Her neck exposed, her head lolling, loud against the glass—it was as if she were reaching a hand down my throat for the words. I wanted to give them to her, to pull her back from where she was drifting, to put something at stake, to find out if anything could ever be at stake for her. I wanted to make her truly want what she already had, for she had so much and I hated her for not knowing it. But if I spoke, I would lose forever what she had allowed me to share. If I spoke, she would make everything seem bland and predictable, and it was that, more than anything else, that stopped me. She would take it in with a look of terrible pity, as if I'd been badly duped. This was her way, to make it seem that her emotion, the one she had at any given moment, was the only appropriate one.

I told myself it was because I had to clean the kitchen that I remained and didn't walk away, but this wasn't true. As much as I resented and envied and scorned Nicole, I stayed there at the counter, trembling slightly but refusing to confess, because she intrigued me, and because I dimly sensed movement, as if the ground beneath us were about to shift.

"It was a happy month in my life, on that train." She pulled back from the window and faced me, the cup of tea warming the bone between her breasts, the spot Marc had claimed, as he kissed mine, was the center of your soul. Surely he'd told her the same thing at some point. Maybe she'd told him. "I was just a little girl. Our schoolhouse was being repaired, so all the kids from Plaire were supposed to go to the next town over for a month. But that town was Protestant so my father sent me to a nun's school three towns east. At six every morning he drove me down in my blue-and-yellow uniform to the train station, bought me a ticket, and put me on the regional to Alt." Her gaze went back through the glass.

"I'm not sure my father ever knew," she went on, after a long sip, "and I surely never told him, but it wasn't a commuter train. This one at six-ten ran from the Spanish border straight across France through Italy, so it was full of travelers—foreigners. At first I was frightened to get in a compartment with all of those faces so different from what I had ever seen. Plaire was small and everyone looked pretty much the same." Her face flushed a coppery color, from her tan and the tea and the memory. "Women wearing baggy pants and men's hats. I couldn't believe my own father had put me on this train. Women sleeping with their heads in men's laps. Groups of four or six or eight, young men and women—no older than my sisters—traveling together unchaperoned, sitting outside the bathrooms sharing cigarettes when there were no seats, and me standing among them. I got used to it all within days, and pretty soon I was seeking out the most exotic people I could find."

I wished she would stop. I looked down at the dishes in front of me, hoping that she would apologize and let me carry on. But I'd never seen her apologize for anything. Whatever she did was calculated. She had probably never regretted one thing she had ever done in her life.

She went on. "When I boarded the train every morning, I stepped out of the only world I knew. My father would have driven me the whole way if he'd ever found out, so until the train pulled out, I just sat in the window, if one was free, looking straight ahead and sleepy, but by the time the train arrived in Alt, I'd be playing cards with some Moroccans or teaching a group of Italians the 'Marseillaise' or eating bratwurst. The foods I ate on that train! People were always rustling through their paper bags to feed me."

I don't want to know these things, I thought, but I heard and saw without listening or looking. It was like reading a book and losing consciousness of the barriers of pages and words—being shoved right to the edge of the scene. I could see Plaire at dawn through the window, the yellow platform lights, her father opening the door of his truck, giving a last wave before he got back in. I could feel the movement of the train, smell the odor of sleep in the carriage, hear the sound of a little girl's step in the aisle.

"I remember one couple vividly. They were Dutch. They had been working in Rhodesia and were traveling to Athens. She was reading Chekhov. She'd read a passage aloud in Russian, then translate it into French for me and Dutch for him. She had long legs that she had to stretch across his lap to the window ledge. The passage was about death, I remember." She smirked at the window, then turned toward me with a quick, unfamiliar shake of her head, as if trying to dislodge the images.

I wondered what shades of blue and yellow the uniform was. I wanted to be able to picture more than just the train station in Plaire. When she spoke, I could feel how it must have been to have a hometown and a childhood in which solitary events stood out in stark relief against the comfortable monotony of years. "Did you ever tell anyone?" I asked softly, coaxingly, before the topic was scared off like a skittish animal.

"Yes, I had an aunt—not really an aunt but a friend of my mother's."

There might have been lots of aunts and uncles and cousins and, on top of that, people you called your aunts and uncles and cousins. There would have been people always watching over you, guiding you, loving you. You would have been part of something large and alive and important. You wouldn't have had just one sister, and when you lost her you wouldn't feel like you'd lost everything in the world.

"I told her because I couldn't keep it to myself, and anyone else would have told someone in my family. I told her everything."

I tried to imagine a Nicole who couldn't keep things to herself, who was bursting with life, and who wore the bright, eager, illuminated face that was showing now, dimly, through the adult mask. This was the second time I'd ever heard her speak of the past, and even now she spoke reluctantly, as if something was pushing her on. This wasn't calculated, I realized, and it had everything to do with Spain. The trip had loosened things inside her. And something else had happened there, something perverse and unsought and terrible: Nicole had come to trust me.

"She's still alive, that aunt. She writes me," she said, and I knew then that those were the yellow envelopes she read in private, "although her writing—" she put out a trembly hand to help me understand the word, *frémit,* she was about to use.

With this gesture, I felt a wave of resentment and suffocation; she knew precisely the borders of my comprehension. The feeling came back to me, the suspicion that she could not be deceived, that she knew not only my vocabulary but the very contours and possibilities of my mind. And the old feeling conflicted with these other newer emotions, this strange affection for her, and my unworthiness of her attention.

"She lives alone. I don't know how she manages now. She must be close to ninety. In Spain, I had a nightmare that I went to her. I could never go back there. But she is so alone, and in the dream I was finally going to help her. I'd promised to take care of her rotting garden and clean her filthy kitchen. I was going to make her delicious, well-balanced meals. But I never arrived. I got in the car and drove, but I could never reach her. Days and days, and I never left Paris. It was such an awful dream because it's the way I feel all the time." Her lips quivered as she spoke these last words.

Was I being manipulated again? Had Nicole orchestrated all of this— the rolling of her head, the memories, the painful remorse—in order to bring me to this point? I didn't care if she had. This was it, my chance for absolution—and escape. I had to take it.

"Let me go," I said. "Let me go be with her."

"Don't be silly, Rosie."

"I want to go. I want to leave here."

I was easily replaced.

The new *fille* arrived a few hours before my train left. She was Austrian and her French was already quite good, for she had been in the city with another family since the *rentrée,* and I found myself speaking as quickly and colloquially as possible while I took her through the rooms and explained the routine. It was evening—my train didn't leave till midnight—and the house seemed small, and faces and furniture close and oversized. The new *fille* kissed the family smoothly, chatted blithely, and tucked a short curl of hair behind her ear whenever she paused for a word to come to her. She seemed so young, so young and so well rested. Of all the fresh, uncomplicated qualities I perceived in this new girl, it was her well-rested face I envied the most.

Nicole had arranged things in a letter to the old aunt and had told the rest of the family about my departure. How she explained it to them I never knew, for she vacillated between feelings of deep gratitude and hostile abandonment. As the day drew near, she settled on the side of abandonment, frequently complaining about the great disruption of training a new *fille.*

Of the children, only Odile had expressed any genuine sadness. Guillaume had come to me immediately, asking if I was sure I wanted to go, but in the same breath he wondered about the new *fille* and where she would be from and when she would arrive. Lola hadn't mentioned it at all. But Odile seemed truly affected. Because I'd been the only one to support her recent breakup with Alexandre, she had taken to talking to me more freely since we'd been back from Spain.

A few days earlier, I'd gone to set the dining room table and found Odile in her father's seat, writing in a notebook. She put it aside to help me, and as we went around the table together with place mats and silver, I said, pointing to the three women washing clothes in the foamy sea, "I'll miss that painting."

"Why?"

"Because of the color of the water." I stepped closer to it. "And the song they're always singing."

Odile smiled, not the snide, dismissive smile she'd given me most of the year but an unexpected pleased and prideful smile. She placed her finger in the bottom right corner of the canvas, just below the tiny initials: o.t.

"May I read you something?" she said, before I had time to express more than surprise.

She shut the door into the kitchen and the door into the living room, then went over to the notebook. *"Dear Aimée,"* she began, slowly and softly making her way through one page, then another. I understood then, not from the contents of the letter but from the tender way she read her own words. It was a description of spring along the river, of buds and nests and rising water. I had noticed none of these things. Odile's face was brilliant but also vulnerable as she looked up from the last page. It was the face Nicole had worn when she'd told me about the train. Why, at the moment I'd proven myself utterly untrustworthy, were people now clamoring to confide in me?

Odile came to my room that last evening to say good-bye as I was finishing packing. She kissed me on both cheeks, and I asked her if I could give her a big American hug. Odile laughed. There was a chance Lola would never tell her, and I held her tightly, with the hope pounding through me that to Odile I would always remain innocent.

After she left, I zipped up my suitcase and sat on the bed. The new *fille* was sleeping in Lola's room that night, and I could hear them through the wall. Guillaume was bouncing from his room to theirs and Lola shouted at him each time to stay out. It was way past his bedtime but I was done with discipline and the new *fille* hadn't begun, so he remained at large. Eventually he bounced into my room, panting and flushed with hysteria.

"Good-bye, Rosie," he said, putting his sweaty face up to be kissed. It was clear that Odile had told him to come do this.

"Good-bye, Guillaume."

"I'll miss you."

"I'll miss you too."

He looked around the empty room. "It's hot down south."

"I know."

"Are you taking everything?"

"Yes."

"And she's moving in here?"

It was as if he'd never had a new *fille* before. I thought of the first day when he and Lola had imitated a whole slew of them, and how I'd wondered what they would remember of me. I was certain now Lola would make sure they forgot me. It was like writing in the sand, my life, each segment necessarily washed away.

I lifted him up by his scrawny, scarred arms and gave him an exaggerated squeeze. He yelped as I knew he would, and I dropped him.

"I'll miss you," he said again, this time sincerely.

Lola had told me to come say good-bye just before I left for the train, but I knew how heavily she slept and how awkward it would be to get to her with the Austrian in the trundle bed below, so I went to her room directly after Guillaume left mine.

They were sitting cross-legged on Lola's bed. They stopped talking when I came in, and it seemed to take several minutes for me to cross the room to them. There were the usual posters on the wall—the French soccer team, Paul Belmondo lighting a cigarette, a lion carrying three cubs by their napes—and the usual smell of artificial flavoring and rubber erasers. I had spent far more time in this room than in my own, and it seemed impossible that these were my last moments in it.

"She has a boyfriend in Vienna," Lola said.

I tried to smile at the girl, who was wearing Lola's Snoopy nightshirt. "Don't you have a nightgown?"

"Yes, but it's in my bag, at—" She hesitated, looping that curl around her ear.

"*Au fond,*" Lola and I said at the same time, but Lola wouldn't acknowledge it. Her face was implacable.

"Good-bye," Lola said in English, with her perfect British accent, when I stepped closer.

I leaned down to kiss her stone cheeks. I hugged her clumsily and got nothing back, but just as I began to pull away, she gripped me hard. It felt so good.

"I'm sorry," I began, "I'm so—" but was politely pushed away.

"*Hasta la vista, Señor Perez,*" Lola said, when I was back across the room. They were still laughing, Lola and the ignorant new *fille,* as I shut the door.

Marc was to drive me to the station since, Nicole had said, we were the two insomniacs. But she was still up when it was time to go.

We said good-bye in the coatroom.

"You can leave this on the train when you get there," Nicole said, helping me on with my wool jacket. "It'll be too warm."

I nodded. So much of my clothing had always embarrassed her.

I was desperate to be free of her, yet I stalled now, fastening each button as if it were winter, asking if there was anything I could send her from Plaire or any messages I could deliver. Not a thing, Nicole told me, watching with impatience as I struggled to push the top button into its too-small hole.

Finally she reached over, shoved the button through with one thrust of her thumb, kissed me, and thanked me for eight months of invaluable something or other. I didn't understand the word and was pleased Nicole was too distracted to know this. Marc was somewhere behind me, closer to the stairs, waiting beside my bags.

Then Nicole was the one to stall. "You know it's the Gare de Lyon, not the Gare de Sud," she said to Marc.

"I know," he said, coming closer.

"And it's the train to Avignon. It won't say Plaire or Alt."

"Yes." He was smiling at her. "Is there anything else you'd like to mention a few hundred times?"

She shook her head. It seemed almost coy.

There was a strange thickness there in the coatroom, but it wasn't like the thickness that had spread over us in Spain after lunch. It wasn't easy or warm; it was debilitating, as if none of us could speak or move without tremendous effort. I wanted to turn and go, but I felt there must be more punishment than just leaving. I wanted Nicole to slap me, or Lola to come running in, screaming out the truth. Instead there was only silence and a sad, grateful expression on Nicole's face.

"It's time," Marc said.

Nicole brought the loose watch on her wrist around to where she could see it. "It is." She raised her eyes to meet his over my shoulder. Her expression changed. *Yes,* she seemed to be telling him, *I'll wait up.*

Marc held his arm out toward the stairs and I climbed them obediently.

The house sealed up behind me as I stepped off onto the quai. The long row of windows on this side of the barge were all dark except for the master bedroom at the far end, and this became, as we drove away, the only part of *La Sequana* that remained in sight from the avenue above. It was as if the rest had broken off and all that remained was that square of light which held, unseen but vivid, a woman waiting up in a large room full of silk stockings laid flat in a shallow drawer, chocolate in silver boxes, a long rack of hourglass dresses, and a cookie tin of letters beneath the bed written on lemon-colored paper—the only thing that bound her to the past and me to the future.

But by tomorrow morning, the rest of the boat would be visible again, and the new *fille* would put jam on the table and bread under the broiler and linger at the window in silence after the children had gone to school. Traffic would begin on the river and the water would be stirred, carrying, then shattering, the reflections of gray-roofed buildings and wide-arched bridges, one after the other.

Marc and I hadn't been alone since Spain.

"She seems nice," I said.

"Who?" But he knew who.

"The Austrian."

"Ah," he said, not agreeing.

"She speaks well."

"Too well. I'm sure she already knows how to say *toes*."

He looked straight ahead, into the glare of an oncoming stream of yellow headlights released from an intersection up ahead. I knew those two tight fists on the steering wheel and the slight protective curl of his shoulders. How many times had I seen this same posture from the back seat of this car?

We moved swiftly along the river across the city. The streetlamps in their fragile glass cases on wrought-iron stands seemed laid out exclusively for the course of my thoughts. I could still see Nicole lifting her eyes from her wrist to Marc and how her face had changed. Whether she was conscious of it or not, Nicole had watched me fall in love with her husband and then, in Spain, watched me perceive all of his qualities that enraged her. He had a terrible sense of direction. He had trouble making decisions and often suffered even after they were made. He was self-conscious and wouldn't attempt a word of Spanish. He was defensive and thin-skinned. He had a small range of focus. He liked to be pampered and reassured. He had dark, sullen moods. I learned all these things, and still I loved him. And because I did, he'd stopped asking so much from Nicole and given her more room to love him. I saw that in the coatroom. She would be waiting up for him tonight.

I felt how I could complicate this good-bye. I could reach out and he would accept me still. I could tell him the words that were careening inside me, reopen what was closing between us. He sat waiting for this, in his slouched blend of accusation and self-pity, but he didn't really want it. What he wanted was for his wife to love him. I clenched my heart and did not give him what he could never wholly receive.

He walked me to the train.

"Let me," I said, reaching for my bags, but he insisted on carrying them, which left him no arms to touch me with. We stopped outside the door to my compartment. It was brightly lit, through the windows, but empty. No long-legged woman reading Chekhov, no small girl in a blue-and-yellow uniform.

Marc put down my bags. His mouth made a crooked attempt at a smile. He wanted to apologize, but I intercepted it with a shake of my head. We didn't use the words *love* or *if* or *always*. Our parting, one slow kiss on the cheek, was grave and silent, tinged with the slightest antici-pation of release. Afterward, he stood on the platform beneath my win-dow with his hands deep in his coat pockets and his arms straight and tight to his body as if it were very cold in the station. I knew he was trem-bling like I was. I wasn't sure how well I could be seen through the brown glass, but he was perfectly clear to me. I remembered Leslie saying he looked like Abraham Lincoln. I could see that now, and I laughed out loud. He smiled back at me. Had I never told him this? My body jerked forward, to leap up and run to the door that was just now closing. Then I stopped myself, for it was going to be like that from now on, and re-mained in my seat.

The train shuddered once, then pulled away gently, a needle ex-tracted from an arm with routine tenderness. Within seconds he was quietly out of view, replaced by a long procession of abandoned trains lying on their sides. Sprayed onto many of the cars were fluorescent swas-tikas. I was alone in my compartment and reached to shut off the light.

We sped quickly out of Paris into darkness. Beads of light swarmed on a faraway hill. A piece of tinfoil squeaked across the compartment floor. We passed without stopping through station after station. I did not sleep.

Dawn, when it finally came, glistened on the red leather of the empty seats. Outside there were blue-green fields, with tiny pearls of mist popping and vanishing above them, and the woolly, slumbering shapes of hills beyond.

Midmorning, the sky held a hot sun. It beat down on my legs through the windshield of the truck I rode in. An old man who'd said my name at the station was driving. The roads were thin and twisted like the ones outside Paris in the d'Aubrys' village. Up ahead, two boys rode girls' bikes, slaloming. The man beeped once and they parted, staring into either side of the truck as it passed. Everyone waved but me. A tear of sweat traveled down the length of my stomach. As if he knew, the man said something about the heat. His accent seemed like an impediment, as if he had something jammed under his tongue. I could barely understand him. I nodded anyway. *"Ouai."* Hearing my pronunciation, he muttered something nasty about Paris. I was rocked into a half sleep, then jolted awake by a child wailing in the back. I turned, but there were only my bags on the seat.

We veered onto a rough uphill road. The man whistled. At the crest there was a gauzy view of vineyards and orchards that stretched to dark blue hills. A lean old woman stood in the dirt ahead, then moved slowly into the driveway when she recognized the truck. Her long cardigan fluttered below her bent back. She pointed for the man, indicating where to park. I carried a heavy bag in each hand but the woman took my arm anyway. It had rained the night before, and we navigated the steaming brown puddles slowly toward the house.

Home

TO GET TO THE TRAIN STATION IN ALT FROM PLAIRE, YOU TAKE A RIGHT AT THE fork where Paco Paniagua's brother was killed on a borrowed motorcycle. You pass the restaurant in Limne where Marcelle celebrated her sixteenth birthday, and then the field where Yvonne Nief was struck by lightning. On the outskirts of Alt is the prison where collaborators were held. Closer to town is Notre Dame de Nazareth. It is vacant as Henri and I drive by; school won't be in session for another few weeks.

One large headlight can be seen down the tracks. For a long time it hovers there in the distance, quivering in the heat; then all at once it rushes at us, whistling before it crosses the intersection and whistling again just before it reaches the station. The front cars race past. Travelers hoist bags on shoulders and move closer, trying to guess a spot on the platform that might align with a door. It is always a moment of exhilaration and possibility, a train rushing by, loud and gusty, full of perpetual strangers. And then it slows and slows, its last cars whining to a halt before us. I am not ready. I hope with all my heart that Nicole will not be on this train.

But there she is, first off, accepting the aid of a uniformed arm and stepping down. She wears a fitted cranberry blazer and matching pants. She approaches us slowly, taking in the station not with the acute, discriminating glances with which she normally enters a room, but with a dull eye that seems unable to fasten onto anything, not even on the two people moving forward to greet her.

"Henri," she says, dropping her suitcase. It is one of the green leather ones she took to Spain. Its brass bolts are the shiniest objects in Alt. "You're an old man."

"And you're a fancy Parisian snob!" He laughs hard, his mouth open so wide I can see that he does have teeth, way in the back. Then he crushes the linen suit in his arms.

I feel her stiffen but Henri just keeps rocking her back and forth. "She'll be so glad to see you," he croons in her ear.

When he sets her free, Nicole turns to kiss me. She holds on to me as if for balance. "How is she?"

"Hanging in there."

"Thank you for calling."

We head toward the parking lot. "How was the trip down?" I ask.

"Fine."

"Any Moroccans to play cards with?"

She shakes her head, not seeming to understand the allusion. If she's come with recriminations, she clearly is in no shape to discuss them yet. This thought soothes me, and my pulse slows slightly.

In the truck, Henri chats away, listing for Nicole—who hasn't asked a thing—all the fortunes and failures of the families in Plaire. Squashed between them, I want him to ask about Nicole's family, but he doesn't. I know it would be perfectly natural for me to ask myself, and even strange if I didn't, but each time I practice the words, they sound rehearsed. If I ask about the kids, it will seem like I'm avoiding Marc, but I can't ask about him first. And if I ask about everyone all at once—*Ça va tout le monde?*—it will sound deliberately unspecific. Every sentence I try in my head feels like a confession.

Very loose attention is paid to Henri's stories. I've heard them all already, told more compellingly by Lucie, and Nicole is distracted by what lies beyond the truck's windows. The first part of the drive from Alt to Plaire is along a plateau that curves above fields of purple fans and taller golden stalks: lavender and wheat. Nicole rolls her window all the way down, flooding the cab with the sharp smell of the perfume distillery nearby. She shuts her eyes and breathes it in; I'm not sure what the smell of lavender oil reminds her of.

In Goulle, we drive along the deep ravine. Bright shorts of climbers splayed against the opposite rock face flicker through the trees. More climbers with belts and jangling clips walk on the side of the road into town. I've never been through Goulle without seeing them, but today the gear, the muscles, and the fluorescent clothes seem preposterous. I can feel Nicole's contempt for their neon invasion. After Goulle, the road straightens out and we pick up speed. At the top of a rise, the towns of Bourne, Limne, and Plaire can all be seen, each clump of buildings blanched and clinging to its own hillside.

Henri pats my leg. "Anything we should stop for?"

"No, we're all set. I've got enough till Tuesday at least."

"Listen to you," Nicole says, without turning from the window. "You're a real Provençale now."

It's true. I no longer speak like a thirteen-year-old from Paris but like an old woman from Plaire. I dread Nicole's scrupulousness— her judgments and labels. Everything will be changed by it; I will be changed.

At the house, I take the green suitcase to the downstairs room I've prepared for her while she lingers in the driveway. She isn't looking out at what used to be her father's land or at anything but the gravel in front of her. I watch her through the window, standing there with her hands in her blazer pockets, her arms straight, and her shoulders raised. She stands just as Marc stood on the platform in Paris, as if something might fall on her at any moment. I feel desperate for news of Marc. Has he lost Lola for good because of me? This is one thing I can never find a way to ask.

From the kitchen I can hear Nicole finally stepping into the house, then pausing again. Everything would be the same: the framed daisies, the low cherry table with the knot on one side, the empty green bowl, the sound of shoes on the flagstones, all the mingled smells.

I hope she'll go straight upstairs to Lucie, who will have heard the truck in the driveway, but she doesn't.

"Let me help you," she says, stepping down into the kitchen.

"No, I'm just making a salad and reheating some soup." I'm embarrassed by what we eat: soup and salad nearly every meal, most of the ingredients from the vegetable garden in back. It's all we can afford. When I found out what little money Lucie received every month, I stopped accepting a salary. "Why don't you go up and say hello?"

Nicole has already started slicing tomatoes. "Isn't she sleeping?"

"Even if she is."

"In a minute. These too?" She lifts a bowl of yesterday's boiled po-tatoes. They are small and bruised, but if I'd tried to cut around the dark spots, there would have been no potato left.

"Yes, please." The potatoes are also badly peeled. I've nearly forgot-ten the agony of working beside Nicole. But Nicole quarters the potatoes as if they are blemishless.

"Have you been all right here, Rosie?"

"Fine."

"This can't be much fun for you."

It strikes me as odd that Nicole, who never took fun into consider-ation, not even as a child, would ask me this.

"But maybe you've made some friends?"

Nicole, who has no friends.

In place of an answer, I ask my question: "*Ça va tout le monde?*"

She looks up at me in sudden delight, as if she'd forgotten the four people in Paris we have in common. "They're very well. And they all send you big kisses."

Before she can go on, I say, "Go up now. I can do the rest."

She sets down the knife but doesn't move immediately. For Marc, most transitions—from car to house, kitchen to study—involved an idle moment or two, a reflective, regenerative pause. How many times did I watch him push back his chair from the table, then sit there still, hands stretched to the table's edge, caught in a necessary realignment. It makes me miss him terribly, seeing these unexpected fragments of him in his wife's body.

Nicole climbs the stairs and I'm glad to miss the reunion. I block out the noise of it by singing the song about the ladybug Lucie taught me and finishing the salad and bringing the soup to a boil. I wait for Nicole to come down for it. The vinaigrette grows a brown ring in its bowl and the soup a firm skin. The bruises on the potatoes darken. I set aside a plate for myself, then make up a tray for them and carry it up.

The door, which Lucie prefers shut, is propped open, and the win-dows have been lifted as high as they will go. A strong current of warm air sweeps through the room, flapping dust out of the curtains.

Nicole has left my chair empty, the chair I sat in most of every day and night for the past month, and pulled another around to the other side of the bed. She's propped Lucie up with extra pillows and changed her nightgown. The old one, which I didn't dare disturb her to remove, has been tossed near the door along with pillowcases.

They sit like lovers, with flushed faces and clasped hands. I place the tray on the arms of my empty chair, pick up the dirty laundry, and leave. They call after me to stay, but I keep moving down the stairs. I drop the linen in the kitchen and go out the back door.

The air is turning, finally. The leaves make a sharper sound when they rustle. Even the grass feels older and stiffer. Before France, I never felt the change of seasons, never paid attention. Today it's inescapable: there is the same rattle in the trees, the same hot but exhausted sunlight as when, a year ago, I delivered my sister's child. It has come back around. Will the end of summer always mean this now, for the rest of my life? He is a year old. Walking, maybe. Uttering a few words that only Sarah understands. For him there will be no memory, no season of loss. He will never ache for me as I will always ache for him.

I can hear Nicole inside, banging cabinets, taking charge.

"Rosie." Nicole comes quickly to the back steps. "I can't find the washtub. It isn't under the sink anymore."

"There's a machine," I tell her. "But I'll do it."

"No, you will not. You've been working here thirty hours a day as usual. And you haven't touched your lunch."

That evening Nicole and I share the foldout table I put beside Lucie's bed, all of us crammed in at the far side of the bedroom as if on a heeling ship. We speak only of the present. Lucie's curiosity about Nicole's family in Paris is ravenous, and Nicole is far more willing to speak of them than anything else. Lucie listens with closed eyes and a temporarily sated smile, though she has not eaten anything on her plate.

There is no mention of her dying, not by Nicole or Henri or the doctor who stopped in this afternoon. I listened to his instructions about food, liquids, and dosages but asked for no information beyond that, not a name for her condition or a prognosis. And neither did Nicole.

Two days later, Nicole rises early—too early, is my guess, to do anything but catch a train back to Paris.

"I've asked Henri to come by around nine," she says. "There's someplace I'd like to go and I don't want to go alone." I wonder where she'll take him. "I mean, if you wouldn't mind, Rosie, I'd like you to come with me."

She leads me out past Lucie's five rows of table grapes, past the vegetable garden, over a small stone wall, and onto her father's land, which was sold just after his death to a fruit company in Avignon. We ignore the men, who stop working to watch two women disappear into the overgrowth, and set out on the old path to the quarry.

Though we both knew it had been drained, it is still a shock. The chasm is enormous. After a while, Nicole moves forward and stands at the edge. Then she climbs down the shallowest slope all the way into the basin. At the bottom there are crumpled cigarette packages and empty liquor bottles. It's still a popular place for parties on summer nights. A few plastic cups, some half full, sit on a rock of coffee-table height. The quarry is a perfect outdoor living room. There are couches, recliners, love seats. A hat has been left hanging on a crag.

Nicole squats and brushes the loose dirt with her palm. "Even though I was told differently, I always thought it would be flat and smooth down here, with soft grasses, like a field. I don't know why." She speaks softly, but her voice carries straight up to me. She remains in that one place, her hair falling forward in two sharp triangles, her chin on one knee, stroking the ground. For the first time I see both the child and the woman as one uninterrupted being.

When she stands up, she raises her eyes to where the water once reached. I strain to see what she sees: the boy and the stone, Marie-Jo diving in on a dare, or Marcelle hesitating. I wish she'd get out of there. Something is strange. Sunlight spreads along the sides in long swaying fingers; the hat on the crag bobs slowly. It's as if the quarry has never been drained at all. Nicole suddenly seems to feel it too. I have never seen her move so quickly. She falls twice, scrambling up the rocks. I put out a hand for her, but she shakes her head and goes past me toward the bushes. Halfway there, she throws up. When she's through, she just hangs there, hands on her knees.

I remember how Sarah used to rub my back and wipe my face with a towel in the mornings.

Nicole hears my steps behind her and says, "I'll be fine." When I don't stop, she says more sharply, "Please. Leave me." But when I pass my hand lightly along the small bent frame, she lets out a long breath and says nothing more.

On Tuesday afternoon, she insists on walking into town with me.

"You two take your time. We'll be fine here," Henri says to me outside the bedroom door. "She seems better today, doesn't she?"

I nod, though I sense no change at all. She still has a fever and no appetite.

I wait for Nicole in the driveway. Through the open windows I can hear her primping: a brush being set down, a cosmetic case snapping shut, perfume being pumped twice. She'll be overdressed for the streets of Plaire and for the weather. Directly above there are flaky white clouds, but to the west, close to the horizon, the sky is dark and the valley is cast in a sickly yellow-green light.

"There's a storm on its way," I call in.

"Coming!"

Nicole appears in another suit, this one slate blue. Around her waist is a leather belt with a big gold buckle. Her shiny purse bounces at her hip.

Accustomed to speaking to Lucie, I say, "We're not going to the Place Vendôme."

Nicole stops to dangle a foot in the air. "I'm wearing flats. And no stockings."

"No stockings beneath long pants. How scandalous!"

It's nice, I have to admit, having someone to walk into town with again.

The clouds are massing, and the moments of bright sunlight grow fewer and briefer until they cease all together. Still, I figure we'll make it back before the rain.

Jean-Baptiste, the dairyman's son, comes barreling up from town in his van, then slows when he sees me. "I was just on my way to drop off a few things."

"Thank you. That's very kind. Henri's there."

He doesn't try very hard to conceal his disappointment at the timing. He nods to Nicole and asks about Lucie.

"She seems better today," I say, mimicking Henri, wanting it to be true.

The car behind him that has been waiting patiently gives a toot.

"You always manage a few admirers, don't you?" Nicole says, as he drives off.

"He's not—"

"I've already heard he is."

"She has a pretty big mouth for a sick person."

A few admirers. Was this her accusation?

She stops in the road. "My house," she says, at the foot of her old driveway.

"Do you want to take a look?"

"No."

We stop first at the pharmacy to fill the doctor's latest prescription. At the sound of the door, the pharmacist looks up from his magazine. As with many in Plaire, his devotion to Lucie now includes me. His features, which were bunched in concentration, widen across his face. Nicole assumes the greeting is for her.

"Monsieur Dudon," she says, in the accent of the child who knew him.

He makes no effort to disguise his confusion so that by the time she reaches the counter, she's slipped back into her Parisian lilt as she holds out her hand and reintroduces herself. Her maiden name unclouds his face only slightly.

The incident doesn't seem to thwart her sudden enthusiasm for Plaire, and as we walk up the street she points to a doorway she claims used to be the newspaper office where she worked one summer collating sections. I never heard about this job, and I thought the newspaper office used to be up next to the police station.

"No, it was right here all my life."

We're alone in the street except for a lean dog that has been trailing us.

"Go home, Greco," I command, though I don't mind the dog. I just want to say his name in front of Nicole and reclaim this town she's taking back from me.

I didn't need to. At the grocer's, the baker's, and the butcher's, the warm reception I receive confirms my place in Plaire. Nicole hangs back near the door of each shop. The women give her no more than the brief acknowledgment they give all foreigners, a sort of *humph* of the eyes, and the men admire her beauty with the same unengaged glance they'd give to an attractive woman on a poster at a bus stop.

The sickly light has arrived by the time we finish our errands. My guess is we have no more than fifteen minutes to make it the two miles back. I head swiftly down the incline. Nicole falls several paces behind.

"I am a ghost," I hear her say, but keep walking.

Then the steps behind me cease. She calls out as if I'm already far away. She's turning that loose gold watch around on her wrist. "I was thinking of making a phone call."

It might be to the train station. Perhaps she'll arrange to leave this evening. "Go quickly. It's about to pour."

"It's still up in the square, isn't it, the post office?" What she's really asking is for me to come with her.

The telephone cabins are at the back of the building. I take the farthest seat from the phone Nicole chooses, but the place is empty and all I can hear is Nicole's voice, though not many individual words. I hear her laugh loudly, groan a little, deny something. She speaks for a long time in a low voice, then laughs again. The door has a thin strip of glass through which I can see a thin strip of her. She swivels in her chair. Then she stands up and opens the door.

I reach for our shopping bags, hoping we can still get ahead of the rain. But Nicole is holding the receiver out to me. "Would you like to speak to Marc?"

I put the bags down. No, I think loudly. "All right." Did he ask or did she offer?

Nicole steps out and I step in.

He would be at work now. "*Ça va, Rosie?*" It was definitely Nicole's idea. He sounds distant, like he's trying to create more distance than there is between Paris and Plaire.

"*Oui, ça va.*" I duplicate his tone, wanting to give the impression that Nicole is still beside me, though in fact she's disappeared from the waiting room.

We speak at the same time, pause, and do it again.

"You first," he says.

"No, you."

We're using *vous.* I want to hang up.

"Have you been okay there?" he asks.

"Yes, fine."

"Should I believe you?"

"How is Lola?" It's all I really want to know.

"Good." He sounds defensive. I give him time, and he says finally, "We've talked. A lot."

"Good."

"I think so."

It's incredible to hold the sound of his voice in my hand. It feels so necessary, so vital. I don't want to let go. But he does.

"We miss you," he says.

"I miss you." Again the *vous,* safe in its ambiguity. "It's going to rain. We'd better go."

The last thing he says is *Au revoir,* but I will never re-see him. It is a deceptive way of saying good-bye.

I find Nicole looking through the doors out into the square. It's started to spit, and by the time we go a half block, rain is shattering on the pavement. We stop in a doorway while it thuds hard above us onto the canvas awning. It falls faster and faster, the wind sweeping it one way, then another. Soon the road is braided with fast-flowing streams. The air grows warmer, as if the rain has lifted the heat out of the earth.

Nicole touches my arm. "Smell that," she says, and takes in a deep breath. "That's the smell"—she pauses, taking in more—"of everything."

Her face is radiant. Despite it all, she is home.

Up and down the street, people stand in clusters under cover. Every so often someone makes a diagonal streak across, protected by a newspaper or cellophane bonnet. No one carries an umbrella.

A waiter darts across the terrace of the Café Plaire to rescue the wooden board that advertises their specialties. Nicole asks me if I'd like to get something in there.

We join the streakers, though our hands aren't free to cover our heads, and our heavy bags make our steps unpredictable. On the threshold of the café, Nicole slips, then rights herself, but not before she lets out a shriek. The sound is launched through the open door, and as we enter, Marie-Jo, standing at the back of the room, is one of the few who doesn't turn our way.

Nicole chooses a spot in the closest corner. "This was where you could always find my father on Saturday afternoons." She strokes the tabletop as if to collect on her fingers a lingering flake from his pipe.

But I can no longer picture Octave or Marcelle. Even Marie-Jo in her coffee-stain smock, now standing there at the bar, isn't real to me anymore. She belongs—like this street and its smell and the phone call to Marc—to Nicole. And all I have to do is point, and Nicole can turn to see her sister leaning on the counter, talking gravely to the bartender.

The waiter who ran out into the rain takes our order, two hot chocolates, his hair dripping onto his pad. I don't ask, but Nicole tells me everything that's going on in Paris. The weather is awful, and Lola and Odile have gone to the movies every afternoon for five days. That's where they are right now. Guillaume is at Arnaud's. The summer *fille* left and the new one won't start until the *rentrée*, still two weeks away. Marc is doing all the cooking. "Tonight," she says, "he's making that pasta dish of yours. With the fennel and the meatballs."

"Bacon."

"I think he bought meatballs."

We grin at Marc's mistake. I imagine being there in my kitchen again, with just Marc and the children and my radio mysteries, a place where I once belonged.

"I was thinking of staying here awhile," Nicole says, in the same way she mentioned the phone call, as if asking for permission.

"Of course."

"And I was hoping you'd consider going up there, to help out until the *rentrée*."

This is my chance, my chance to explain things to Lola, or to hold Marc again. It's my chance to escape Lucie's death.

"No." It shoots out before I can stop it. It shoots out from a place that cannot be tempted or weakened, a place that is not afraid: a place I didn't know existed inside me. And though this isn't at all the answer I want to give, it feels good to say something clear and level and unambiguous to Nicole.

I wonder if it's a test, if Nicole wants to know how fast I'll jump at a chance to return to Marc. Does she know? She seems to know everything and nothing. Maybe knowing has never mattered to her. I remember her in the phone booth, swiveling, giggling, teasing, being teased. It didn't matter at all.

"It wouldn't be for long. Just until the new girl arrives."

Behind her, Marie-Jo pushes off the counter to leave.

"That's your sister."

She turns just in time to watch Marie-Jo take three steps and go out the door.

Nicole remains with her mouth half open, like an American. Then she says, "I thought she lived—"

"She's come back."

Marie-Jo, one hand clutching a brown bag, the other trying to cover her head, runs past the window. The rain has already wet her face but she looks ahead expectantly, as if the next step will be onto dry ground. Nicole jerks to stand, then sits again.

"You should stay longer, Nicole."

"Then you'll go to Paris?"

I shake my head. "They'll be fine on their own."

Beside us, the window is empty again. Rain lashes the panes in long gusts, then briefer, harder spatterings. The waiter removes our cups and brings us two more, though neither of us remembers ordering them. The café is full now, hot and thick with smoke, and all the extra chairs against the walls have been dragged out. Across the room, a child wakes up from a nap in his mother's arms and begins to cry. It's a noise like any other noise in the room, like the steady clatter of plates and saucers, the click of dominoes, the snap of cards, the chatter and the slow peals of laughter.

Once again, I remember it is fall. I think of the word *rentrée,* the return. For nearly a month now, I've slept straight through each night. In my chest I feel a small unrecognizable swell of pleasure at the memory of a pain that has diminished. I think of all the unopened letters outside in the wood bin. Some are so thick she had to tape the envelopes shut. The rain is coming down hard, and the box is cracked, but it's protected beneath the eaves. The letters will still be dry. It will take me all of tomorrow to read them.

"Did Lucie have a sister?" I ask.

"No. She had brothers."

"Brothers," I repeat, and we look at each other in mutual bewilderment.

"Two sets of twins. And all four of them fell in love with my mother's cousin, Laure," Nicole begins, and she speaks until the rain eases, the clouds travel east, and the hour, when we step out onto the terrace, has turned a dark gleaming mauve.

ACKNOWLEDGMENTS

I would like to thank the following people for their kindness, generosity, and unending support of this book: my sister, Lisa, and her husband, Lanny; my husband, Tyler; Laura and Tom McNeal, Cammie McGovern, Jeff Darsie, Kathie Min, Naeem Murr, Lucie Prinz, Tobias Wolff, Don Lee, the MacDowell Colony, Beth Gutcheon, Wendy Weil, and my excellent editor, Elisabeth Schmitz. I would especially like to thank my mother for her daily, unswerving encouragement, enthusiasm, intelligence, and faith.